THE
RUINS
OF
WOODMAN'S
VILLAGE

THE
RUINS
OF
WOODMAN'S
VILLAGE

AN LT NICHOLS MYSTERY

ALBERT WAITT

LEVEL
BEST BOOKS

First published by Level Best Books 2023

This novel is entirely a work of fiction. The names, characters and incidents portrayed in it are the work of the author's imagination. Any resemblance to actual persons, living or dead, events or localities is entirely coincidental.

First edition

ISBN: 978-1-68512-236-2

Cover art by Level Best Designs

This book was professionally typeset on Reedsy.
Find out more at reedsy.com

Praise for The Ruins of Woodman's Village

"In seaside communities up and down the New England coast, the mega-wealthy share space with too many people who are struggling to get by. Al Waitt knows this world better than anyone — the glamorous restaurants, the dirt road hovels, the sense of entitlement, the deep-seated resentment. More than anything, he knows the people. And in this book, at once riveting and elegant, Waitt brings it all together in an exquisite and explosive read."—Brian McGrory, *The Boston Globe*. Author of *Strangled* and *The Incumbent*

"As much as the landscape presents a unique regional quality to Maine, so do its residents. The eclectic mix of yuppie, townie, vacationer, and transplant are equally represented with cinematic prose and pulsing dialogue. Set against the backdrop of a small coastal town, this thriller grips you like a riptide, with Waitt encapsulating a tension that will make you devour this book with a page-turning fury."—Joe Ricker, Author of *All the Good in Evil* and *Some Awful Cunning*

Chapter One

"Chief, you better come out here."

I put down the sports page of the *County Star*. Estelle Maynard's eyebrows were in a V, and her chin was quivering. She hadn't knocked, never mind used the intercom. I couldn't even guess what that meant. I sighed as I leaned into the arms of my chair and pushed myself up. Estelle receded from the doorway, and I maneuvered around the metal desk, swearing that this would be the week I started working out again. When getting up from a sitting position required noticeable effort, something had to be done. But before I could get to that little slice of self-improvement, I would have to spend the day stomping out the brush fires that the summer crowd always managed to kick up.

A sheet of sweat broke out across my back when I saw the woman glaring at me from the counter. She could have only come from Woodman's Village. The black hair, thin face with the ski jump nose, and close-set, dark eyes were one indication. Her clothes were the other—a dusty pair of men's jeans that looked to be a size too big and a yellowed version of a plain white t-shirt. The sweat moons over her chest and under her arms told me she'd walked here. It was five miles. She may have been the first person from the Village to ever enter the station not in handcuffs, though even that was a rare occasion. The agreement that existed between the town and the Village was only understood but couldn't have been more clearly defined if in the Constitution: If the Villagers behaved themselves on those occasions when they did venture into town, the town—meaning this department—would stay out of the Village. Something had to be seriously wrong.

1

"What can I do for you, ma'am?" I said, approaching the counter.

"You in charge here?" Her eyes drilled into me.

"That's right. Chief Tim Nichols."

She glanced at the door as if she were having second thoughts, then returned her gaze to me. She wasn't much shorter than my five-seven, and with wispy streaks of gray around her temples, I guessed she was probably five or six years older than my thirty-five.

"I want my girls back," she said. "Right now."

"Excuse me?"

"The twins. You ran them out of town, and they're gone. You had no right to do that. I want them back. Now."

"This isn't the Wild West, ma'am. We don't run people out of town."

"Then you have them locked up. They're not even eighteen, so you can't do that. I know the law."

"Did we pick anyone up last night, Estelle? I don't recall seeing anything in the log." The truth was I'd gone straight to the newspaper and hadn't glanced at my reports yet. But even if one of my three seasonal men had a run-in with someone from the Village, they would have known to call.

"No, Chief," Estelle said, keeping her eyes on her switchboard. "And neither has the county sheriff. I checked."

"How old are these girls you're talking about?" I asked the woman.

"Sixteen."

"Who told you we had this encounter with them?"

"They're gone, and everyone knows you people do anything you want around here. Maybe you don't like them going into your pretty little shops like they do. Told them to get out and stay out. Or maybe you have them penned up like dogs."

I suppressed another sigh. Typical backass Woodman's thinking. They'd even kicked up a fuss when I was in kindergarten, and the Board of Education made them start sending their kids to school. For the five years that I'd been Chief, we'd had very little trouble with the Village. That streak appeared to be over. I could feel the muscles in my neck beginning to tense.

"I'm sorry, but we don't have your daughters and haven't ever asked anyone to leave Laurel. How long have they been missing?"

"As if you don't know."

"Believe it or not, we aren't in the habit of picking up random teenagers, no matter where they're from. But I will help you find them if they are actually missing. That is something we do. Why don't you come into my office and let me get some information?"

"You're a goddamn liar."

"Please," I said. She would never believe me if she didn't see for herself. That's just how those people were. I walked up to the end of the counter and opened the gate. Teenage girls, they could be anywhere these days, especially if their alternative was going home to a shack that probably didn't have hot water and might not have electricity.

"You going to lock me up now?" The woman's voice had lost some of its bite, but I wouldn't have called it conversational.

"Certainly not. Please, come this way."

She stood still, pulling on the green elastic that held her ponytail.

"I can help you if you let me." I took a step back toward the office and tried to smile. It wasn't easy. But if I couldn't diffuse some of her anger, I'd never get anywhere. She finally moved forward. "That's my office, but I want to show you that outside of you, me, and Estelle over there, we are the only ones in the building."

I took her behind the desk and down the hall past the conference and squad rooms. At the end were three empty six-by-eight holding cells, cement plastered over the original wood paneling. I couldn't remember a time when they'd all been occupied at once.

"You got a cellar here?" she asked. "How do I know they aren't down there?" We trudged to the basement, which contained nothing but boxes of old files, outdated radio equipment, and a refrigerator that held the beer we confiscated from underage beach parties.

"I'd like to get some information from you that will help us locate your girls, so let's go into the office."

"You better not be using me," she said, continuing to follow.

"Like I said, we're here to help people, and I'm glad to do it if you'll let me."

I stopped short of asking what she thought I could be using her for. In the office, I pulled one of the folding chairs from the wall and put it in front of the desk. I motioned for her to sit and went to my own seat. I didn't find the expanse of metal between us to be a bad thing.

"You better know that I'm not having anything funny," she said. "If Boomer hears, he'll come down and clear this place out, and you know it."

"Boomer is your husband?" Boomer Woodman ran the Village. Rumor had it that the day he'd come home from Vietnam, he'd paraded around Laurel from bar to bar wearing a string of Vietcong ears as a necklace. I'd been off at UMaine that fall, so hadn't witnessed it myself. Though I'd had plenty of folks tell me they'd seen it, I found it more likely that the VC necklace was one of those small-town rumors that get repeated enough to be taken as fact. That it was somewhat believable was all one needed to know about Boomer Woodman.

"He's my brother."

"Let's start with your name?"

"Rory."

"Connolly, Woodman, or Sampson?" There was not a lot of diversity in the Village, which created its own strain of problems.

"I'm a Connolly." She sat with her hands folded in her lap.

"Married to?"

"Jake Connolly."

"The girls who are missing, they are your daughters, correct? What are their names?"

"Yes, Holly and Maisie."

"Connolly?"

"That's right, Sherlock Holmes." She looked less happy when she noted my surprise at her reference.

"When was the last time you or anyone saw them?"

"Thursday afternoon, they went off to town."

"Last Thursday?" I couldn't keep my voice from rising. Five days had passed before Woodman's ignorance would let their mother come for help.

"Yes."

I told myself to get the facts, just get the facts. My getting worked up wasn't going to improve the situation.

"They went by themselves? Were they walking?" There weren't many cars down there, as far as I knew, and I doubted they'd let a couple of teenage girls take one.

"That's right. Walking, just them."

It was three miles to the town square from the Village.

"Could you describe them, what they look like, I mean?"

"I speak English just fine. I went to school with you, Mr. Big Time Wrestler."

"Timbercoast Regional?"

She nodded. "But you don't remember me."

"I'm sorry, but my memory for that kind of thing isn't very sharp. I see too many people in this job." I tried to chuckle, but it sounded like a hollow cough.

"Funny," she said, "that you'd forget folks you tried so hard to dodge in the hallways."

"Are you sure it wasn't the other way around?" I did recall a small group from the Village at Timbercoast. We'd had little to do with each other. That's just how it was.

She shook her head and sighed. "I didn't come here for your help."

"I can find your daughters," I said. I was not a master of deduction, an expert in forensics, or knowledgeable in criminal psychology, but I was capable. I could track down a couple of backwoods girls who'd run off. "You're going to need to cooperate some for me to do it, however."

"Have at it then," she said, leaning back and folding her arms across her chest.

"It's important that I get the details correct, so please bear with me. The girls, they're identical?"

"Pretty much can't tell them apart if you don't know them." They had long black hair, and were thin, and I assumed they had the same curve in the nose, younger versions of their mother. She told me that they'd left walking on Thursday afternoon, headed downtown to get ice cream at Scoops.

"Did they go into town often?" I asked.

"Twice a week. They like their ice cream."

"And they had money for it?"

"What do you take us for? Yeah, they had money. They work digging sea worms and getting night crawlers. Sell them to Blink's General Store."

No, the Village wasn't an island. You did see their people out and about. If someone was walking toward town and they were in jeans and a flannel shirt, whether it was August or January, and it looked like they needed a bath, it was someone from the Village. They'd be in a store, three of the wives with one of the husbands watching over them, buying products they couldn't make at home or barter for, but always keeping to themselves. Never a "Is it cold enough for you?" or a "Hey, how are you doing?" They avoided eye contact except for Boomer, who would stare anyone down if they tried him. Mornings, you could see a group of men crammed into a green Plymouth Fury headed up to the Bates Textile Factory in Milltowne. They'd stop at Bartley's Store on the way home on Fridays and buy cigarettes, beer, and whisky. Some of the women did sewing for a shop in Brookeville. They traveled in a red Pinto. I couldn't recall seeing any twin girls.

"What would they do after getting ice cream?"

"Come home." She sat eerily still as she answered the questions.

"They go to school?"

"Of course."

"Any friends in town, maybe from school?"

"No more than we had, and you know how many that was."

"Are you sure? Times have changed."

"Not from what I've seen."

"How about boyfriends? Anyone in the picture?"

"They are nice girls, Nichols."

"I don't mean to imply otherwise."

"I don't care what you mean. I don't like the way I'm feeling when I think about them. Something ain't right."

"When did you first realize they were gone longer than expected?"

When the twins didn't come back Thursday, Jake had told her not to worry,

CHAPTER ONE

that they probably went straight to grabbing crawlers overnight. She said
they did that sometimes on weekends and would then come home late, well
after midnight. They still hadn't turned up Friday morning, and Jake had
left for the mill, so she went to Boomer, who said that he might have heard
about them going down to the flats for sea worms. On Saturday, she'd gone
back to Boomer, and he told her that the police had probably picked them
up for doing nothing but being who they were and told them to get the hell
out of town and not come back. He'd said that them being young girls, they
didn't know better than to just come home, but ran off scared. Her hands
pressed against her flat stomach as if trying to hold down nausea.

"I can assure you that we did not tell them to leave Laurel. It's my guess
that no one in this department was even aware they were downtown. As
you know, there's a few people around this time of year." She bit her bottom
lip, looking like she was about to burst. I motored down. It was my job to
help her, no matter how difficult she chose to make it.

"I hate to say this, Mrs. Connolly, but your twins are legitimately missing.
I'm going to file an official Missing Person's report for both of them."

"What's that going to do?"

"It will get their information out all over Maine and New England. Police
will keep an eye out for them, and if they get picked up, they'll notify us."

Rory's jaw opened wider, then she held her tongue between her teeth. She
said nothing.

"Do you have a picture of them, like one of those yearly school portraits?"
I said. "We can put it out on the wire, give police a visual to go by, rather
than just a description."

"I don't know that we have anything like that," she said, taking a deep
breath and shaking her head. I wouldn't have been surprised if she believed
that photographs took your soul, like the old Indians did.

"Anything would help," I said. "Maybe the school or the yearbook might
have something. I can check."

"If you really didn't make them leave here, what could have happened?"
Lines came out on the corner of her eyes and around her chin. Her voice
lost its ire.

"That's a tough question. Teenagers do some crazy things these days. We got kids hitchhiking all over this country, they take off, they come back. They take off again. Did your girls ever talk of going anywhere? Portland? Boston? Hollywood?"

"No. Their family's here. Why would they want to go unless you made them?"

"The Sixties may have ended fifteen years ago, but that free-spirit thing is alive with the youth, that's for sure."

"Do we look like hippies to you?"

"Of course not."

She didn't want to hear what I thought they looked like, and if I told her, she'd have gotten up and left. If that happened, her girls would likely stay missing. Neither of us wanted that. I would do what I could.

"Who do they talk to the most?" I said. "Do they have friends in the Village?"

"Sure. They have their cousins, plenty of them. But you can't talk to them. Maybe you could speak to their brother. He works at Ned's Service, fixing cars."

"That's Caleb?" I'd seen the guy—some sort of mechanical savant—but according to Ned Ferguson, the kid was as spooky as a rabid fox.

"Yes, that's him."

"And who would the cousins be?"

"I can tell you, but it won't do you any good."

"Why is that?"

"They won't say nothing to the police, for one thing. That's even if you could go down into the Village and ask them."

"What do you mean?" I straightened up.

"Boomer won't allow it."

"He's got nothing to say about it. This is a legal matter, and we have jurisdiction. If I need to go to the Village to question people, that's what I'm going to do."

"You come to the Village, Boomer's going to beat your ass. And if anyone is stupid enough to talk to you, the same thing will happen to them. You should know that."

Even if all her girls had seen of the world was Scoops, Blink's, and Timbercoast High, they had to know more of it than their mother, who thought the police picked up teenagers and ran them out of town for kicks. Holly and Maisie Connolly had likely seen the life waiting for them in that Village and said, "No way." They'd probably put their thumbs out and jumped into a summer kid's convertible. To them, a honky-tonk like Ogunquit would seem like Malibu Beach. Parents were often the last to know what their kids were thinking. I'd been lucky to get height, weight, and hair color. So I let it go.

"A mother's intuition is nothing to sneeze at, Mrs. Connolly. I'm going to start looking into this today. I'd like to begin by giving you a ride home and having you check on a picture. It also wouldn't hurt if you at least talked to some of their cousins and see if they'd speak to me. You'd be surprised at how willing people are to help."

"We both damn well know they won't say a word, and Boomer will go looking himself before he'd let anyone talk to you. He'll find them, too." She was glaring again, the way she had when she'd first walked into the station.

I leaned my elbow on the desk and covered my mouth. I didn't have the heart to point out that if she truly believed that, she wouldn't be sitting in front of me. She was thrashing about now, the way even a person who can swim does when they're unexpectedly thrown in the deep end. Over the years, I'd seen plenty of hurting people. She was as bad off as any of them.

"Maybe you had a hand in what happened, or maybe you didn't," she said. "But I don't want you having any part of it from here on out."

"I can't ignore what you've told me," I said.

"The likes of you have never done anything for us," she said, tugging on the sleeve of her shirt. "And you aren't about to start now."

I tried to count to ten, using what they taught me in the course. I made it to three.

"I'll do my best to find them. I mean that."

She rolled her eyes. "Can I go?"

"Sure. I'll be glad to give you a ride back to the Village. Maybe you could give a quick look for a picture?"

"You must not listen too well. I'll walk."

"It's hot."

"I'm no delicate flower."

"Fair enough," I said.

I breathed in and got out from behind the desk to open the door for her. I wanted to mention that if the twins had an ounce of brain in their thin heads, they'd already be halfway to Los Angeles, and if that were the case, she should be happy for them. I walked her out to the front desk, banged into one of the office chairs with my stomach, and opened the gate so that she could leave.

She paused at the door. "You been doing a lot of talking, Nichols. If you come out to the Village and you don't have my girls with you, you better be prepared for Boomer, because he's not going to have it."

"He doesn't concern me."

"He should, because you're just a little bit of a thing." She nodded and opened the door.

"I was a fucking state champion, you know," I said, loud enough that it echoed.

"Yes, you were," Estelle said, smiling widely. "Still the only one in the history of Timbercoast."

Rory Connolly kept walking.

Chapter Two

I returned to my desk, took out the newspaper, unfolded it, and threw it in the waste basket. The '86 Red Sox had an eight-game lead, and I couldn't even enjoy reading about it after getting Pearl Harbored by a crackpot from the Village. I didn't need to prove myself to anyone, but I did have a job to do. I swiveled left to my typewriter, pulled out the appropriate forms, and completed Missing Person's reports for each of the girls. Rory was right that Boomer would not welcome an incursion into the Village, even to help. If we rolled in and started interrogating the Woodmans, Sampsons, and Connollys, he'd be sure to answer. Boomer and his misfits would spill out all over town and upend business the only time of the year we had people here. They'd hit the bars and leer at anything that moved, hoping someone would challenge them. Stores trying to sell hundred-dollar lamps and three-hundred-dollar paintings would be cluttered with folks in need of deodorant, crowding tourists and touching everything they could get their hands on. That left me to learn as much as I could without lighting that spark.

Four years earlier in Ogunquit, an Admiral's daughter had gone missing, and the Defense Department had put every officer in the state on red alert, only to find that she'd eloped to Vegas with a waiter from Kittery. This case would not be so neat and easy with Woodman's Village involved. Laurel had one thousand year-round residents and our share of bar fights, car accidents, marital disputes, and an occasional breaking and entering. What we didn't have were missing teenage girls. While I'd never dealt with anything like this, that didn't mean I was lost. Common sense could go a long way.

I phoned the departments in Wellport, Milltowne, Brookeville, and Portland, as well as the State Police. None had anything on a set of twins or even a single girl meeting their description. That meant I'd need to get the photo that Rory wouldn't provide. I called Vince Marcucci, the principal at Timbercoast Regional. I got no answer there or at his home. I tried the superintendent's office and requested a yearbook, hoping that the girls had made it into at least one photo. They said to come on in. It was a start.

I radioed my sergeant, Cole Crowley, who was out on patrol, and gave him a description of the girls and let him know that they'd been missing since Thursday. Then I told him where they were from.

"Are you yanking me, LT?" he said.

"No, sir."

"Who wouldn't want to get the hell out of that shithole? They're long gone if they have half a brain, but you can't count on that, either."

"Just keep an eye out, okay Crowley?"

"Right-o. If I come across an identical pair of teenage hosebags, I'll do my best to haul them in without starting World War Three."

"Over and out," I said, clicking off. Crowley's attitude came from a few places. Many said it predated his belief that he'd been passed over for Chief because my father had been a twenty-year selectman in Laurel. Crowley just enjoyed being a dick. The next traffic warning he gave for a violation would be his first. If I or Nate Trout caught a lobsterman driving home a little weavy, we'd follow him and make sure he got there. Cole would have him out on the road shoulder standing on one foot trying to touch his nose, hoping he faltered. In this case, however, Crowley's approach might prove useful.

I gave the Missing Persons reports to Estelle to post in the station log and put out to other departments and the State Police. It figured that despite my scheduling shifts to avoid this kind of thing, with Trout in Boston for a Red Sox-Blue Jays series, my patrols for that evening would be Kevin Martin and Jeff Regan, two of my summer officers from the criminal justice program at New Hampshire Tech. While I'd briefed them on the Village when they'd trained at the beginning of June, going so far as to drive them by Woodman's

Lane, they'd need further instruction. I contacted each of them, and Joe Griffin, the third rookie, and told them that if they saw the girls, to pick them up and bring them in—and call me first thing. I wasn't worried about their ability to do that, but wanted them wary of encountering Boomer or one of his minions. While those of us who lived here knew what we were up against, these three were green. Things could go south in a hurry.

I rode patrol for much of the year, but in summer, I turned into an administrator. We integrated our three seasonal officers with our year-rounders and tried to keep things rolling until Labor Day. I'd usually put the kids on day shifts and would have them patrol the beaches and downtown, where they could write enough parking tickets to keep the town funds above sea level. Crowley and Trout would patrol nights. Experience allowed them to deescalate potential brawls at the Port Tavern and keep things quiet so the hotel and B and B guests could sleep. We employed a simple philosophy: Be reasonable and look out for our people. If there was a Mass or New York plate busting the speed limit, they were stopped. Locals got a little more rope. We put out unpermitted fires on the beaches at night, which kept the downstairs refrigerator stocked. We didn't bother bringing folks in for drinking in public unless they were making an ass out of themselves or disturbing others. If anyone smoked dope or did a line, or tried to move either drug, that was just stupid, and they were arrested. Laurel was a place where everyone mostly got along. My father had told me that this job would be more about peace-keeping and glad-handling than law enforcing, and he'd been right, God rest his soul.

I'd been on the force for eight years when Ray Dederian announced he was going to retire, and I took over. He was the one who had brought me on the force. My father might have put him up to it, but neither would admit to it. I'd dropped out of college and was working as a bartender. Dederian showed up one night and asked if I were going to sling drinks forever or if I had an interest in doing something with my life. I answered honestly. I told him I hadn't given it much thought.

He nodded as he considered what I'd said, then exhaled.

"Here's the thing," he said. "I need people who can earn the public's trust.

There's too many who see this job as a license to be a prick. People here already respect you, and we can build on that. You can handle yourself, but you don't strut around town like a goddamn rooster. That tells me it won't go to your head. You might even be able to help some folks. You think you could do that without turning into an asshole?"

"Probably."

"I'm going to have a position open when Canfield retires. We can start you up at the academy in Waterville, and then you take your spot by next summer. You want in?"

I didn't know what kind of beer I wanted to drink after work. I asked him if I could think about it. He said I'd be a fool not to.

I hadn't considered a possible career since I'd aged out of Little League. I had determined academics weren't for me, and while I liked bullshitting with people across the bar, I'd spent fifteen minutes one night sweating it out when someone ordered a kir, which I didn't know how to make or even spell to look it up in the Mr. Boston guide. I sat down with a Molson Ale that night and deliberated. When I looked back on my twenty years of living, I realized that I did best when I had a purpose. That's what Dederian was really offering me, so I signed on. It didn't take long to find it was a good fit, even if it wasn't playing shortstop for the Red Sox.

I liked to think that if I sat at my desk long enough, I could come up with the most logical actions that Holly and Maisie Connolly had taken. When I was a rookie, I'd been to the Village with Chief Dederian and seen its shacks, outhouses, and rusted husks of ancient pickups. If I knew anything, those girls wanted out. Maybe they dreamed of being actresses in Hollywood and were headed west, or their desires could have been more modest, and they'd landed in Boothbay for a long weekend with some college boys. I was almost certain they'd walked the mile to Route Nine, chose a direction, and dropped their thumbs. Unfortunately, there was always a chance they hadn't. That's what sent me to the pegboard for the keys to my cruiser.

Chapter Three

T he aroma of fresh-baked bread welcomed me as I opened the door to Blink's. I'd spent a lot of time in that store. Deacon Blinkedakis was my best friend growing up and our wrestling team's heavyweight. Though in season he was the only one of us who got to eat what had to be the best Greek rolls in New England, that didn't stop us from hanging out there. The two years I was married, my wife and I lived just around the corner and popped in on a regular basis. I'd visited less frequently after I moved back into the house I'd grown up in, but since I'd started up with Suzanne Anderson a few months ago, it had again become a favorite lunch spot.

Blink sat behind the counter on his stool and smiled widely, exposing the gap between his front teeth. When Blink was a smoker, he'd wedge a Camel in there to free up his hands while baking or dressing a deer. To my left, a middle-aged couple was ordering at Suzanne's sandwich counter. That didn't stop her from grinning when she saw me. She'd been Deac's high school girlfriend and after he left for the west coast, she'd stuck around and wound up running Blink's food service. The three twenty-foot aisles were empty. Blink carried just enough items and priced them just low enough to make one question the drive to the IGA in Milltowne. No one was surveying the beer and drink coolers that formed the back wall of the store.

"Well, if it ain't Little Tim Nichols, the baddest man this side of the Piscataqua," Blink said, patting the stomach that rolled into the denim overalls he wore every day. "Been at least forty-eight hours since you've graced this fine establishment."

"I can see that wit of yours is keeping the place packed," I said, walking past him to the reach-in for a Coke. Suzanne smiled again when my eyes found her, and I nearly clipped a potato chip display.

"You got a keen sense of observation, LT." LT stood for Little Timmy. The nickname emerged after I'd knocked Jim Boxford's front tooth out in fifth grade for calling me Tiny Tim. That act resulted in a reduction in name calling rather than an eradication. I'd been somewhat of a runt and had a bit of a temper about it. Once I found wrestling in sixth grade, however, I stopped caring.

I popped the top on my drink and flicked it into the wastebasket behind Blink.

"Help yourself, Chief," Blink said. "Must be awful hot out there fighting crime."

"Don't you know it? How's that son of yours doing, Blink?"

"Just called the other day. That outfit he's working for got a contract to build a string of cantinas, or whatever they call those Mexican restaurants. I ain't never had a burrito, but I guess they're big business out there."

"You know, when we're all freezing our asses off in the winter, you might think about visiting the poor kid. He could probably use some guidance."

"Then who'd butcher all the poached deer for Christmas dinners?" Blink laughed. "Did I just say that?" It was common knowledge that folks around here did some off-season hunting for the holidays. Technically, that was the Game Warden's problem. What I knew that I wasn't supposed to was that once the Drydock and Port Tavern closed on weekend nights, if you needed a case of beer and had Blink's number, you could pull around the back door, slip Blink the regular price plus ten bucks, and he'd throw a case in your trunk.

"You still peddling sea worms and night crawlers, Blink?"

"Why? You hungry?" Of course, this was said just as the couple was walking out with their sandwiches, raising their eyebrows as they passed. Suzanne laughed.

"Not quite that hungry."

"Don't tell me there's regulation on goddamn bait now," Blink said, coming off his stool. "The Fish and Game got you out looking for some sort of license?"

"No, it's not that. Do you still get them from those girls from Woodman's?"

"I do. They stock me up once a week, bring me a good supply."

"When's the last time you saw them?"

"They was here yesterday."

"The twins? Holly and Maisie Connolly?"

"They're not twins, LT. One's got to be at least twelve or thirteen, and the other's a half pint, maybe ten. Filthy little things, but they get their worms. Must be some special kind of soil out in those fields. Course, they do have the black hair and the nose, but there's about half a foot difference in height. Wouldn't doubt they're sisters."

"You ever see any twins from the Village?"

"My worm girls last year was a pair of them, spitting images of each other. But all those women look alike, as you know. They were older than the two I got now."

"Last year?" I said, louder than I should have. I'd been fed bullshit right from the get-go. Either Rory Connolly had no idea what her daughters were up to, or she'd been feeding me false information. I didn't know which was more likely. Yet.

"You been taking too much target practice and can't hear, LT?"

"Thin, black hair, dark eyes, the ski jump nose? Identical?"

"That's them, likely as anything."

"You recall their names?"

"Not too sure about that, but for Village folks, they were pretty talkative. I can't barely get a word out of the ones I got this summer."

"What did those girls have to say last year?"

"I can't remember nothing specific. They'd ask about business, try to get me to pay more if they'd slip in extras, a side deal between me and them. But I'd worked out the price with Boomer, so that wasn't happening. They were different though, than most of them from there. They'd look you in the eye, and when I wouldn't give 'em more money, they'd still try to get a Pepsi or candy out of me. If I offered a Snickers to my girls this year, my

17

guess is that they'd run out screaming."

"They ever say anything about going anywhere?" Not only were these sisters a possible mystery to their mother, they were also engaging and outgoing. Things were already starting to not make sense.

"Doubt I could remember if they did. I haven't seen them since last summer. Why, what'd they do?" His eyes focused as if he were actually interested.

"I'm just looking for them." I wasn't giving out any more information than I had to. People talked in this town, especially Blink. I didn't need anything getting back to Boomer or any other of those jackasses, should someone actually speak to them.

Blink nodded, went to say something, and then stopped. His eyebrows raised. "Why?"

"There any reason you think I might be?"

"You know me. I mind my own business." He started rocking on his stool. He knew everyone's business.

"You know Rory or Jake Connolly from the Village?"

"Nah, Boomer's the only one of them I know by name." He looked down, patted his thighs. Then he raised his head. "You dealing with those folks, you better watch yourself, LT."

"You deal with Boomer on a regular basis, and you look okay, Blink."

"I ain't had no trouble with him, but we ain't comparing notes about the country club." Blink stood up and came right up to the counter. "You investigating these girls for real?"

"It's my job, Blink."

"They must have done something dandy then. They were a bit lively, but I never took them for the criminal element."

"Did I say they did anything wrong?"

"I don't believe you did." Blink ran a hand under his chin and picked up a magazine to swat a fly. It could be that his interest came from their being outgoing and different than the usual Woodman's resident. One didn't need to be Sherlock Holmes to see how that might play into their disappearance.

"Do you remember how those girls got here last year? Walk or someone drive them?"

"Sometimes they'd be in the tan Malibu with the mechanic from Ned's, and sometimes they might've walked, I guess. You know if it ain't too serious, what they did, I'd just let it rest because I know this town ain't shelling out for combat pay."

"You ever go down to the Village, Blink?"

"Not a once, but we don't deliver, as you know."

"Lucky you."

"Is this crusade taking you there?" Blink said.

"Maybe." I felt like I was now being mined for information. If it weren't a habit of his, I'd have asked why he wanted to know.

"Back in the day, I never had to worry about you and Deac getting into anything that you couldn't handle." Blink shook his head. "You think you're as tough as you used to be?"

"Probably not, Blink," I said, "but in theory, I'm a hell of a lot smarter."

"I'd debate that last point," Suzanne said from across the room. Then her smile disappeared. "Those two you were asking about were a pair of skanks, like the rest of them down there." Suzanne had never liked Analisa, my ex, either. That made me think that she was a sharp judge of character. On the other hand, her ex-husband Derek was a real piece of work, and she'd chosen to take up with me after her divorce, which might be enough for anyone to question her intelligence. Regardless, she did offer to make me lunch. I was sorry to decline, but I had things to do.

Chapter Four

I parked at the Congregational Church outside downtown and walked
in past the Captain Farrell Inn and post office. The town square was
actually a trapezoid. Route Nine ran through it north and south, and
Nine was bisected by Old County. But across from where Old County
should have continued cleanly along the Abenaki River was the pharmacy
and a restaurant, Allie's. River Road ran in front of them and then hooked
to the river, leaving just enough space for a small park and bandstand. The
off-kilter layout required posting a traffic officer every Saturday and Sunday
all summer, possibly the worst job on earth to work with a hangover.

I paused at the end of Old County. As it was beach weather, there weren't
many tourists hitting the shops. A few camped out having breakfast on the
picnic tables on the Port Tavern's deck, but that was it. I strolled through
the square toward Scoops. I could have stopped to shoot the shit with Brian
McGrath at the pharmacy. He sponsored the youth wrestling team I coached
every winter. And I made it a point to bypass Rita and Karen French, the
sisters who ran Allie's, as I was determined to cut weight. Since my divorce,
they'd concluded I never ate enough unless I was in their restaurant. But
the sooner I got this investigation completed, the better. A problem with
the Village was like a B-movie ticking time bomb.

Scoops was around the corner on River Road. Freddy Greenwell, the
owner, had a similar place in Fort Lauderdale, and lived six months in
each spot. Greenwell looked like he had a body built by ice cream, and
he frequented the bars from Memorial to Labor Day. He'd buy me a beer
whenever he ran into me, but I assumed he considered it good business

more than a gesture of friendship because our conversations never lasted more than three sentences.

The ice cream shop was small. Stands painted like buoys with ropes running between them corralled and directed the customers to glass-fronted freezers. There were eight tables to the right. A mural of a smiling lobster holding cones in each claw covered the wall behind them. I didn't recognize the teenager working the counter, so assumed she was a summer person. Her calling me sir confirmed that. She went to the office to get Greenwell. When we sat down at one of the tables, and I asked him about two black-haired, thin, kind of poor-looking teenage girls, he rose to the edge of his seat.

"Oh yeah, I know who you mean," Greenwell said. "They come in on Tuesday and Thursday afternoons every week. That's when Jimmy Goodwin works, you know, Earl's kid, the quarterback. I think they're sweet on him."

"Do you see them this Thursday?"

"Nope, missed them."

"You weren't here?"

"No, they were here Tuesday but not Thursday. I make it a point to be here when they show up. Those two, they can put on quite a show."

"What do you mean?"

"They can lick an ice cream cone, let me tell you."

"Like they're starving?"

"No, Chief, like they could suck the chrome off a tailpipe."

"I'm not following." I gave him "the stare" in the hopes that he'd watch himself. He was well in his forties and describing girls barely old enough to drive.

"Jesus, I've seen you walking out of the Tavern with some talent. You know what I'm talking about."

"You're telling me they eat their ice cream, *sexually*?"

"Yeah, and they're good at it. The thing is, have you ever seen these girls?"

"Not exactly."

"I'm no creep. I mean, they're high school girls and all. But they come in those cut-offs, and for skinny little things, they got some nice tits and they

21

don't feel the need to restrain them, if you get my drift."

"Are you sure we're talking about the same girls? Ski-jump noses, dark eyes?"

"I've seen those eyes. The heart of darkness, Chief. They watch me watch them, and they like it. When you catch up with them, imagine them in the shower, cleaned up, makeup, miniskirts, halter tops. They'd be smoking. I think they like the challenge of being hot without trying." Greenwell shook his head and sat back in his chair.

I wanted to reach across the table and throttle him. He had no clue that the girls he was gushing over lived in something barely more than a tent city. They'd make it through high school if they were lucky and end up marrying a third cousin. Greenwell expected me to believe they got him off on purpose by deep-throating ice cream cones.

"You don't wear glasses, do you, Greenwell?"

"Good one, Chief." Greenwell lowered his voice. "Just what are they up to?"

"They're missing." I was sure that one person Greenwell would never speak to was Boomer.

"I wouldn't put anything past those two," he said, laughing.

I walked back to the car, shaking my head. I'd made two stops, and everything I'd learned conflicted with what Rory Connolly had told me, not to mention the nature of folks from Woodman's. Whether their mother was clueless or playing me remained to be seen. The girls may have come into town that Thursday and gone somewhere other than Scoops, freaked out by a middle-aged pervert drooling at them. If I had pictures, it would be easy enough to take them around and see if anyone had noticed them. Their brother did work at Ned's Service, so perhaps there was something in that, too. Maybe this generation of Connollys was different than their predecessors and assimilating into Laurel and the rest of the planet. As I climbed in the cruiser, I tried to determine how likely that was. Given steep odds, I still wouldn't have bet on it.

Chapter Five

I headed south through town on Nine toward Ned's Service, located in West Laurel. Once I passed the driving range on the top of the hill, there wasn't much to see, just oaks, maples, and pines, with a few houses scattered among them. I knew who lived in each one. The few people that had settled here, away from the coast, earned their living on the water. Maybe they were sick of looking at it. I came to an intersection where a spike on the left led to Bishop's Beach. I took the right, Brown Street, which shot inland. A half-mile later, I slowed at an S-turn, and as I came out of it, passed a dirt road. Woodman's Lane didn't have a sign. I stopped the car and stared down twenty yards of gravel encompassed in a tunnel of varying greens: hemlocks, poplars, and overgrown field grass. From the street, it looked like the road stopped and went nowhere. But that wasn't the case. It veered sharply to the right, then cut back on itself, hiding what lay behind it. If I didn't find those girls and quick, I might be forced to drag the Village out into the open. That wouldn't happen without casualties.

When we had learned about the history of Laurel in school, we read accounts of steadfast settlers, seafaring clans, and shipbuilding icons. But not a single word addressed the origin of Woodman's Village. Stories did pass through town, however. The old-timers at the VFW maintained that after the turn of the century, a Woodman started a family with his first cousin, who also happened to be a Woodman—though some claimed it was actually a sister. This resulted in the god-fearing denizens of the Cape Laurel Church running the entire clan of three households out of the town proper and upriver into the mosquito-infested marshland they now inhabited. An alternate tale had it that during prohibition, the Woodmans saw opportunity and moved there to produce corn liquor, as if in the woods of Kentucky. One would think, given the current habits of our townspeople, that this would have made them local heroes. Unfortunately, that was only the beginning. Eventually, being Woodmans, they were caught and then turned in their distributors to avoid the pen. This made more sense, as a dry town would have surely angered more citizens than unacceptable romantic practices. Both stories followed a simple pattern: Something bad happened, it got worse, and then it stayed that way. If the history of the Village was dubious at best, its results were well woven into the fabric of the town. Keeping the Village and its people at a distance was as much a part of Laurel as lobster buoys, fried clams, and getting sand in your shorts.

I hadn't forgotten my one trip there. My first year on the force, Boomer had a run-in with a doctor from Boston at Bartley's Store, the result of which was a trash can being projected through the windshield of the doctor's Triumph convertible. As one might deem reasonable, the physician had gone to the police station up the road and filed a complaint. Chief Dederian told him to forget it and claim it on his insurance. The doctor, who had recently purchased a cottage at Gray Gull Beach, insisted on justice. Deciding it would be best for everyone if this went away, Dederian brought Dr. Finley to the Village for an identification. He assumed that once Finley saw who and what he was dealing with, he'd find letting the matter drop a wise course of action. We went in two cars, with me and Trout following in the backup cruiser. Dederian had armed me with a shotgun and given me instructions not to get out of the car unless he specifically ordered me to do so.

Despite living in Laurel my entire life, I'd never talked to anyone besides Dederian who'd seen the Village. Word was you didn't go there unless you wanted to get skinned alive. As a boy, I'd always pictured it as log cabins with smoking chimneys like in the Daniel Boone television show. Older and wiser, as I drove in with Nate Trout, I envisioned a somewhat neglected 1950s motor court. We came out of the woods and into a field, and my grip on the shotgun tightened. The houses weren't anything more than shacks, and most looked less stable than the shed that housed our lawnmower. Some were sided in plywood, others had shingles. None seemed to possess a clean right angle. They were painted a variety of colors. The roofs were patch-worked corrugated iron or tar paper, and canvas was not in short supply. In the middle of the shacks, which were arranged in a hundred-yard oval, a fire pit smoldered. There wasn't a utility pole in sight.

Dederian's car pulled up in front of the biggest shack at the end of the oval, and Trout pulled up a little behind at an angle. Trout was forty then, a fifteen-year veteran who'd taken me under his wing. It didn't ease my nerves as he sat there repeating, "Shit, shit, shit, shit, shit." After a few minutes, Ramm Woodman, Boomer's father, came out with his son behind him. I worked the Remington's safety back and forth. As if on cue, men poured from every shack. I watched as they walked past us to join Ramm and Boomer. There must have been ten of them, all in green work pants and gray t-shirts. We'd been badly outnumbered.

Dederian got out of the car. Crowley stayed behind the wheel. Neither he nor Trout had turned the engines off. Dr. Finley was in the Chief's backseat with Frankie Kelly, our summer help.

"You're interrupting my supper, Dederian," Ramm said. He wasn't quite as big as his son and looked old, maybe sixty or so. His dark eyes took us all in. "I hope this is something of grave importance."

"Might be," Dederian said. Trout told me to sit still and got out to join Dederian.

"What brings you down here?"

I kept my eyes on Boomer, who was grinning and staring into Dederian's car at Dr. Finley.

"It seems that your boy, Boomer, got into it with one of our summer citizens and tossed a garbage can through this man's windshield yesterday."

"Boomer wouldn't do nothing like that without reason, would you, boy?" The boy was a man in his twenties who looked like he could have picked up a whole car and thrown it, never mind a trash barrel.

"Hell, no. I do recognize the fellow in the back seat, though. That's the guy with the real nice car who don't like nobody looking at it. Bought the old Noble place out on Gray Gull. Friendly enough, other than calling me a sheep fucker, which I don't believe is a nice thing to say."

Dederian shook his head. Dr. Finley had left that out of his account.

"Well, Ramm, I've got an eyewitness here in my car, and I've seen the windshield myself. You know I can't abide those kind of disturbances in town. It doesn't do anyone any good. I think we can agree on that."

"I do agree, Chief. But you heard what Boomer said, and he ain't a liar. We ain't inclined to take shit like that, and we may be less happy should you try taking him out of here, no matter what some tourist says."

"It don't matter, Pop," Boomer said, stepping forward. "I'm sure if I could stop by the fellow's place someday and talk to him, he'd see it was nothing but a misunderstanding."

Dederian put up his hand, halting Boomer's movement and the conversation. The stock of my shotgun was slick with sweat.

Dederian walked to Dr. Finley and made a hand motion so he'd roll down the window. They conferred briefly. Dederian nodded and then informed Ramm, Boomer, and their entourage that while a mistake had indeed been made, he would personally appreciate it if no more cars were assaulted for the duration of the summer. Ramm stated he didn't have a problem with that. Thirty seconds later, we were backing up. To say I was glad to get out of there would have been a colossal understatement.

Unless I turned up something on Holly and Maisie Connolly, I might be making that trip again. A vintage car windscreen could be replaced. Two girls could not.

Chapter Six

I popped out of the car at Ned's and patted my holster, something I used to do as a rookie. I could thank the goddamn Village for resurrecting that tic. There were two bays to the left and an office on the right. I went in through the office. Ned had the neatest mechanic's office on Earth. Ferguson's desk was free of dust and oil, with a pile of white slips in an 'in' box and a stack of yellows in one labeled 'out.' The cash register was clean and fit for a grocery store. I moved to the door that led into the bays and waited.

Ned pulled at the front left tire of a Ford Maverick in the area closest to the office. At the far spot, Caleb Connolly leaned into the engine of a Satellite. A transistor radio sitting on a workbench behind the two mechanics played the Rolling Stones. The tinny guitars bounced off the concrete blocks. Caleb hadn't picked his head up, but Ned noticed me and stopped working. Caleb finally looked and eyeballed us as we walked into the office.

After bullshitting about tourists and the percentage of them who had cars that broke down, I took one last glance at the doorway to make sure Connolly wasn't there and asked what Ned thought of the kid.

"Best mechanic I've ever had," Ferguson said, rubbing a greasy hand on his bearded chin. "You know he does the maintenance on your cruisers, and you folks never have a problem."

"Does he talk much?"

"Hardly. But he shows up on time, and he can fix just about anything. So I wouldn't care if he didn't speak at all."

That made him unlike his sisters but typical of the Village.

"Have you ever seen any of his family?"

"We ain't social, Chief."

"He ever talk about them?"

Ned shook his head. "What's going on?"

"He's got twin sisters, high school age. Did you know that?"

"I did. He's got parents, too."

"Well, the sisters are missing."

"First I've heard about it." Ned's large head came to an angle as he scratched his ear. "Boomer came to you with a problem from the Village?"

"I didn't say that."

"Then how do you know?"

"It's my business." I could see the confusion on Ned's face, but didn't feel a need to explain. "You mind if I talk to him? See if he knows anything that might be helpful?"

"Fine by me, long as you don't tie him up all day."

I had asked to be respectful. But if I needed to question Caleb Connolly for eight hours, that's what I'd do. The well-being of my town took priority over some tourist's failing muffler.

Ned went into the garage and came back with Caleb loping behind him. He looked to be six feet, but was thin with a concave posture—his body seemingly bending backwards behind his head and boots. You could count the individual hairs on his moustache.

"Caleb, this is Chief Nichols. He wants to ask you a few questions about your sisters." Caleb glanced at me, then lowered his eyes and looked to Ned, who nodded that it was okay.

I motioned for Caleb to sit down in one of the plastic waiting room chairs, and I moved Ned's papers and sat myself on the corner of the desk, folding my arms across my chest. Ferguson leaned in the doorway.

"If you don't mind, Ned, I'd prefer to talk to him alone."

"Okay. You're the boss. Caleb, if you get confused or need me to explain anything, you just yell, okay?" Caleb nodded, his lips tight.

"How're you doing today?"

He shrugged for an answer. I knew that if I went straight at him, he'd

28

stonewall. I figured I'd start by lobbing him some softballs. I got him to confirm that he was nineteen, and that Rory and Jake Connolly were his parents, and Holly and Maisie were his sisters.

"When's the last time you saw your sisters?"

He shrugged and pulled a Marlboro pack from his shirt pocket, tapped one loose, and fired it up. "I don't know," he said.

He seemed more confused by the question than adamant about not answering, so I retreated to more background. I got him to admit that he'd finished high school two years earlier, hadn't liked it much other than auto shop, and that Mr. Graham, the shop teacher, had recommended him to Ned, who had taken him on.

"Your sisters. Have you seen them this week?"

He shrugged again. He wouldn't look me in the eye, but that wasn't unusual for someone from Woodman's.

"Do you all live in the same place in the Village?"

He nodded.

"That's a yes?"

"Yeah."

"I've got a report that they're missing. So, it's important that we find out the last time anyone's seen them. It matters when the last time you saw them was. Do you understand that?"

"How do you know they're missing? Maybe they're just at work."

"Where do they work?"

"They was digging worms."

"Who do they sell them to?"

"Blink's Store." That was true at one time, if no longer. It was yet to be determined whether he and his mother didn't know what the girls were doing or were putting me off on purpose.

"I thought that was last year," I said.

"I don't know everything them two do." He threw up his hands as if exhausted by the questioning.

"Not many folks from your Village are like your sisters. I heard they like to talk."

"I don't know nothing about that."

"I haven't seen you around much, but they're downtown quite a bit. Why is that?"

"I don't know."

"You ever bring them there or to Blink's?"

"Sometimes."

"Do you know what they like to do in town?"

"I don't pay attention to kids."

"So you never go with them?"

"I'm a man. Why would I be running around with them girls?"

"What you're telling me is that even though you live with them and they're your sisters, you really don't know anything about them. Is that right?"

"That about sums it up."

If I was certain that he was jerking me around and not just thick, I might've tried a more forceful approach. It wouldn't have bothered me to put him up against the wall.

"When you brought them to town, where did you drop them off? Or would you wait for them?"

"Left them at the bridge." He rubbed out his cigarette in the clean ashtray on the desk.

"You don't like ice cream?"

"Not like those two."

I tried not to grin. At least I'd confirmed that.

"When was the last time you saw them?"

"I don't know. Last week, I guess, now that you mention it."

"What day?"

He shrugged. His shoulders were going to be worn out if he kept this up. I took a different tack.

"What kind of things do they like to do?"

"I told you I don't know. They're dumb girls. They do what they want. I don't hear none of their shit."

"Were they popular at school?"

He rolled his gray eyes, and ran a hand through his stringy blond hair.

"How many times do I have to tell you we ain't hanging out together?"

"Any boyfriends?"

"Them two? That's a good one."

"Why?"

"They got bad attitudes. Think they're something special."

"What do you mean by that?"

"They liked to make fun of things. Always bitching."

"Did they make fun of you?"

"Not if they wanted a ride." He lit up another cigarette.

"What did they complain about?"

"You name it."

"Can you give me a specific example?"

"Nope." He shook his head as if he couldn't think of one. I was tempted to put him through the wall.

"Do you have any idea where Holly and Maisie would go if they wanted to get away from here, even for a little while?"

"Nope."

"Are you aware that no one's seen them since Thursday?"

"I didn't have nothing to do with that."

"I didn't say that you did. Is there a reason they might take off for a few days?"

Caleb sighed. His right foot began tapping, and he clasped his hands together in his lap. "I don't know anything about what they might be up to."

"If you don't, who does?"

"Ask them."

"You see the problem with that, right?"

"It ain't my problem."

I still couldn't decide if Caleb was nervous, stupid, or intentionally dodging the questions. If he knew anything, he wasn't telling me now. I let him go back to work. Ned came through the door.

"He didn't have much to say, I take it," Ned said.

"That's a pretty good assessment."

"Well, he barely talks to me, and I spend fifty hours a week with him."

31

"Have you noticed anything different about him this past week?"

"Can't say that I have."

I thanked Ned for his help. This had likely been a preview of me questioning anyone from the Village, whether they cared about the girls or not. Rory had nailed that part of it: If someone knew something, I'd be the last person they'd talk to. They'd be even less inclined to do so on their home turf and amongst their people, which is about the only place I'd be able to find them. To make matters worse, the information I'd received from their mother didn't match up with what I'd heard from Greenwell and Blink, and their brother tried to come off as knowing less than anyone. I'd known from the start that this was going to be messy, but could have spent the last four hours banging my head against the wall and felt better about things.

I drove back to the station, not bothering to slow down as I passed Woodman's Lane. I took the left on Route Nine and, as I headed back into town, passed John Trent's house. If the girls had walked to Scoops, they would have passed by here. As usual, the old man was sitting in the shade of his garage in a lawn chair. An empty chair sat next to him. It was his wife's, who had passed away that winter. Even Crowley had mentioned how tough it was to drive by and see it. Since Trent had retired from lobstering five years ago, that's where you'd find them just about every afternoon. He'd spent nearly his entire life with one woman. I had a marriage that hadn't lasted twenty-four months, and while Suzanne and I made eyes at each other like kids, it was hard to say where that was headed. I slowed and pulled in the driveway. Trent was standing by the time I made it over to him. The blue polo shirt he wore didn't match any of the colors on his plaid shorts. I had a tough time turning down his offer of a cold one. When he asked me to sit down, I didn't feel right taking Tricia's chair, so remained standing in the shade of the overhang.

"You aren't going to sit on the ghost's lap, LT. You might as well have a seat."

I sat and asked Trent how he was getting on. Typical for someone who had fished into his seventies, Trent wouldn't say that anything was too bad that he couldn't stand it. As my willpower to stave off a beer was diminishing, I got to the point.

"You're still out here every day, Trent?"

"Sure am."

"Do you see many people walking by?"

"This ain't exactly Fifth Avenue. Now that long-haired kid who runs for the college goes by, but he's not walking."

"How about two girls, look like twins. You ever see them?"

"As a matter of fact, I do. Not the most done up women in world, but I'd guess they're coming from Woodman's. I do see them every now and then."

"Do you remember what days?"

"Ha. Now that I ain't working, I can't tell one from another."

"They say hi to you or anything."

"I wave, they wave back. That's about it."

"Do you remember seeing them last week?"

"I do, because they got picked up right over there in front of the tree." He pointed to a big maple at the north corner of his lawn.

"By a car?"

"Yes, sir. They were just about out of sight when this big old car stops in the middle of the road right next to them, not even with the sense to pull over. The girls got all excited, waving their arms around and such, but they must have worked it out, because they hopped in, and then the car did a U-ee and went back the other way."

"What kind of car did you say it was?"

"I'm not sure other than it was something big, maybe an old Impala or a Lincoln. It was a dark color, too, like purple or black. I've never owned anything but a truck myself."

"Did you see the plate, Maine, or somewhere else?"

"I don't recall, but if I had to guess, I would say Maine, because if it was out of state, I might have noticed."

Trent couldn't remember anything else, but at least I'd confirmed they hadn't made it to town and that there was someone else involved. It was progress and I wanted to keep it moving. Instead of heading back to the station where I had my usual stack of paperwork waiting, I drove to the regional Superintendent's office in Brookeville.

The photograph I found in the "Candid" section of the yearbook showed two girls with black hair and ski jump noses sitting beside each other in the cafeteria. They were in the background of what I guessed was a more popular kid—maybe that quarterback—who had chosen a spot in front of their table to do a Hercules pose, flexing his biceps. One of the girls stared straight at the camera as if annoyed, while the other appeared to be gazing at the boy and smiling. Although it wasn't captioned, there was no doubt it was the Connolly twins. I commandeered the office's photocopier for a good half hour, copying the picture at first, then using scissors to cut out the athlete, and then adjusting sizes so that I ended up with several copies of a slightly grainy and oddly shaped picture of the twins. It would certainly be enough for people to identify them, and I did leave a request with the secretary to see if I could get the negative and have a professional take a run at it. The look of the one enjoying herself made me think it might be worth tracking down the boy and maybe some other kids from Timbercoast. I had a feeling that Holly and Maisie Connolly were better integrated into the community than their mother had been—or that anyone in the Village realized, another factor in the disappearance that could not be missed.

Back at the station, I called Rick Pettibone, the State Police detective for our county. He was never short of advice and always willing to provide direction. At times he was even helpful, and helpful might be needed. While Estelle had sent the information out, I wanted to be sure that he'd seen it in case this did turn out to be a kidnapping or abduction rather than two girls on a road trip. After listing off a series of steps that I could take, most of which I'd already done or planned to do, Pettibone let me know that giving the girls a five-day head start would make things difficult. "Gee, Rick, I hadn't realized that," I wanted to scream. He did, however, share my opinion that it was hard to rule out that the girls had just gone off the reservation to get out of Woodman's. Then I called the DMV and asked for a search of all dark-colored Lincolns, Impalas, Caddys, and the like in the area.

I made some flyers with the girls' pictures and information on our Xerox machine and had Estelle send it out to the State Police and departments in southern Maine. It was just the basics—names, age, missing since date, last seen getting into a dark-colored sedan, and if seen or recognized, call this number. Half the time we went asking questions, the person we needed wasn't there. However, we could always get lucky with a random citizen if we made information available. I grabbed the staple gun and made a circuit around town, posting the flyer outside stores and restaurants and at the toll booths on the turnpike and the bus station in Milltowne. No one I questioned at either transportation hub had seen them. That surprised me. I wondered if there were anything else I could have done.

It was a poor time for Trout to be in Boston. Though Crowley was a career man and second-in-command, it was Trout who I leaned on when I had something to think through. To the flat-topped and mirror-sunglass-ed Crowley, everything was black and white. Trout, on the other hand, could work angles around a problem. Our best strategic discussions were reserved for evenings on my front porch, where he and I would sit down, have a beer, and kick something around until I could make sense of it. With him gone for another day, that left Crowley as my sounding board. I met up with him at Gray Gull Beach on my way back to town. Even if Crowley could be obstinate, he'd been dealing with Woodman's before I had become a cop. He thought everything I'd done so far was sound, which was unusually agreeable for him. While he didn't have anything pop into his head, something about the car scratched an itch, though he couldn't say what that was.

I did have other things to get done. Back at the office, I reviewed our logs for the last week to see if anything came up that could be connected to the girls. There was nothing but the usual traffic stops, bonfires on the beach, a near-fight at the Port Tavern, a dispute over a parking spot between lobstermen at the pier, a few cars taking wrong turns onto private property, and a house party that had gotten too loud. That was a standard week-long crime wave in Laurel.

I spent the remainder of the afternoon determining assignments for the holiday weekend and writing up a timeline for the Fourth of July parade in two days. What had started in the 1950s as an excuse to show off the high school band was now a full-fledged event backed by the support of the Chamber of Commerce. It started south of the bridge and then crossed over into downtown, and proceeded down River Road to the Bluff Hotel. When Martin and Regan came in for their night shift, I briefed them on the Connolly case, and what they should do if they came across Boomer, Jake Connolly, or another stray from Woodman's. If they were up to anything more than buying cigarettes or beer, they needed to call or radio immediately. They didn't seem to be too worried, a benefit of being young and inexperienced.

Chapter Seven

I made it home at six-thirty, and all I wanted to do was pop a beer and flop onto the couch. That hadn't been allowed when I'd had an over-achiever for a wife, but since then, the pendulum had been wedged in the other direction. I climbed the stairs to the bedroom and pulled running shorts from the drawer. The blue and white pair of Air Pegasus in the closet looked new. My last effort to get in shape hadn't made it a week. I took off my uniform and threw it on the bed. Usually, I laid out my badge, belt, and holster carefully, so that in the morning, I could get ready in an orderly manner. Any hesitation now, and I'd never make it out the door.

Four telephone poles down the road, I had to cut back the pace, and I wasn't burning it up, to begin with. Only pride kept me from retreating to a walk. My house was a mile from the water on Magnolia Avenue, a dirt road on the backside of Gray Gull Beach. It led to Shore Road, which took me to the beach, and then I'd run the hard sand to Front Street, the main access road, which also led back to Mags. That would be three miles. But I wasn't going to make it. I hopped onto an old deer trail that triangulated the loop and cut it down to two miles. Twenty years earlier, I could hammer the three in the time it was going to take me to do two today. To make matters worse, hitting the trail left me the prime target of horse flies, and my feet clipped every rock and root. I came in at a crawl.

I dragged the welcome mat onto the middle of my small front porch. I made twenty-five sit-ups, my stomach restricting the movement designed to save it. The pushups were worse. I'd been able to do two hundred in two minutes as a senior in high school, but now could barely make one for every

37

year of my life. It did feel better when I stopped.

The Red Sox game wasn't on television, and my refrigerator was empty except for some scattered Budweisers and half a loaf of bread. At least it wasn't filled with Analisa's kale, bran, wheat germ, and yogurt. If I'd been paying attention, I could've grabbed a sandwich at Blink's that morning. But working as hard as I had seemed to justify dinner at the Port Tavern. I didn't have to make a night of it. If I stayed home, I'd polish off all the beer and choke down a few peanut butter sandwiches. I'd actually be coming out ahead by going to town.

The Tavern wasn't bad for a Tuesday night the week of the Fourth. I could've gone upstairs and had a table on the deck, but this time of year, I tried to stay under the radar. While the folks from town respected me, I didn't want the summer people getting the impression that I was a rummy. It was another of those conundrums that went with the job. When there were enough people here that there was fun to be had, it wasn't in my interest to have any. So I slipped into the small, dark downstairs bar that didn't have a view of anything except for bartender Wesley Rogers' wide forehead and a blurry television perched in the corner. The first beer of the night tasted better than usual after all I'd done to earn it.

I'd speared my last piece of baked haddock—I did know how to eat properly—when I felt someone behind me. I turned slowly, hoping it was a tourist with poor spatial skills in search of a rum punch rather than an aggrieved stray from Woodman's Village.

Suzanne, drink in hand, waited, biting her lip.

"Hey, Suzy," I said, relieved, though she was smiling like she'd caught me doing something stupid.

"Didn't think to invite me to dinner?" she said, as if asking how my meal had been. She was right. I hadn't. I was slow to relearn the girlfriend experience.

"I'm here only because I forgot my refrigerator was empty. If this was a planned event, I surely would have asked you this morning."

"You could have, if you weren't in such a rush to get out of there." Her cheeks rose in a sarcastic smile.

"Jesus, Suzy, I was on official business."

She rolled her eyes. "You had plenty of bullshit for Blink."

"You can't get out of there without that happening."

"Lame." She drained the bottom third of her drink in one pull.

"You didn't call me," I said, "and yet, here you are."

"Robin invited me out. I've been drinking all afternoon."

"I can see that. Do you need a lift home?"

"I don't need a fucking ride, LT."

"Okay."

"I have a question for you," she said, sitting down on the stool next to me, which had just been vacated. I waved Wesley over and held up my empty Bud and nodded to Suzy's hurricane glass. Her green eyes had a glimmer to them.

"Well?" she said.

"Well, what? You were asking me." She had a fine buzz going.

"Okay, let me spell it out for you. What are we?"

I would have preferred she poured her drink over my head rather than ask that question. After two months of dating and an obvious mutual attraction, we were more like handsy drinking buddies than anything else. There were reasons for this, of course, which I thought we'd been gladly skirting. The way she was looking at me, she was expecting an answer.

"Friends who are getting friendlier and taking it slow?" I said.

"Too slow." She cocked her head to one side and sipped her Planters Punch. "Don't you think?"

"You might have a point," I said. We had yet to sleep together, which was either hard or easy to explain. Hard because she was sexy as hell, and we may have been the only year-round single people in Laurel our age who still possessed all our teeth. Easy because I hadn't dated anyone in years and had clearly lost my fastball. She'd only been divorced since March, and neither of our exes had done much for us other than to leave us with a truckload of baggage.

"Why do you think that is?" she said.

"I'm not sure." I was positive, however, I'd botch any attempt to put it into words.

"I'll tell you: It's because we're pussies." She smiled and slapped her drink down on the bar.

"You have been drinking all afternoon, haven't you?"

"Look, your ex was a monumental bitch who thought she was too good for you and this town. Derek is a massive piece of shit, who I apparently deserved because it took me ten years to figure that out."

"So they've screwed us up?"

"That's what I'm saying."

"And being red-blooded Americans, we should just let it go and do what we should've been doing from the first night at the Dry Dock when we made out like a couple of teenagers in the Bronco?"

"Exactly," she said, leaning into me and planting a kiss, swirling tongues and all. My hand on the small of her back sent a heat wave up my spine.

We came apart and smiled at each other. "Now buy me a nightcap," she said, "and then let's get the hell out of here."

We left her car, and she climbed in the Bronco with me, sliding over into the middle of the seat. Her hair smelled of henna. We had the windows open, and the unbuttoned top of her shirt gave me a glimpse of cleavage I'd first noticed in eighth grade. Weak people couldn't help themselves, I used to tell myself during wrestling season, but this was exactly what I should be noticing. I goosed the gas pedal. She grinned.

"No one would believe this day," I said. "It started with Woodman's Village and it's ending with this."

"And you didn't even have to buy me dinner," she said, leaning over and running her tongue up my neck. I tried to keep the Bronco on the road.

I'd chosen to make my life in this town. Maybe things weren't less complicated anywhere else. I looked over at Suzanne. She gazed out the window, hair flowing in the breeze. I'd ridden around with her plenty in high school, usually in Deac's Mustang. My view had been from the back seat, sometimes with a date of my own, but mostly as the third wheel. She'd had long hair then, down her back. Now it was feathered and rested on her shoulders. Where once she'd been tight and angular, she was now soft and curvy, but not in the horse-out-of-the-barn way I'd crashed myself. She patted my thigh as we pulled into the driveway. It was a miracle that I saw the black truck backed up to my garage.

I yanked the wheel and skidded to a sideways stop. I put the Bronco in reverse and swung its tail onto the lawn. The headlights swept over Boomer Woodman seated on the pickup's hood. My ninety-minute respite from thinking about the Connolly girls was over. I reached across Suzanne and grabbed my .38 out of the glove compartment. I slid it into my belt and covered it with my shirt.

"Who the fuck is that?" Suzanne asked.

"Stay here, Suzy. Leave it running, and if anything happens, and I mean anything, put it in gear and get the fuck out, and don't stop until you get to the station."

"Okay," she said, her voice cracking.

I stepped out and walked around so that I faced Boomer. He slid off the truck and dropped an embering Marlboro to the driveway. We were ten yards apart. He leaned forward, a defensive tackle gone to pot. His shoulders were wide, and his frame pushed his plus-sized black t-shirt to its limit. The jeans he wore would have gone up to my chest. There was enough moonlight to make out the wide, flat nose, the male quirk of Village inbreeding. Five o'clock shadow darkened his face, and the whites of his eyes glowed yellow.

"You're going to ruin your grass, parking on it, Little Man." The voice was deep.

"What the fuck are you doing here, Boomer?"

"I ain't here to break up your action with that blond strap monkey, if that's what you're worried about."

"You have something to say, spill it and get the hell out."

"You know why I'm here." Boomer Woodman came out of the garage's shadow, lumbering two steps toward me.

With one day of physical training under my belt, I was barely confident in my ability to subdue a frat boy at the Tavern, and a psychotic veteran twice my size stood in front of me. If this turned into anything more than talk, I was screwed. My only hope would be to get him to the ground where I could

41

put him in a hold and break an arm or snap an ankle. But grappling with a gun in my pants wouldn't be smart, either. It would be just as available to him as it was to me. If he came at me, I'd have to use it. I rested a palm on the butt of the pistol.

"You always carry around your own house? You got some chipmunks you're scared of?"

"On second thought, I don't give a rat's ass what you have to say. Get in your truck and go."

"Where do you get off ordering me around?"

"You're trespassing, for one thing."

"That's what happens when you poke your nose in business where it don't belong."

Of course, Boomer knew something was up. There was no way his nephew hadn't run straight home from Ned's and told him what had happened. It had only been a matter of time before Boomer and I faced off. I just hadn't expected it would be that night in my own damn driveway.

"You've got two girls missing from your tribe, and it's my job to find them. A concerned citizen like yourself should be grateful."

"You let me worry about my people. That's how things work around here. That's how it's always worked."

"This isn't poaching deer or digging clams on closed flats. Lives could be at stake."

"Our lives, and none of your fucking business." A meaty finger pointed at my face.

"Those girls have been gone almost a week, and you don't know where they are."

"Says you."

"Bring them in so I can verify they're okay, and I'll drop it."

Boomer glared, grinding a massive fist into his other paw.

"I'm going to do you a big ass favor right now and tell you that those girls done left. You can forget about them."

"Yeah, where'd they go, and how do you know that?"

"You don't worry about that. You just listen real good."

Though he had obviously thought that she'd never do anything about it, the question was, 'Why did you tell your sister that we ran them off?' Asking it now would only result in a beating for Rory. Boomer was not one of those sensitive, understanding modern men.

"Why don't you stop by the station tomorrow?" I said. "I'll take an official statement. Then after we track down them down, the investigation goes away."

"You fucking know that ain't happening. We handle our own business. You crossed the line today. If you don't get back to your own side, you're not going to like what happens. Not one bit. You get me?"

"You want me to back off, bring the girls to the station."

"You're not hearing me, Little Timmy. I'll turn your precious town into a pile of rubble. Is that what you want?"

"Time to go, Eugene."

Boomer's real name straightened him up.

"You let me take care of my bitches, I'll let you take care of yours." Boomer nodded over my shoulder at Suzanne, who had to be wishing she'd made some different choices, at least for tonight. "Maybe she'd like to be with a real man after I'm done with you."

I couldn't threaten him anymore without pulling the gun, and if I did pull it, I'd have to use it. I could shoot the trespassing bastard, and it might make finding the girls that much easier.

"Go back to your shack, Eugene, and try to get your people right. If you want to be smart, you'll bring these girls in or let me know where they are so I can verify they're okay."

"I got no idea how you come to put your nose into our business, but if you want it to stay on your face, you better forget you ever heard about them."

"This department will be investigating until we find them."

"You couldn't find your own pecker under that gut," he said, laughing. "So you stay out of our business, and that slut in the truck might get to help you with the looking. Have we got an understanding?"

I stared him down as he turned and walked back to his truck. He climbed into the cab, started it, pulled ahead slowly, then spun his wheels on the gravel without looking back.

My legs were shaking as I wiped the sweat off my forehead. The pre-match tingling and tightness I used to feel before competition were redlined. I needed to call Martin, the rookie on night patrol, and warn him. The murmur of my idling Bronco brought me back. Suzanne's hands gripped the wheel. I went over to the driver's side and opened the door.

"Was that Boomer Woodman?" she asked.

"Sure was."

"What the hell is going on? I nearly had a heart attack."

"He's not too happy about me looking for those girls."

"Jesus, LT, are they worth it?"

"They better be." My eyes shot up the road to where Boomer's tail lights had disappeared. If I backed off now, I might as well hand him the keys to the town.

She slid over so I could get back in. We didn't have to say it. The moment had passed. I could only hope there'd be another. I drove Suzanne home, the radio playing, my mind trying to settle on why Boomer had the balls to show in my driveway. It could have been general principle like he said, but my mind kept tracking in another direction—there was something he didn't want me to find.

Chapter Eight

I woke with a start, at the point in a dream where you're falling and about to crash, only I couldn't remember any dream. A gray light filled the room, the sun having yet to rise. A layer of dried sweat covered my skin. My alarm was still an hour from going off, but my temples were pounding, and I wasn't going back to sleep. I rolled over, landing my feet noiselessly on the floor. I crept to the front window. There was no mammoth black truck in the driveway. A squirrel sat on its hind legs under the big oak. Birds chirped. Boomer had more to do with my pulsing temples than the beer I'd drank. He'd nearly pushed me to pulling my gun, something I'd yet to do as a police officer. That wouldn't have ended well. Was he calculating or psychotic? I was sure I'd be finding out.

I needed to clear my head. After choking down four aspirin, I grabbed my running shorts out of the laundry pile. I guzzled two glasses of water and, with no intention of anything more than survival, started jogging up the driveway. I was even slower than the day before. I made it halfway to the beach before I puked up the pills and a brackish trail of stomach acid. By the time I finished the two-mile circuit, my shirt was drenched with toxins, and my hair soaked as if I'd gone swimming. I felt better.

I stepped into my office at seven-thirty, a half-hour early. A stack of reports covered my desk, the topmost being a log entry from the previous night's patrol. The town had been quiet. That was a relief. I'd had Martin and Regan get Suzy's car from the tavern and drive it home for her, then had them patrol extensively on Langford Road to keep an eye on her house. I wasn't taking anything for granted with Boomer. Honor among thieves was more of a myth than Bigfoot.

The DMV report had come in, and I found it at the bottom of the pile. There were close to ten pages of full-size cars listed from Laurel, Wellport, Brookeville, and Milltowne. If things ran true to form, the car that Holly and Maisie Connolly were seen getting into was on that list. Though I couldn't count on that with the Village involved, it was worth checking. I'd scan it, then cross-reference for men who were known to be a little off, established criminals in the county, and considering what I'd learned about the girls, students from Timbercoast. It was going to be another long day. As I started to work through it, Estelle put through a call from Henry Glennon, a fund manager from Boston who had a vacation home up here. A bi-weekly call from Henry was a staple of summer law enforcement.

Five years earlier, the Glennons bought one of our historic buildings on the north side of town, the old Kent place. They'd doubled the size of the house, which sat on a ridge surrounded by two hundred acres of field and woodland. One of its features was a half-mile long driveway that people often mistook for Oak Ridge Road, just fifty yards past their entrance and also dirt and deserted-looking. Henry and Kate frequented Laurel's restaurants, usually with a horde of friends not from here, but otherwise kept to themselves. They weren't a problem, except that Henry Glennon did not like people coming up his driveway, even if by accident and meaning no harm. Maybe he had some Picasso's or priceless art back there that concerned him. I continued to page through the DMV report and punched up the line.

"Chief Nichols here. How are you, Henry?"

"Fine, Chief. Other than I'm getting tired of these people coming up my road every other day."

"I understand that you had someone enter the driveway around eight last night?" I had scanned Griffin's log on my way to the DMV report.

"It was right when we were sitting down for dinner. They almost reached the house before they figured they weren't on a public street."

"From what I understand, our cruiser was there by eight-fifteen, and the offender was gone."

"This has been happening at least twice a week since Memorial Day. And at all hours. I know you think we make somewhat of an issue of this, but it's quite unsettling."

"As I've mentioned, Henry, you could put up a gate. We've got some real craftsmen in town who could come up with something nice for you."

"The reason we're up here is because we shouldn't need a gate."

"A 'private way' sign might help, as well."

"That would only reduce the authenticity of the rustic setting, wouldn't it, Chief Nichols?"

"I wouldn't argue that, Henry, but it might keep people out of there."

"Well, something needs to be done."

It was the same conversation we always had. I was about to mention that I'd increase the patrol of the Old Milltowne Road when something jumped off page nine of the DMV report: 1974 Ford Galaxie 500XL, purple, registered to Caleb Connolly, Woodman's Lane, Laurel, Maine, in December of 1985. I hung up on Glennon and radioed Crowley to come here instead of going out on beach patrol. The tourists could park at will. We would ride out to Ned's garage, only this time, I'd be hauling in that junkie-looking bastard and getting some answers. The girls last being seen getting into his car made him at least a material witness and, considering the way he'd evaded answering my questions, a suspect. It hadn't taken long, but I'd already had enough of this Woodman's bullshit. Crowley and I drove out together. He turned red when I told him that Boomer had visited me. "Too bad he didn't rush you so you could have popped him," he said. Of course, Crowley would have advised that if Woodman had shown up with Girl Scout Cookies. There was no telling how he'd react when we brought his nephew to the station. We pulled into Ned's Service at nine-fifteen. No purple Galaxie sat in the line of cars arranged neatly in the yard.

I walked into the office and had Crowley swing around by the far bay in case Caleb had ideas of avoiding us. A white Ford pickup was raised on the far lift, but no mechanic attended it. Ned Ferguson's black boots poked out from under a Camaro. The wheels of his rack squeaked when he heard his name called. When he came clear, he looked up and sighed.

"Get a move on, Ferguson," Crowley said. "We don't have all day."

"You're looking for the kid?" Ned said, walking to the workbench, where he picked up a rag and began wiping his hands.

"That's right," I said. "Where is he?"

"Don't know."

"Why not?" Crowley said.

"Don't start on me, Crowley. That kid hasn't been late once in two years. LT stops by yesterday, grills him, and today he's a no-show. I'm screwed. I got five cars to get out of here, and I got two hands instead of four."

"That's a tragedy," Crowley said. "Maybe you should've hired a real person instead of a backwoods deviant."

Ned looked like he wanted to tell Crowley to shut up, then thought better of it.

"So, do you have any idea where he might be?" I asked.

"I told you yesterday, we don't talk."

"Ferguson, just answer the question," Crowley said.

"He hasn't been acting strange at all this past week?" I asked. I shot Crowley a look to get him to stop with the bad cop routine.

"He's been a good employee. But he's Woodman. Both oars ain't always in their water."

"In that case," I said, "has he been stranger than usual?"

"It's a simple fucking question," Crowley said.

"He's a skittish kid, and I told you he doesn't say much. Comes in and does his job. Leaves. Shows up the next day."

"So he had nothing to say after I left yesterday?"

"Not much."

"Not much isn't nothing. What did he say?"

"He said that you people like to bust their balls just because they're from Woodman's. That you're all assholes and that no one from this town likes him. That he can't even live his goddamn life without someone up his ass."

"What a load of shit," Crowley said. "I never hassled that kid, ever."

"I'm just telling you what he told me, like you asked."

"So if we aren't up his ass, who is?" I said.

"Why are you asking me? I told you he barely speaks. That was the most he's talked about anything that wasn't a carburetor, brake pad, or transmission since he's been here."

"Does he ever have friends come by?"

"Not really."

"What the fuck does that mean?" I said, my voice rising. Over the last twenty-four hours, I'd had too many tap-dancing answers. Two girls were missing, and Ferguson was only worried about losing his mechanic. That didn't sit well. "Just spit it out, for chrissakes, instead of this bullshit stumbling and bumbling." Crowley grinned.

"I like the kid well enough, but I don't want trouble with that crew. Boomer comes around and talks to him every now and then. I think he has him running errands when he gets out sometimes. I don't know. But if the kid ever asks to leave early, he makes up the hours without me having to ask."

"When's the last time you saw Boomer?"

"Last week, came by in a real beautiful Chevy pickup."

"Well, la-ti-da. You get a hard-on looking at trucks?" Crowley said, snickering.

"I didn't do nothing wrong," Ferguson said, looking at me. "I don't have to take this from him."

"If either one of those two said anything and you heard it, stop wasting our time," I said.

"They go outside and talk. It was last Thursday. I didn't hear them."

"What time?"

"I don't know, around noon."

"Did Caleb leave early that day?"

"Yeah, for an hour or so, and then came back, worked late."

"You didn't think to mention that yesterday when I asked if anything unusual happened?" I wanted to put him through the wall now, too. This confirmed our thinking that it was Caleb's car that had picked up the girls. I started worrying that Crowley was going to have to hold *me* back. "What fucking time did he leave?"

"Probably around two-thirty or three."

"And when'd he come back?"

49

"He was here by the time I left at five."

"How do you know he stayed late?"

"The car he was working on was all finished when I got here in the morning, and the job after that and the job after that were done, too."

"Is there anything else you can tell us, Ned?" I said, taking the bite out of my voice. The information was the important thing, and if I had to go smooth to get it, that's what I'd do. "We aren't here because he ran a stop sign."

Ned looked down, then back up at us. "I borrowed a tool from his kit one Saturday when he wasn't here. The bottom drawer of his case has got some well-worn skin mags."

"So, are you telling us that he jerks off in the corner?" Crowley said.

"Look, if you ask me, the kid just wants to get laid, only no one in this town would touch him with a ten-foot pole."

"What?" Crowley said. "He's got plenty of cousins over there in the Village, doesn't he?"

"See what I mean?" Ned said, turning to me. "He's not that type of kid."

"But you wouldn't let your daughter date him, would you, Ferguson?" Crowley said.

"With all due respect, fuck off, Crowley."

"Watch it, Ferguson," I said. "You haven't covered yourself in glory helping us." We'd gotten all we could from him. Crowley grinned and rocked on his feet. We walked out a minute later.

"You know what this means, right, Crowley?"

"We're going to the Village to get the hillbilly?"

I nodded, my mind already working out the logistics.

Chapter Nine

I drove in with Regan. He stared out the window under his brown bowl cut like a tourist gazing upon the harbor. That was less than reassuring, though his biceps, the size of my thighs and stretching the short sleeves of his uniform shirt, provided a small measure of comfort. Even those monstrous arms could offset only a limited number of foaming-at-the-mouth woodsmen. My hands sweated as I turned onto the dirt road. I hadn't outfitted him with a shotgun. In the car behind us were Crowley and Martin. Martin, with the pudgy hairless face of a twelve-year-old, was the lucky devil playing me, armed with a twelve gauge and instructed not to use it. Neither of the rookies had been able to keep still back at the station. Their smiles were small and phony as they climbed into their respective passenger seats. Crowley and I acted like this was no big deal. Experience allowed us to hide our nerves.

It darkened as we entered the tunnel of trees as Woodman's Lane doubled back. The road turned, then straightened, and we came out into the field. I was blinded for a second, but did not slow down. My eyes went down the road, where the cluster of shacks looked like the long-abandoned ruins of a summer camp. They were as I remembered them, with some differences. Warped utility poles carried single phone and electric wires past the shanties to Boomer's place at the end of the oval. His shack almost resembled a real house as a second story had been added—a penthouse for this neighborhood. The gleaming black pickup sat beside it. The buildings were all painted a battleship gray. Even as heavy as they were coated, you could still pick out the mismatched siding panels of steel and plywood. I could only imagine how much the roofs leaked. The remnants of a fire pit smoldered in the middle of the oval, and the sour trail of smoke that rose from it indicated it was used for trash removal rather than toasting marshmallows. I considered gunning it to the clustered hovels and skidding to a stop to kick up a cloud of dust. Instead, I slowed to a crawl. I had no idea which of the shacks could possibly contain Caleb, so decided to get to the point and headed for Boomer's palace. Then I spotted the purple Galaxie parked between the second and third shacks on my right and hit the brakes. It wasn't exactly out in the open, but if they had wanted to hide it, they could've done better. They'd thought we wouldn't come here—or didn't care if we did.

I passed the Galaxie and cut the cruiser at an angle across the lane so that no other vehicle could pass. Crowley noticed what I did and parked the same way, bookending any possible exit by the Ford. I told Regan to get out with me and look mean, but say nothing. I motioned for Martin to remain in his car and hoped he remembered my instructions. I stepped out into the heat. I watched Boomer's place as I waited for Crowley to join me. Then I started up the plywood steps of the shack in front of me.

Before I could put a foot on the porch, the slap of a screen door turned my head. Forty yards away, Boomer stormed out and started toward us.

"Here we go, LT," Crowley said.

Behind Boomer came four others. On any other day, they probably would have been at the mill. I did not continue to the door. The real threat would come from Boomer. I stepped down in front of the cruiser. Crowley was a few yards behind me. We waited. Two more men came out of the next place as soon as Boomer reached it. At least none of them were carrying pitchforks or torches. If any appeared behind us, we'd be surrounded. And if that were the case, I hoped Martin would have sense enough to step out of the cruiser against my orders and let them all get a good look at that pump Remington. Boomer approached, taking his time. I took my hand off the butt of my gun. I assumed he'd push me further than he had last night now that he had his pack of hyenas behind him. He stopped a few yards away, close enough that I could smell him, a ripe combination of garbage smoke and Old Spice.

"Little Timmy," Boomer said. "You must have lost your fucking mind." The six men behind him nodded. They could have used a shave. While none appeared to be carrying weapons, I couldn't rule out that there wasn't a deer rifle pointed at us from somewhere. "You got your whole department out here with you. Two pissants who've only fired a gun on the range and probably wet themselves doing it, and Officer Cole Crowley, who'd just as soon suck a cock as fuck his mother."

I didn't have to look and put a hand out to stop Crowley. He'd come up next to me but had enough sense to slow his ass down before he let Boomer get him to do something stupid. There had to be a way that this didn't end up in a brawl or shooting, but Boomer wasn't going to help me find it.

"Always good to see you, Eugene," Crowley said. "Of course, I did learn how to suck dick from your mother. Used to see her every time I had a spare nickel."

Boomer's nostrils flared. His men's eyes were trained on his back.

"Eugene," I said, "do you know the whereabouts of Caleb Connolly?"

"Have you got a warrant to be on our land?"

"We don't need a warrant to be on your land. We do need one to go into your domiciles, and I have that right here." I pulled it out of my pocket and held it out to him. I could have been holding a list of parking violators at Gray Gull Beach. He wasn't going to come read it. I returned it to my pants.

"I do believe that piece of paper will fit right up your ass, even with the stick you keep up there."

"Regardless of where this important legal document ends up, it is in effect, and if we have to, we will search each of these fine homes." I couldn't rise to take the bait, no matter what.

Crowley laughed.

"Like hell." Boomer leaned back, letting his hands rest on the top of his stomach, as if we were haggling over the price of steamer clams.

"How about any of the rest of you? Do you know where Caleb is?" This was met by quiet. Most looked down at their shoes. Some watched Boomer. None would meet my gaze. "Okay, what about his sisters, Holly and Maisie Connolly, who've been missing for a week now. Any of you know where they are?"

"I speak for them," Boomer said, smiling and raising his arms to encompass his people, "and no one knows shit."

"Obviously," I said, then raised my voice: "Caleb Connolly is wanted for questioning, and if you don't bring him to us, as I said in case you missed it, we will search every one of your homes. In the process of that search, if we find anything illegal, we will be obligated to take further action. There could be a whole lot of you spending some time with us unless someone smartens up and tells me where Caleb is."

"Your balls must be the biggest part of you, Little Timmy, to come down here and threaten us with this bullshit. Remember, we ain't the lilies you got running around in town. You'd have to be smoking some of the hooch you take off the high school kids to think anyone's talking. What I'm getting at is that you can turn your asses around and leave."

"We'll go when we can take Caleb Connolly with us. Or you show us the girls."

"I'm going to do you a favor, Little Timmy. I'm going to tell you where those girls are, and then you can get the fuck off my land."

I wouldn't give him the satisfaction of asking.

"I've done my own investigation and found that they left. I heard it was for sunny Mexico."

"Really?" I said. "How do you know that?"

"They told me that's what they were going to do."

"When did they leave, and how are they getting there?"

"Don't know when they left, and how does any broad get around when they don't have a car? Probably jiggle their tits on the turnpike and get a ride."

He had just offered me the out I didn't think was coming—but one we all knew was a complete fabrication. I was being asked to forget about the missing girls, and in return, we'd be spared the trouble that Boomer and his posse could render. If I were going to roll over for that, I would've had to hand Crowley my badge and go back to tending bar.

"Would you like to come down to the station and make a formal statement, for which you would be legally accountable?" I said, offering Boomer his own untenable path.

"I would not."

"Then you can tell me where Caleb Connolly is."

"That ain't happening. What is happening is that you're leaving. Now."

"Martin," I yelled, hoping another player on the board would break the stalemate. He got out of the car, brandishing the pump across his body like he was strolling downfield on a pheasant hunt. He was following instructions, but I wished he looked a little itchy. Boomer laughed. My eyes stayed on Boomer, but my peripheral could see his men watching him. They were dumb enough to believe they could take us.

My choices weren't great. I could leave one of the rookies with Crowley and take the other as I went through the cabins. The men I left would be badly outnumbered, and Crowley's rookie would be in over his head. Another issue was Crowley's temper, worse than mine, and if I weren't there, Boomer would be more able to push his buttons. It was a great time for Trout to be off enjoying himself. My only choice was to search each of the shacks alone. I'd be lying if I said that wasn't a frightening prospect, because I had a hunch more of Boomer's henchmen lurked out of sight.

I turned to Crowley. "Watch these nice folks while I search the homes. No one moves. Martin, Regan, remember what I told you." I hoped Boomer took that the wrong way.

"Yes, sir."

"You got it, Chief." They sounded confident. I was surprised.

I turned toward the place to my right.

"Don't take another step, LT," Boomer said, his voice a growl.

I stopped and looked back. "Do you know where he is, Eugene?"

"Yeah, let me show you." He charged head down, as if on an all-out blitz. I hadn't wrestled for eight years for nothing. Without having to think, I dropped my center of gravity and shifted my feet and hands into position. I'd use his momentum against him, pivot to his side, pull his leg out behind him with mine, get my arms up under his shoulder, and take him down to the ground where his size wouldn't be an advantage. It was a move I'd done a thousand times in practice, in meets, and even on Deac. I waited for him to take one more step and sprung. I got my right leg inside his left. But as I reached up under his shoulder, he swatted my arm away, and my left foot slid on the dirt. I was going down, steamrolled. I hoped that the rookies wouldn't have to shoot anyone to save my ass. I grabbed at Boomer's sweatshirt to prevent getting completely slammed, thinking there'd be a chance I could scramble out from under him. Then I got lucky. As I latched onto his collar and my momentum slid beneath him, my flailing left leg inadvertently tripped his right, and I sling-shotted him forward. Boomer flew over me like a fat-filled missile, and the thud of his head torpedoing the cruiser's front fender was as sweet as anything I'd ever heard. I was back on my feet as if I'd never touched the ground. Boomer lay face down in the dirt. Neither he nor his minions moved.

I brushed off the back of my pants and started breathing again, putting a "Who's next?" look on my face. The group of Villagers stood slack-jawed. Martin's shotgun was leveled at their midst. I hoped the safety was on.

"You've got two choices, guys. Tell me where Caleb is, or I toss every house until I find him."

"Ain't you going to see if he's all right?" one of them, long bearded, spit out, nodding at his fearless leader.

"He just tried to assault a police officer. That's not very smart." I doubted that even a car could truly damage that thick skull of Boomer's. And we now had reason to bring him in if we wanted. I looked at Crowley, then to Boomer splayed out in front of us. Crowley read my thoughts. He got on one knee and checked on Boomer, rolling him back just a bit so he was facing us.

"He's breathing, Chief. The bigger they are, the harder they fall." He looked at the pack facing us and smiled. "Ain't that right, boys?"

"Let's stay focused, fellas," I said. "I know Caleb's here. His car's sitting right there. Who's going to bring him out?"

Having their leader flat out had a negative effect on their powers of speech. No one told me to fuck off.

"You're going to let me take a tour through all of these plywood mansions and see what I can find?"

Now they wouldn't look at me. I waited for a full minute. The door of the shack beside us squeaked open. Standing on the sagging boards of the porch were Caleb and Rory Connolly.

"Jesus Christ, woman, what the hell are you doing?" one of the men said. I followed her stare to what must have been her husband, a scrawny, balding man in the middle of the pack.

"You can shut up," Crowley told him. Martin's shotgun hadn't moved.

"Caleb, come down here and keep your hands where I can see them." He looked at his mother, and she nodded. Then she stared at me like she wanted to go off, but thought better of it and dropped her eyes. He stepped down from the rickety porch with his hands above his head. Rory followed him, as mad as she looked in my office. When he reached the ground, I nodded to Regan, and he opened the back door to the cruiser.

"What are you doing with him?" Rory said, more an accusation than a question.

"We're taking him in for questioning."

"Why? What for?" Her hands were balled into fists.

"We have probable cause. That's all I'm going to say."

She frowned and pointed to the car, where Caleb was paused outside the door. "Jake, you go with him."

"That's not going to happen," I said.

"He's a boy," Rory Connolly said, a flush coming to her white face. "He doesn't know about these legal things."

"He's nineteen," I said. "He's an adult." Crowley kept his eyes on the Villagers.

"You can get in the car, Caleb," I said.

"You can't get away with this," Rory said, glaring at me. "You're taking away someone who didn't do anything, and look what you did to Boomer. You can't come in here and do that, like we did something bad."

"Speaking of Eugene, Chief." Crowley said, "Are we bringing him in for assault, too?"

"I think if Caleb here comes along peacefully, we can assume that Mr.

Woodman has learned his lesson."

It might have been smart to arrest Boomer to get him off the street. But that would only mitigate the level of intimidation we'd just established. And if they were smart enough to get a lawyer and it did get to court, there'd be us saying one thing and ten of them saying the opposite. We'd proven our point with Boomer, if by luck. Once we had Caleb in the car, I got in myself, giving one last look to the horde watching with eyes bulging out of their heads. With Boomer sprawled on the ground, there wouldn't be any trouble. We backed up, turned around, and drove out. Caleb didn't say a word, and neither did we.

Chapter Ten

Caleb was locked in one of the cells that his mother had thought held his sisters. I'd sent the rookies out to patrol our neglected beaches, and Crowley and I had collapsed into chairs in my office. We were drinking iced coffee loaded with cream and sugar, waiting for Pettibone and hoping for a second wind. We slumped as if we'd worked twelve-hour shifts. The clock had yet to reach noon.

"Jesus Christ," I said.

"Hey, we got out of there with what we came for," he said.

On the surface, it seemed like an accomplishment. In reality, it wasn't much. We wouldn't be cracking the champagne for bringing in a person of interest, like departments all over the country do every day. Caleb wasn't the goal, only a means to move forward. We'd come out of a tough spot, but it was only worth anything if it led to Holly and Maisie Connolly. We needed him to tell us what happened after he picked up his sisters.

Once Pettibone arrived, the handlebars on his moustache waxed solid, we updated him on pulling Caleb out of the Village and asked him to send a crew to impound the Galaxie. Crowley, who was for once impressed with something I'd done, told him that I'd left out the best part of the story, running Boomer Woodman head first into my cruiser and that if he went outside and looked, he'd notice a sizable dent. Crowley smiled, his teeth as wide as dimes.

"That's going to be a problem," Pettibone said, as prescient as ever.

"He showed up at the end of my driveway last night to tell me to mind my own business, too," I said, and then sent Crowley to go get Caleb.

"You should have shot him when you had him on your property," Pettibone said, fingering the curls of his moustache. "You had cause. Now he's going to have to get back at you, no matter what comes of these runaways. The only one in more jeopardy than you is his sister if he finds out she's the one who started all this."

He was right about that. Rory had nearly given herself away, furious that we were taking her son. But she'd managed to pull back before saying anything to reveal she'd spoken to me. Pettibone did make valid points on occasion, and my shooting Boomer may have been another of them.

"You think they're runaways?" I said.

"It doesn't matter. Those sisters aren't your biggest problem if this guy is anything like I've heard."

"What's done is done."

"Keep it locked and loaded, Chief, that's all."

* * *

We put Caleb at the desk in the conference room. I sat across from him, and the two larger men stood looming behind me. I explained his rights to him and asked if he understood them. He grunted. I took that as a yes. Then I spelled it out as clearly as I could that the girls were missing, and he'd been seen picking them up on Route Nine. We didn't know what happened after that, but he did. He was going to tell us. He looked at me like he hadn't understood a word I'd said, his eyes flitting about in their sockets.

"Did you hear me, Caleb?" I said.

"Yeah."

"Why did you pick them up?"

"You said I picked them up," he said, smirking. "I didn't."

"But you did, didn't you?"

"So now picking up sisters in a car is some sort of illegal thing?"

"They've been missing for a week." He didn't have anything to say about that.

"So you did pick them up?" Pettibone's voice shook the room. He had energy like a stick of dynamite.

"Maybe I did, yeah." He couldn't spit that out fast enough.

"Why?" I said.

"They was walking, and I had a car," he said with conviction. I was coming to believe he was that simple, and not a natural wiseass.

"Where'd you take them?"

"To town."

"Where in town?"

"I dropped them off at the bridge."

"Cut the shit, Caleb," I said. "You left work early, which you rarely do. You drove by where they were walking. They argued with you, then got in your car. But you didn't take them to town. You turned around and went the other way, south on Nine. We know all this. Where did you take them?"

"I don't remember."

"Try hard," Pettibone said, slapping the table.

Caleb jumped in his seat, then looked down at the tabletop.

"Did you have it planned to pick them up?"

"I don't know."

"So you were just driving around and happened to see your sisters, and then picked them up?" His lips came together, and he looked like he was trying to hold his breath.

"Mr. Connolly," Pettibone said, his voice grave and vibrating. "Do you know what happens in jail?"

Caleb shook his head.

"There are some bad men there. They like to do things to other men that they'd normally do to girls. Do you get what I'm saying? They like skinny guys like yourself, because they're the closest thing those men will get to a woman in a long, long time. Does that sound good to you?"

"No." He stared at the table, his mouth open.

"Why did you take off from work?"

"I was taking a ride."

"No, you weren't," I said. "How did you know to get them where they were?"

He shrugged.

"You better start answering these questions, young man," Pettibone said. "You are the prime suspect in the disappearance of two women, and that could keep you locked up for a while."

"I don't know if this is the kind of thing you people are into in the Village, but you might just find yourself becoming some jailbird's girlfriend," Crowley said.

"I didn't do nothing but drive them." His bottom lip twitched.

"To where?" I asked.

Caleb kept his eyes down.

"Start talking, son," Pettibone said. "If you want to get back home."

"What if I don't?" he said, straightening up as if he'd finally lit on something.

"What if you don't what?" I said.

"Want to go back there."

"To the Village?" I said. That hadn't occurred to me. I'd believed it for the girls but hadn't considered it for him.

He nodded.

"Does this have to do with your sisters?" I asked.

There was a knocking on the door behind us. In the thin vertical window, Estelle waved frantically. Crowley opened it.

"There are people here to see you, Chief," she said.

"We're kind of in the middle of something. They can wait."

She didn't shut the door. "They're here because of him." She half-pointed at Caleb. "It's Boomer Woodman, and he's got that lawyer, Dan Reynolds."

Crowley and I left Pettibone with Caleb. Reynolds and Woodman waited for us at the counter. I couldn't suppress a grin when I noticed the mark that ran across Boomer's forehead like a swath of red paint. He glared when he saw the smile. Reynolds stood next to him in his gentleman lawyer uniform: chinos, white shirt, red tie, and blue blazer. His top button was loose, and his tie was more scrunched than knotted. His gut made mine look like a crater, and although he was only a few inches taller, he must have outweighed me by a hundred pounds. The lines on his face and drooping chin had me placing him close to sixty, but his hair was jet black and slicked as if he were in his twenties.

"I understand that you have Caleb Connolly in custody, LT." I wasn't a formal person, and the people I'd grown up with called me by my nickname on a regular basis. That wasn't Reynolds. In this professional setting, I took it as an insult. Maybe he was trying to impress Boomer, who stood with his arms folded.

"That's correct," I said.

"Under what grounds?"

"We're holding him for questioning."

"In regards to what?"

"A missing persons case, as I'm sure Eugene has informed you."

"Don't assume anything, Nichols," Reynolds said, as if delivering a lecture. "His uncle here, who I know you are acquainted with, has secured me to represent him. Before you ask him another question, I'd like to talk to him, as would his uncle, in private."

"I don't think so," I said. Crowley smiled.

"It is his legal right to have an attorney present for questioning, as you know."

"He was advised of his rights. As of yet, we haven't charged him with anything. He's not under arrest, and he hasn't asked for representation."

"So are you considering him as an ordinary witness, and thereby he has the right to leave? Can you even prove there's been a crime committed?"

"A missing persons case is a serious matter, Reynolds, as I'm sure your knowledge of criminal law would allow. Caleb Connolly is the last one to see those girls alive."

"You said, 'alive.' Are you presuming they're dead? Do you have evidence of that?"

"Just stating a simple fact." I did not presume they were dead. I believed they had just enough brains to realize they were better off leaving the hell hole they lived in.

"I happen to know that Mr. Woodman has provided you with information as to the girls' whereabouts, in that he informed you they left on a trip."

"I'm sure your client informed you that he also refused to issue an official statement, and that this information came about only after we had arrived to question Caleb. So what does your legal mind tell you about that?"

"You need to release Caleb Connolly, immediately," he said, using a courtroom summation voice.

"I don't answer to you, Reynolds. It's standard that if two teenage girls go missing in one's town, it's the police's job to find them. I've gotten zero assistance from Mr. Woodman and his people. If you truly want to facilitate Caleb's release, why don't you convince Eugene and the rest of them to cooperate?"

"Is it also your job to harass an entire community and physically assault one of its members?"

"Are you referring to when that oaf behind you tripped and fell and somehow head-butted the town's police cruiser? He's lucky he's not getting a bill for the bodywork."

Legally, the argument could have been made that Caleb was a material witness. He also qualified as a suspect. But I wasn't about to get tied up by debating the law, even if Reynolds wasn't F. Lee Bailey. As far as I knew, he dealt mainly with real estate, probate, and divorce. The closest he got to a criminal case was the occasional drunk driver, which he always had his clients plea out of. I hadn't known he'd had a connection with the Village, but Boomer had been able to get him here in no time. I told them that if Caleb requested a lawyer or we charged him, I'd be right back out to let them know. They didn't look happy when we left them standing there and returned to the conference room.

Pettibone raised his eyebrows as we came back in and nodded to Caleb. The pale of Caleb's skin flashed even whiter. His eyes shot up to meet mine, and then he shook his head.

"The kid hasn't said a word since you left the room," Pettibone said. "Literally won't even move his lips."

"Did your sisters want to leave the Village?" I said.

Nothing.

"Where did you bring them?"

More nothing. He kept his head down. His hand on the table was shaking. He put it in his lap.

"What do you think Boomer's worried about, Caleb, that made him rush down here with a lawyer?" I said.

A foot tap.

"When we search your car, Caleb, are we going to find blood in it?" Crowley asked.

He kept staring at the table.

I told Crowley to bring him back to his cell. We could hold him for twenty-four hours as a material witness, and that's what we were going to do. I let Boomer and Reynolds talk to him for fifteen minutes and positioned myself at the end of the hallway. They spoke in low voices, and I couldn't hear any of it. When they left, I told them that they could pick him up in precisely twenty-two hours and ten minutes, if we didn't arrest him. We'd clearly need more evidence for that. That was not only because the District Attorney, Charles Laurent, was a "by the book" piece of Wonder Bread who probably thought twice before taking a right on red. We just didn't know what had happened. But I would be finding out.

Chapter Eleven

I was glad to see Trout walk through the office door at nine the next morning, though he did look spent from his days in Boston drinking beer and watching baseball. He'd been on the force for almost forty years, full-time, since I'd taken over as chief. I immediately sat him down, and we went over the case point by point. He nodded along, occasionally scratching the bald crown of his head or patting down the wings of white hair over his ears.

"Jesus," he said when I was through. "I picked a good time to get away, didn't I?"

"All time off requests for next year will be denied," I said. He laughed.

Two explanations for Caleb's behavior were stuck in my head. The first was that he'd done something to his sisters. That was the most logical explanation for silence. The second was he'd brought the girls somewhere but didn't want to say. There could be a number of reasons for that, from not wanting anyone to know that he'd helped them leave to possibly implicating others in their disappearance. Either way, we needed to get it out of him. Crowley and I hadn't had any luck, so I let Trout have a run. His calm, easy-going manner might go over better with our skittish suspect. I picked up sandwiches from Blink's for lunch, and the three of us went into the conference room. Caleb salivated over his sub like it was a hunk of prime rib. At least his jaw was getting a workout with the chewing. I planned to keep quiet and let Trout work his magic.

"I know this must be hard on you," Trout said. "Your sisters being missing and all."

Caleb kept right on chewing, his face blank. He looked over at me, then back at Trout. His expression didn't change. We were all the same to him.

"Can you help us find your sisters? I don't think we can do it without you."

"Then why did you put me in jail?"

"We'll let you walk right out that door if you help us." His voice was sing-song as if reciting a nursery rhyme.

"I don't know anything."

"Are you sure? You told us last night you gave them a ride. Where'd you take them?"

"I don't know."

What I didn't know was how Trout could stand it. I was in there to take notes, but the pen in my hand was one more stupid answer from being snapped in two.

"You don't like it here, do you?" Trout said, smiling.

"Course not." Caleb's forehead came forward, and his jaw sunk as he frowned. That was apparently a stupid question.

"Then help us, and we'll let you go."

"Maybe you will, and maybe you won't."

"I promise you." Trout turned to me. "The Chief's right there. He heard what I said, and he's good with it, aren't you, LT?"

"You bet," I said.

"He don't like me," Caleb said to Trout, nodding at me. That may have been the first truth he'd hit on since we'd picked him up.

"You didn't hurt your sisters, did you?"

"Like I told them last night, I didn't do nothing wrong, and I don't know anything."

"Are you sure about that?" Crowley gave him a pleading face and soft voice.

"I don't know anything."

"Enough of this," I said, unable to echo Trout's tone. I stood and tossed the pieces of pen into the corner wastebasket. "You're going back to your cell. I guess you can get used to it."

Reynolds must have advised him not to say a word, and if so, Caleb was executing that to perfection. There was the Boomer factor to consider, as well. Last night we'd been able to chip away to where it looked like he was ready to open up, then his uncle had showed. It wasn't hard to figure out that Caleb was more afraid of him than he was of us, and that apparently encompassed becoming someone's prison wife. At first, I'd thought those girls had just made a run for it. But I was far from sure now. The shadow of intimidation Boomer and the Village cast was impossible to escape. They were hiding something.

That afternoon Trout and I hoped for a lucky break and canvassed the town from Woodman's Lane to downtown in one direction and Wellport in the other. We knocked on doors at every house between Ned's Service and the bridge, showing the picture of the girls. No one had seen them other than Trent, and if he hadn't seen them, I would have believed they lived in a universe parallel to our own.

We kept on. A stop at the Goodwin's house on River Road resulted in Cindy Goodwin nearly having a meltdown until we told her we only wanted her son to identify people in a yearbook picture. It was close enough to the truth. Once she could breathe normally, she told us that Jimmy was in Foxboro at a one-day quarterback camp run by Steve Grogan. We searched the places Holly and Maisie had been known to go: the clam flats where they'd dug sea worms and the fields where they'd gotten their earthworms. We drove the roadside from the Village to the north and south tollbooths at five miles an hour, scanning the shoulders for a glimpse of anything. When questioned, the toll booth and bus station employees again supplied us only with blank stares. As we pinballed from one part of town to another, Trout gave me a play-by-play of every run scored and given up by the Sox in the two games he'd seen. There were twenty-four of them. A list of bars to hit around Fenway was provided, as well, should I get to a game, along with listings of the charms of the female bartenders who worked them. He also pumped me for information on how I'd been making out with Suzanne. There was no progress to report in any area.

We returned to the station to find that the flyers I'd posted resulted in zero calls. There'd been no communication received from other police forces, and when I called them to double check, I'd found the reason was because there was nothing to report. The state crime lab had found no traces of blood anywhere in the car. The long, black hair they discovered in the front and back seats of the Galaxie told us nothing. We knew they rode in it on a regular basis, and Caleb had admitted picking them up. According to lab techs, there were no signs of struggle, not even as much as a quarter-inch tear in the faux leather seats. We'd been shut out. When I had to release Caleb to Reynolds and his uncle that afternoon, he wouldn't look at us. Boomer had a good laugh when I told Caleb not to leave town. I had to work hard not to go after him right then and there.

Trout came over to the house after work, and as was our process, we sat outside drinking beer and discussed the case. It was hard enough dealing with Woodman's Village, but it riled me that if the girls had been from anywhere else in town or cheerleaders at Timbercoast, the day's results would have been different. People in Laurel didn't care about Connollys, Sampsons, and Woodmans. They didn't even see them. We'd have to turn over every rock ourselves if we were going to find out what happened. Trout agreed and handed me another Bud.

"Don't get yourself all worked up, LT," he said, watching me pace back and forth. "We'll get to the bottom of this eventually."

"What I feel like getting to the bottom of is my emergency bottle of Jack Daniels."

"Shit, that hasn't come out since Analisa hit the bricks. We're not there yet, are we?"

"I guess not," I said, shrugging.

We kicked through possible explanations of the girls' disappearance again, most of which revolved around Caleb. The first was that he'd brought them somewhere as a favor, maybe to the turnpike or bus station, so they could get out. Of course, none of those workers had recognized their picture. He could have given them a ride somewhere else, and then they left on their own. But in either case, there's no reason he couldn't have just told us what he'd done and cleared himself. He was just about to explain his own issues with the Village when Boomer arrived, and it could have been he didn't want Boomer to know he'd done it. The other possibility was that Caleb had harmed them. It was something to be considered given the circumstances, though we didn't have a motive. He didn't seem like someone who possessed the balls to pull a trigger, but there was something off about him. "Squirrely as shit," Trout said. A suspect reluctant to talk usually indicated some level of guilt, but clamming up in the presence of authority was normal for any dope from the Village—and probably normal too, if you'd done anything that might piss off Boomer. The only thing we didn't consider was that aliens had abducted the girls and erased the incident from Caleb's brain. Unless he opened his mouth and could tell us otherwise, he'd remain the prime suspect. How jail wasn't as bad as what Boomer could do to him was beyond us. The case, less than forty-eight hours old, was a dud. We needed to learn where he brought his sisters. Unfortunately, the one person who could tell us that wasn't talking. It was almost enough to send me to the hard stuff.

Chapter Twelve

The Fourth of July fell one week and a day after the Connolly twins had vanished. It was usually my favorite day of the year, this despite the monumental levels of corniness on display in Laurel. The parade was its centerpiece. It began assembling in the Port Tavern parking lot at eight o'clock and started at ten. We had high school marching bands from all over the state, elementary school versions that couldn't get through Yankee Doodle, veterans from World War Two to Vietnam, the Elks, Rotarians, Boy Scouts, Girls Scouts, the town's Little League and Babe Ruth teams, and floats put together by local businesses. It ended at the Bluff Hotel. There, Randolph Grimes—a real United States representative who had a summer place just north of the hotel—would stand on the veranda and address the whale pants and alligator shirt crowd to rousing applause. Everyone would then disperse to their various beach outings and cookouts. Because of the parade's long-standing tradition, one of the state's three television stations always filmed for the six o'clock news. As a child, the parade was only surpassed by Christmas in my book. It was still great when I marched several years as a shortstop for the Laurel Tigers, and being afforded my own convertible as State Champion following my senior year was something I would never forget. We had more people in town than on any other day, but there were rarely problems. Not one drunk had blown off a finger with an M-80. Everyone swam in the nostalgia of simpler times, as if they'd actually existed.

By the time I sat down to breakfast at the Port Tavern at 6:30 to start organizing, I'd already put in an hour's work at the station. When you spend

71

half the night lying in bed thinking about missing girls, it makes sense to just get up and go into work. I was getting accustomed to dragging ass, anyway. I'd gone through the night's reports and checked to see if anything new had come in from other departments. It hadn't. As I mopped up my yolks with wheat toast, I tried to clear my mind of Boomer Woodman and his big black pickup. I kept seeing him roaring out of Old County and mowing down the twelve-year-old ballplayers in their black and orange uniforms like a scene from *Animal House* crossed into the *Amityville Horror*. I'd even prepared for that eventuality. Usually, I led the parade in one of the town's cruisers and had another officer pull up the rear. This year we were all on duty. I had Trout leading the parade, with Crowley trailing. I had Martin, Regan, and Griffin stationed at posts four hundred yards apart in the middle of the route. I'd be walking it myself, somewhere between the Girl Scouts and this year's Tigers. I finished my breakfast, one which mandated another run that night before I took Suzanne to dinner, and went out to put the groups in the marching order that Link Johnson, Laurel's Head Selectman, and I had finalized while stuffing our faces. I was glad to give the Village a rest from occupying my every thought.

The parade went off without a hitch, and the people lining the town square applauded as the bands marched forward. Everything in the midst of the scouts and ballplayers was fine. They waved to their friends and families. Parents implored kids to look this way and that for pictures. My eyes were trained on side streets, from which nothing sinister emerged. I passed Martin, stationed at the intersection of Elm Street and River Road, home of the town hall, and received the all-clear sign. I spotted Earl Goodwin, the town's real estate king and father of the star quarterback, in the crowd. I stopped and asked him if his kid had returned from his camp in one piece and if he knew where I could find him.

"Cindy said you wanted him to ID some kids from a yearbook picture?" He looked skeptical.

"That's all, Earl. He's the big man on campus, a leader, right? He must know everyone." Bringing the Connolly girls into it would only raise a red flag in the Goodwin or any other Laurel household. The town wasn't perfect.

"He's right there, LT," Earl said, pointing to a tall kid in a Timbercoast Baseball t-shirt. "He's helping coach the Tigers this year. Been thirty yards behind you all morning." I thanked Earl and let the team catch up. I introduced myself and asked Jimmy to walk with me. I put my hand on his arm to slow his pace and drop behind the kids.

"Do you know Holly and Maisie Connolly?" I asked straight out. I didn't bother buttering him up by parroting tales of his prowess in football and basketball.

"They go to my school," he said, his eyes on the back of his team bouncing along in front of us.

"Do you know where they live?"

"Woodman's." He looked at me, confused that I'd asked such an obvious question. He was blue-eyed with a wave of brown hair across his forehead. I came up to his dimpled chin.

"When's the last time you saw them?"

"Last week sometime." I pressed him to be more specific, and he got it narrowed down to Tuesday. "They come to where I work."

"That's what I've heard," I said, just to let him know that I wasn't to be snowed. "Are they friends of yours?"

"What do you mean by that?" he said, stopping. I stopped with him.

"What do you think I mean? Do you talk to them?"

"Sure. They're cool."

"Even though they're from Woodman's?"

"You sound like my dad."

"Would you say that you know them well?"

"Is this getting back to my parents, or is this, what do you call it, off the charts?"

"I think you're looking for off the record. And yeah, it can stay between us."

"Because they'll hold it against them that they're from there. A lot of people do around here."

"I'm aware. But you don't?"

"Why would I?"

"Do you know they're missing?"

"I've seen the flyers. There's one up at Scoops. And Mr. Greenwell told me. Do you know where they are?"

"I was going to ask you that same question." He started walking again, and I went with him.

"No idea," he said. "Are you sure they're not stuck in the Village or something?"

"They're not," I said, shaking my head. "Do you think they may have taken off for somewhere?"

"Like where?"

"I don't know. Portland, Boston, New York, some summer kid's house? Do you know anywhere they wanted to go?"

He shrugged. "I do, but they were chilling for now."

"Where's that?"

"California. Holly wants to go to college out there. One of those state schools has a program on women's rights, and that's what she wants to study. I guess it's cheap if you get a place there. They're going next year after graduation."

"Could they have left early?" I could feel my pulse starting to race.

"No way," he said. "They needed to save a lot more money. And they needed to graduate."

"Have they been talking about this recently?"

"No, it was this year at school."

"Did they ever talk about their brother?"

"The guy who works at Ned's? Yeah, he's a dick." His face got tight. If he knew how right he was, he might have stormed the station and gone after him himself.

"In what way?"

"He could've given them rides to school and games, helped them out with shit like that. He got to have a real job, but wouldn't speak up for them. You know their parents and uncle made them dig worms last year, and they didn't even get to keep the money. That blows."

74

"What did they say about their uncle?"

"That he's a jerk and dumb as a stump. They thought their dad was a wimp and full of shit, too. What they told me makes my folks look like Ward and June Cleaver."

"What about their mother?"

"They thought she was lame. They never heard of Women's Lib in the Village, I guess, so she just went along with whatever their uncle or father told them to do."

"And what was that?"

"I don't know," he said, throwing up his hands. "Isn't making them dig worms bad enough?"

I nodded. "How'd you get to know them so well?"

"I had a chemistry class with Holly last year. Teacher assigned lab partners, and she was mine."

"And you got her through?"

He laughed. "No, sir. It was the other way around. I would have never passed that class if she hadn't helped me. I could tell she was a little weirded out at first having to work with someone she didn't know, but it doesn't hurt to be nice to people, and she warmed up. After a while, things got totally cool. We'll be seniors this year." A smile stretched across his face.

I thought of what my reaction would have been had I received Rory as a lab partner. It wouldn't have been something I'd be proud of now. I would have protested and sulked and sat as far away from her as possible at the lab bench. Probably made fun of her to my friends. I was glad the kid didn't ask how it was in my day.

"Do you think they might've taken off for some other reason?" I said.

"I know something happened, but they weren't that pissed." He adjusted his Tigers cap, so it sat a little lower on his head. "They really want to graduate, and they want to go to the prom and to some of my games this year. Their folks wouldn't let them last year. We are going to get them to homecoming this fall, for sure."

"Are things loosening up in the Village?"

"No fucking way," he said, shaking his head. "But we're figuring it out."

"Are they friends with a lot of people, or just you?"

"They weren't real close to any specific kids, but they were okay if there was a group. People weren't mean to them at least, like I've seen in town."

"Your boss says they have a thing for you. Suggestive ice cream eating and all that."

He blushed. "They liked to fool around and tease me a little, that's for sure. Nothing too bad." He met my eyes, then looked up into the leaves of the oaks lining the road. "You know Mr. Greenwell's a creep, right?"

"I got that impression."

"Holly, she's great. Maisie isn't bad, either. She's got a wicked sense of humor. But they had to do everything on their own." The smile left his face. "The guys from their family were losers, and that Village itself, what the hell? It's so messed up, and no one in Laurel would give those girls a break. They just want to graduate so they can do their own thing. That's all I know." His voice was rising, and he wound up and kicked a rock in the street as if he were booting a fifty-yard field goal. He started to say something and stopped. He adjusted the brim of his hat again and looked over to the river.

"What aren't you telling me?" I said. There was more to it.

"Nothing."

"Look, Jimmy. I get it. But those girls are missing, and we're having a hard time finding them. No one's helping us. Anything you know could make a difference."

He turned to me. "Are you sure they just don't have them locked down somewhere in that damn Village?"

"I'm sure."

He nodded, then took a deep breath and exhaled. "This part really needs to be off the record. The thing is, Holly is kind of my girlfriend."

"What do you mean by 'kind of'?"

"We did the best we could. Her parents, and mainly her uncle, they wouldn't let those girls do anything. If we were hanging around at school, it wasn't my friends who had a problem. Their cousins would go back and tell their uncle that Holly and Maisie were too friendly with us. They'd get in trouble for not staying with their own and hanging out with people who thought they were pieces of shit. But that's not what we thought, and Holly and Maisie knew it. It was their parents and their uncle, that asshole Boomer, who treated them like shit."

"Was it just you and Holly? Did Maisie have a boyfriend, too?"

"No, she was a little different. She was such a wiseass and would roast people. It took a while for my boys to get what she was about. But if they'd been able to go to dances and games, I'm sure guys would have asked her. I mean, they ate lunch with us and stuff and talked, but she kept more to herself until she got to know you. At least when they came to see me at Scoops, we could meet up and not have people throwing a fit about it."

"You always worked Tuesdays and Thursdays? Were you working last Thursday?"

"Yes." I thought it would break his heart if I told him that they were on their way to see him when they were picked up by Caleb.

"What did you think when they didn't show up?"

"I figured their uncle made them do some stupid shit."

"Like what?"

"He had them working for him every now and then."

"Sea worms and night crawlers?" I said.

"No, that's what they used to do." He shrugged. "Something else, I think."

"Do you know what?"

"They wouldn't say."

"There's some other stuff, too, that I should tell you," he said, his facing turning red again.

"We had a real relationship, Holly and I." His face flushed darker and after briefly meeting my eye, he looked away.

"Meaning you went to the movies in Milltowne and held hands, or more than that?"

"More." I imagined that he was talking about sex, but I didn't see the need to push him.

"How did you manage that?"

"Everyone thinks those people are really dumb because they don't have much. But that's bullshit. They got it so they would sneak out some nights."

"Both of them?" It was becoming ever more apparent that these sisters were a different breed for the Village. I'd never heard of any Woodman, Connolly, or Sampson who had dared to cross Boomer.

"It was Holly at first. But after a few times, Maisie came, too."

"And you'd do what?"

"Hang out. This was spring, after basketball season, when we started seeing each other like that. We'd pick a time, and I'd drive up to Brown Street, not right where their road is, but before the turn. She could go out the back way, cut through some fields and the woods, and I'd be waiting. Sometimes we'd go to a house party. Sometimes we'd go up to the gravel pits and, you know, do stuff. We did less stuff when Maisie started coming, but still."

"I get it. Their mother thought they were out digging worms."

"I don't know about that. I got the idea the parents were clueless and didn't know they were gone."

"That went on until last week?"

"I wish. It got stopped in May. We might be good in other sports but not so much in baseball. We'd just won our first game after five losses, so we had a bonfire out in the pits on Oak Ridge, the dirt road up from the Glennon's place. Oh shit." He'd just spilled a party location for the high schoolers. There were a few around town. Sometimes we tracked them, sometimes we didn't.

"Don't worry about it, keep going."

"There were the three of us, plus Jeff Bennet and his girlfriend, Tammy. There were a couple of other guys from the team, too. So we had a few beers and were sitting around, and maybe Holly and I had wandered off into the woods, because usually if it was just the three of us, with Maisie, I mean, we weren't going to, well, you know."

"Go on," I said. I'd known the third wheel role. I felt for the girl.

"All of a sudden, this big black pickup comes roaring into the pit. It stops maybe a foot from my dad's car. Boomer gets out, yelling for Holly and Maisie. I was with Holly, and let me tell you, she started shaking right there in my arms. We came out of the woods, and he had Maisie by the hair, and

Holly left me and ran right over to him. Tammy was crying and the guys were just standing there. We didn't know what to do. He grabbed Holly by the hair, too, and practically took her off her feet. I started over, and he yelled, 'Don't even think about it, Goodwin.' Like a pussy, I stopped."

"That was smart of you." I couldn't believe that Boomer hadn't taken those boys apart, which is something he'd have enjoyed. There had to be a reason he didn't. It wouldn't have been fear of them ganging up on him. That wouldn't have even been a fight. And he wouldn't have cared if it eventually got back to us. But it was something, and I couldn't even guess at it. In the midst of all this hometown All-American happiness, I could feel acid building in my gut. I was letting down those girls. So much of what I should have been able to see was lost to me.

"Do you think that Holly and Maisie had told him about you, and that's how he knew who you were?" That he'd known him was odd.

"Definitely not. They weren't saying anything to anyone in the Village. They were catching shit just for talking to us at school. Maybe he saw my picture in the paper during football season. He said that if he ever caught any of us around his girls again, his girls is what he called them, he'd fucking kill us. We cooled it after that. But we were going to get around him, one way or another. That's why they kept coming to Scoops. I don't know what happened to them, but I know they didn't just take off."

"Damn it, Charlie," he yelled at one of his guys. "Stop throwing shit at the Girl Scouts." The kid jumped. "Just cool it, please," Jimmy added, calmer.

I put my arm around his shoulder and told him that we were doing our best to find Holly and Maisie and that we wouldn't stop. Another promise I couldn't allow to become empty. I thanked him for his time and let him get back to his team. Here was an actual teenage boy you might want dating your daughter, should you have one.

* * *

The parade concluded at the Bluff without incident. I released Crowley, Regan, and Griffin to the beaches. I sent Martin and Trout home, because they'd be patrolling that evening and overnight. I stood around getting congratulated by townspeople, shop owners, and tourists for running such a fine patriotic event. I smiled and shook hands, knowing that if the two girls missing from our town had a different address, this parade would have morphed into some sort of rally to support the family and find them. All they were now was some black ink in a police log, reported along with speeders and runners of stop signs. Jimmy Goodwin, a teenager, had shown more concern for them than anyone short of their mother. That wasn't right.

I watched Steve Russell from the County Coast Star talking to Rex Healy from Channel Six as Healy's cameraman packed up his equipment. With Caleb buttoned up like a clam, it came to me that a missing persons case involving two teenage girls was something that would garner attention. While our questioning and flyers hadn't appeared on the radar of our residents, seeing an anchorman digging into the story might carry more weight and communicate the urgency we needed to get some action. There were plenty of other people out there, too, who didn't know the Connollys were outcasts. This is how we could reach them. I strode to Russell and Healy as they chatted in the shade of the giant pine in front of the Bluff.

"Not so fast, gentleman," I said. "I've got a story for you."

That the girls were from Woodman's Village didn't matter. The story was there. Holly and Maisie Connolly were teenagers who'd been gone for a week, disappearing without a trace. An exhaustive search had turned up nothing. The town had been scoured. Our department needed help finding them. Yes, I left out the details of their background and I didn't explain that they may have just taken off, that they'd have been crazy not to want to. The journalists were all over it.

We left for the station so that I could supply them with pictures. Healy suggested that an on-camera plea from a mother could inspire action, and he was right. But I maintained that the family, worried and concerned, wanted to keep to themselves. He put me on camera instead, a small-town cop asking for neighborly help from all Mainers. I could picture the grave, deep voice of the anchorman, pivoting away from the parade footage to this story—two tales of the same town. With the girls' pictures plastered across the front page of the County Star and the Channel Six news, the odds that someone had seen them and would contact us would greatly improve.

I was not in this job for the glory, if that's what one would call getting on television. Laurel rarely got media coverage. There wasn't much statewide interest in the expansion of a town dump or breaking up bar fights between guys who were friends ninety-nine percent of the time. Our most challenging crime solving meant swinging by Vince Neely's house when someone's place had been burglarized. Vince had the only drug habit bad enough that, when combined with a lack of brains, usually resulted in him ripping off one of his neighbors. The stolen property was always sitting in his living room or hidden under his bed. Missing teenage girls were different, however.

I made it home by six, in time to see I'd been wrong again. They did not piggyback the Laurel stories. While the parade was in the first block, the Connolly girls didn't appear until after the sports at the end of the broadcast. The anchor stared gravely into the camera and presented a "concerning story on this most wonderful of days." The grainy picture I'd photocopied out of the yearbook filled the television. Then there was me behind my desk, my face looking like an overcooked ham, and this after I'd cut five pounds in the last week. I looked grim, saying that we needed the public's help to find these missing sisters. The number of the Laurel Police was plastered across the screen. As the newscast moved on to the weather, I did two rounds of pushups and sit-ups, then went to the basement and did a weight circuit. I was optimistic and not thinking about what could go wrong when I hopped in the shower. I had to pick up Suzanne, and I just knew how great that first drink would taste.

Chapter Thirteen

I sat across from Suzanne and couldn't stop smiling. I had finally done something that might find the Connolly girls. In addition, Suzanne was smiling back. If one allowed that your date seeing you on television and remarking that you looked like a ten-year-old who'd eaten a bucketful of Halloween candy wasn't a horrible thing, we were in great shape. I had savored my first beer, the second had hit the spot, and the third had taken the edge off. I was relaxed enough to notice that Suzanne's green eyes matched her sundress and that when she turned to look out the windows over the Cape, her profile fell into the glow of the sunset, columns of dusty light sparkling behind her. We'd avoided talking about my Connolly girls and weren't even comparing the bitchiness of my ex to the moodiness of hers, formerly an angry staple of our bar conversations. We were laughing about their faults and not taking them on as our own. Perhaps we were headed into a relationship, and it was making things easier. My pulse seemed to be running normal for the first time in days.

Then out of the corner of my eye, I caught Louie Larusa, the manager of the Overlook, speed walking toward our table while tapping his teeth with the eraser end of a pencil. I guessed he wasn't worried about my steak being overcooked. The last time I'd seen him working a pencil like that, he'd called me about a missing deposit that he'd sent to the bank with an employee, only the bank had never received it. Louie feared theft. It turned out that the prep cook, who always believed it was five o'clock somewhere, had dropped it in the deposit slot at Bay State Savings instead of Maine Bank and Trust. Louie's hips swung as he charged across the room. If he'd had to go any further the pencil would have been worn down to a nub.

"LT, I hate to interrupt, but an Officer Martin is on the phone for you and he's having a stroke. He's yelling, and I can barely understand a word he's saying."

If I'd had the foresight, I would've rewritten the schedule and put Crowley on opposite me so that one of us would be active to handle things. I wouldn't have needed to leave phone numbers of my whereabouts at the station. I tried to keep smiling as I stood up, but Suzanne's eyes registered the stress. She let out a breath and frowned. Louie kept hammering his teeth with that overmatched number two. It could be a lead I told myself, hustling to the front desk.

"This is LT."

"Chief, there's a woman here at the station. I think the one from Woodman's. She's filthy, and she won't talk, and when I tried to help her up she screamed."

"Help her up?"

"I don't know how she got here. I found her laying on the grass next to the parking lot on my way out. She's in bad shape."

"What do you mean?"

"Beat up. There's blood down her chin and her shirt. Looks like she was kicked around. I tried to get her into the station, but she won't move."

"Call an ambulance."

"Already did. What do you want me to do?"

"Keep her there. I'm coming." It had to be Rory. Boomer must have figured out how we came to know about the girls' disappearance. I hadn't been able to get on top of things fast enough and now they were going to shit. I went back to the table and told Suzanne that we needed to go.

"What happened?"

"Development in the Woodman's case," I said.

"They found the girls?"

"Not quite. I'll explain on the way."

I would have had to drive past the station to get Suzanne home and then double back, so I asked her if she didn't mind coming along and that we'd get her home as soon as we could. Whatever I needed to do, she replied. We cut backroads, and I asked her if she remembered Rory Connolly. "Who?" she said. I told her how Rory—apparently a classmate of ours—had walked the five miles from the Village to the station to tell us she wanted her girls back, and that her brother, the guy from my driveway, who everyone knew, had probably discovered how we found they'd gone missing.

"Those people are fucked up beyond belief," Suzanne said.

"Jesus, Suzy." I couldn't blame her for thinking that way. She hadn't seen what Rory had gone through physically and mentally trying to help her daughters, no matter how misguided she'd been. Nor had Suzanne been inadvertently shamed by a high school kid with humanity.

She shrugged. "I don't mean to be a bitch, but really."

"They're people and citizens of this town, whether anyone likes it or not."

"Yeah, they're regular All-Americans," she said. "I'm surprised Boomer Woodman isn't representing us in Augusta or maybe we should just send him to the UN."

"You can't judge them by their worst."

She snorted. "You like having them show up at your house in the middle of the night?"

The lights of the ambulance sliced red beacons through the trees in front of the station. I parked the Bronco behind the ambulance that was halfway up the drive. I jumped out and ran to Martin and an EMT, Fred Wilson, who stood over Rory Connolly. She sat with her knees pulled up to her chin, her arms hugging her legs. Blood glistened black on her cheek as the crimson light whipped across her face. Her left eye was swollen.

"She won't let us treat her, Chief," Wilson said. "It looks like she's pretty beat up."

"I can see that."

"Why don't you guys back off for a minute and let me talk to her?" I said. "Move your rig up to the parking lot. Martin, ask my friend to move the Bronco up to the lot, too." I waited until they'd done what I asked. They stood in the parking lot under a spotlight and watched us. Rory looked straight ahead. I bent down into a catcher's stance so that I could be eye to eye. The red beams spun around us like a whirlpool.

"Wilson," I yelled. "Turn the goddam lights off."

Once he did, I asked, "What happened, Rory?"

"Nothing."

"I know you don't think I'm the brightest bulb on the tree, but I'm not buying that."

"I tripped."

"Where might that have happened, and then how did you get here?"

"I asked you to forget about my girls, but you wouldn't. You had to make a big deal of it. You're the one who did this."

"I'm sorry you see it like that." There was some truth to what she said. I could have walked away when she'd asked and no one in this town would have blamed me for it. She wouldn't be sitting in front of me now. But that wouldn't have been right for her girls—or their mother, no matter what she thought at the moment. I'd known there'd be collateral damage along the line, but it was tough to take when it was a woman only doing her best for her daughters. Nothing would make any of this worth it if I didn't find them.

"You wanted to be a big man. Push us around. But you wouldn't even leave it at that. Had to go on television so that everyone knows our business."

"I'm sorry this happened to you, but I'm trying to find your girls. That was the best way to—"

"You've got no idea. About anything."

"I'm not giving up. Getting the word out is critical and I've taken steps to do that. The more people who are aware they're missing, the greater chance we'll come across someone who's seen them."

"So where are they, all these people?" She waved her hand out toward the town and started to list as if she were going to fall. I held her shoulder to steady her. She tried to slap away my hand but winced and pulled back when she tried to raise her arm.

"Let Wilson take a look at you. Where are you hurt?"

"Nowhere."

"It's pretty clear that someone gave you a good going over."

85

She glared.

"Who was it?"

"Like I'd ever tell you anything again."

"Boomer? Your husband?"

She stared straight ahead. I had to do something. The longer I let Boomer run over his people as he pleased, the worse it would get for all of us. But I couldn't just go in there and haul him out if she wouldn't go on the record.

"We can lock up whoever did it. You can be safe. Let me bring the medic over."

"I said no." Her scream faded into the woods behind the station.

"Well, what are we going to do then? Will you come in so we can get a look at you?"

"Leave me alone."

Footsteps clacked on the asphalt. Suzanne approached.

"How's it going over here?" she asked, standing over us.

"Great," I said, rising.

"Why don't you take a walk?" Suzanne said. "I think your rent-a-cop has a question for you."

"That can wait," I said.

"I really don't think it can." She widened her eyes and tilted her head slightly. I got the point.

"I'll be right back, Rory."

"Don't bother. I ain't staying."

"You can barely move."

"LT, for chrissakes," Suzanne said. She was not smiling. I turned and walked.

For a night that had bottle rockets, Saturn missiles, and Roman candles going off non-stop, we had entered a pocket of quiet. From the top of the hill where the station sat, you could hear crickets, leaves fluttering in the breeze, and every word that the two women were saying.

"No one was ever married to a bigger jerk than I was," Suzanne said. "I've been there." We could only see their silhouettes, Suzanne standing over the crouched shape.

86

"Yeah," Rory said. "Is that a fact?"

"My husband broke my hand by slamming it in a car door, on purpose."

"That all? You ever get dragged out of your house, beat up, and dumped at the last place on earth you ever wanted to be? And you can't go home, and you don't have no other friends, and your daughters are gone, and no one can fucking find them?"

"After he did that," Suzanne said, "he cried at my feet and took me to the emergency room where I made up a bunch of bullshit so he wouldn't get in trouble and LT wouldn't make a federal case out of it. So I suffered for three years longer than I should have."

"My husband didn't touch me."

"Somebody did. But what's happened isn't your fault."

"I know some folks that don't agree with that."

If it wasn't her husband, the only one in the Village who could get away with it was Boomer. I'd made a mistake by not bringing him in when I had the chance.

"Why don't you let the medic take a look at you?" Suzanne said. "LT just wants to make sure you're okay."

"He's the one behind all this. I don't want nothing to do with him."

"Then what are you going to do?"

"I can take care of myself."

"That's what I used to say." Suzanne shook her head. "I was wrong."

Rory looked up at her but didn't reply.

"Do you have a place to go?" Suzanne asked.

"I can find a spot." Rory laughed, then winced.

"It'll be okay," Suzanne said.

Rory didn't say anything to that. I told Wilson to head on down there and followed a few steps behind. Wilson looked over at me, and I nodded. He got down on one knee as if he were proposing.

"Where does it hurt, Miss?"

"Where doesn't it?"

"If you could walk up to the station, I could take a look at you in the light. Might be a good idea."

"You figured that out, did you?"

Wilson stood. "Help her up, LT," Suzanne said.

I leaned down and held out my hand. She grabbed it, and her body shuddered in pain. She tried to pull away when I put my arm under hers to steady her, but didn't have the strength. She reached her feet and tried to straighten up, but remained somewhat hunched over.

"Wilson, get the stretcher," I said.

"You're not taking me to the hospital."

"No one said that, Rory," Suzanne said.

"If we're going in, let's go." Rory took a step forward. I walked beside her, my arm under hers. As a group, we shuffled to the station and, once inside, to my office.

In the light, she looked worse. Wilson started with her eye and cleaned that up. He had me make an ice pack for her. He cleaned the cut on her temple. There was bruising on her neck, a red handprint etched on her cheek. It was easy enough to guess where that came from. Dirt was ground into her jeans and the flannel that she had wrapped around her t-shirt. She wouldn't let Wilson look under her clothes. Every time he asked her to move, she grimaced like a movie cowboy getting a bullet pulled. Wilson concluded that she could have cracked, if not broken, ribs and possibly a concussion.

"She needs to go the hospital," he said, looking to me, before turning back to Rory and listing off her possible injuries.

"I'm not."

"But Rory—" I said.

"I'm not going."

"She needs to go," Wilson said. "One of those ribs, if it is broken, and we can't tell that if she doesn't get an X-ray, could puncture a lung. This is potentially life-threatening. Not to mention that if there are additional cuts or skin tears, they could get infected if they're not cleaned and sterilized."

"Not going to happen," Rory said. I looked over at Suzanne, hoping that she would be able to convince her.

"Rory," Suzanne said, "you heard him. You need medical attention."

She shook her head. "Just because they don't want me there doesn't mean

88

I want to be here."

"Jesus Christ, Rory," I said, barely above a whisper. Her chin quivered, and she ran the back of her forearm across her good eye.

"Do you really have a place to go?" Suzanne asked. Rory didn't answer.

"I know that Boomer did this," I said. "If you will verify that for me, we'll go in and get him out and lock him up. You will be safe."

"Are you fucking crazy, LT?" Suzanne said.

"What she said," Rory said, approaching something like a smile.

I understood well enough. The problem was, if she wouldn't go to the hospital, I didn't have any place to bring her. If it were the off-season, I could have her put up in one of the motels around town. But there wasn't an open room in the state this weekend. I might be able to find her a campsite, but then she'd be alone, and she needed a shower and to be cleaned up, and if something happened, there'd be no one there to help. None of our matrons would take her in, as they wouldn't want anything to do with "those people," and with Boomer running around still, I couldn't ask Estelle, who had clearly been terrified all week. And I wasn't about to ask Suzanne to get further involved. It was too dangerous.

"We can keep you here in protective custody," I said. "Either one of my men or I can stay all night to make sure you're okay."

"I ain't staying in jail," Rory said.

"You can't make her sleep in a cell," Suzanne said.

"You wouldn't be under arrest or anything," I said,

"She really needs to go to the hospital," Wilson said.

They were all looking at me as if figuring out shit like this was in my everyday wheelhouse. I'd spent five years as Chief leading parades, chit-chatting with residents, and making sure drunks got home without running themselves into a tree. I needed time to sort this out, which I didn't have. The bottom line was I needed her to be safe before I got to dealing with Boomer and continuing my search for her girls.

"You can stay at my place," I said. It wasn't exactly standard operating procedure or even appropriate. But I had room, and she could clean herself up. Maybe I could call Southern Maine Med and get them to send over a nurse.

"Oh, no," Rory said, shaking her head.

"That wasn't a question, Rory. You go to the hospital, or you come to my place. You'll be safe there. You'll have your own room with a bed. You can take a shower and clean up. If something happens, like Wilson was saying, I'll be there to get you to the hospital."

Rory didn't say anything. She put a hand on her ribs, as if to judge just how bad off she was. She looked over at Suzanne, who wasn't frowning and didn't look like she'd just heard the worst plan ever voiced.

"I'd like you to stay over, too, Suzy," I said. "In case anything of a female nature arises."

"Anything of a female nature?" Suzanne said, eyebrows high on her forehead.

"Jesus," I said. "Don't you think she'll be more comfortable with you there?"

"Of course," she said, smiling at Rory.

"Okay," Rory said quietly.

"We can stop at my house, and I can pick up a few things," Suzanne said.

"A slumber party," Rory said. "Lucky me."

I left the Bronco at the station and took one of the cruisers. We drove to Suzanne's, listening to static crackling over the radio as if it were a station. She ran in to pack a bag for herself and pick up some clothes for Rory. I followed the lights she turned on as she moved through the house. Every other second, I scanned the mirrors to see if anything had come up behind us. I wasn't taking anything for granted.

"I'm guessing Boomer figured out how we learned about your girls," I said while Rory and I were alone in the car.

"You think?" Her eyes narrowed.

"Do you want to tell me that he did this?" I said. "So I can do something about it."

She looked at me in the rearview. "No. I just want my girls."

"I've been trying."

"Where are they?"

Suzanne came out of her front door, checked that it was locked, and started to the car.

"I don't know," I said.

I sighed and reached over to open the door for her.

Chapter Fourteen

e got Rory into the house and settled in the kitchen. I made coffee. Suzanne took out some clothes that she thought would fit her, aspirational clothes she called them, saying she hadn't been able to get into them for a few years. There were some Calvin Klein jeans, a few blouses, some t-shirts, and underwear. I didn't know if wearing strange clothes would be any better or worse than being forced to sleep in a strange place. The bedrooms were on the second floor. Rory would sleep in the room I'd grown up in. Although I'd taken down the Red Sox and Raquel Welch posters, a thirty-year-old twin bed and mattress waited for her. I'd be at the other end of the hall. I'd bought a new set of furniture and moved into my parents' old room when they'd retired to Florida. This had been neatly synchronized with my wife leaving me. Between the bedrooms was the master bath. I imagined she'd spent time in worse spots, though perhaps not under worse circumstances.

We finished our coffee and went to the stairs. I offered to carry her, piggyback or in my arms. The look she gave me, like she'd just as soon have me shoot her, said 'no.' Suzanne walked in front of her, and I stayed behind. We took it one step at a time. In the bathroom, she sat on the closed toilet while I got the shower running. Suzanne asked if she wanted her to stay with her, and Rory said no, thank you. I told her to leave her old clothes in a pile and that I'd wash them for her. She shook her head and asked, instead of told, if I could please not touch them. Suzanne placed Rory's clean clothes on top of the hamper. I put out a fresh bar of soap and face cloth, and pointed out my Johnson's Baby Shampoo. I asked her not to lock the door in case she slipped or had a muscle spasm and needed help. I didn't want to have to break into my own bathroom. Suzanne said that she'd wait outside. I readied Rory's room.

When she came out of the bathroom, she looked like she could have lived on any street in Laurel except Woodman's Lane. I don't know if she'd ever worn clothes that were designed to flatter, but they were certainly an improvement. Without the dirt and crusted blood, her skin was smooth and pink. She looked almost healthy, other than the swelling over her eye, the bruises around her throat, and the cut on the side of her head. It was absurd. I asked if she was hungry.

"I could eat," she said.

We went down to the kitchen and resumed our places at the table. Suzanne opened the refrigerator.

"Jesus Christ, LT," she said. "Do you only shop when you're having me over for dinner?"

The answer was yes, though the loaf of bread was somewhat fresh. There was also a jar of spaghetti sauce, some American cheese, a six-pack, and the assortment that never goes away: jam, olives, butter, and mayonnaise. I didn't have to look long to know what I could offer her. She was okay with a grilled cheese. Without asking, Suzanne opened beers for her and me. Then she checked, and Rory had one, too. She made a tequila face on her first sip, but subsequent gulps went down easier. Beer probably wasn't a great idea on top of the painkillers that Wilson had given her, but anything could help.

The two of them sat at the table while I flipped the sandwich and got out a bag of chips. Rory ate, taking small bites, and by the way she chewed, I guessed the slap that Boomer had planted on her left her jaw sore, if not out of alignment. Wilson's directive for the hospital should have been followed, but this was better than nothing. I emptied my beer before either of them were halfway through. When she finished eating, the question became what to do now. It wasn't a time for small talk, and what I'd wanted to discuss with Suzanne, which was Rory, couldn't be done in front of her. I turned on the radio and got a Beach Boys concert in celebration of America's birthday.

"That's a hell of a sound system you got there," Suzanne said, noting the clock radio that sat next to the Mr. Coffee. It did sound lousy with its tiny speaker. The stereo system had gone south in the divorce, and I'd had no reason to replace it. It wasn't like I was hosting parties.

"I'll shut it off if you want," I said.

"I like it well enough," Rory said. Did they even listen to music in the Village?

I tried to consider the approach I should take trying to get her to finger Boomer for the beating. I settled on waiting until the morning, when she'd be less traumatized but sorer and hopefully angrier. Suzanne placed a hand on Rory's arm and told her things would get better. Rory shook her head. I asked if anyone wanted another beer.

"I think I've had enough of this day," Rory said.

"We'll show you up to your room," I said. We struggled back up the stairs and down the hall to my old room. The bed had been made, unused for at least a year since my cousin Becky and her husband had visited. The time when my relatives wanted to come, summer, was also the time I was least able to host them. Rory stepped into the small room, a ten-by-ten. I had scraped off the ancient scotch tape and repainted it so it didn't look like a complete relic. But while the posters had come down, I had not replaced them with paintings or the like, despite the town being filled on a regular basis with artists drawn by the rocky coast. I went over to the windows that looked out over the back yard. The quiet pop of long-off fireworks drifted in from the beach. There wasn't much of a moon.

"It's nice," she said.

I turned on the lamp on the nightstand and pointed out the bookcase if she wanted to read. I doubted I had anything that would be of interest. There were sports books from when I was in high school, some of my first-year texts like Modern Psychology, and some Ray Bradbury and Arthur C Clarke paperbacks.

"We'll be right down the hall if you need us," I said, pointing through the doorway to my bedroom.

"I think I'll make it okay," she said.

We backed out the door and closed it behind us. I put my hand on

Suzanne's hip and pointed her toward the staircase. We sat at the kitchen table and opened two more beers. As soon as we sat down, I got up and went out to the living room to scan the road. I didn't know whether it was the events of the night or the coffee that had made me jittery. I reached into the cabinet over the sink and pulled down the bottle of Jack Daniels. Good idea, Suzanne said. We each did a two-finger shot.

"I needed that," I said.

"Hell, yeah," Suzanne said, patting my arm. "But I have a bone to pick with you."

I had been caught up in the moment since the call at the restaurant. I hadn't bothered to ask if she'd wanted to help, but had placed her in a position where she'd had little choice. I would be apologizing for a long time, I believed.

"What you just said up there," she said, "indicated that we would be sleeping in the same room, if not the same bed. That's somewhat presumptuous, is it not?"

"I'm sorry," I said. "I didn't even think. I can take the couch."

"Damn, LT," she said, laughing. She took a long draw off of her beer. "Don't you think I need some sort of reward after all this?"

"You consider sleeping with me a prize?"

"It's a small town. I'll take what I can get."

"I'll do my best. But doesn't it seem like the world is trying to keep us apart? First Boomer, then Rory by way of Boomer."

"We have overcome," she said, leaning close enough to spark my leaning as well. We kissed awkwardly with the table between us.

"Let's go upstairs," she said.

"You go ahead. I want to lock up."

Naturally, I did not have an alarm system. For one thing, it was Maine, and the crime rate was ridiculously low. I was also the Chief of Police. Who in their right mind would think of breaking in here? I knew the answer to that one. The four of us who'd been there knew where Rory was, plus Trout, who I'd called. I'd made sure that everyone knew not to speak of our housing plan, and that included Wilson and Martin not mentioning it to girlfriends, wives, or priests. But I wouldn't rule out Boomer or his lackeys putting two and two together for once in their lives and finding her. There were eight windows in the living room, two more in the kitchen, and another in the downstairs half-bath. I emptied the cupboards of Campbell's Soup cans and grabbed a case of empties from the garage that I'd luckily not gotten around to returning. I lined up bottles and cans behind every door and below every window. Should anyone try to come in, there'd be a racket I could hear from upstairs.

I turned the lights off on the first floor and went to each side of the house, pausing for a minute to scan the yard. Then I climbed the stairs, left the light on in the hall in case Rory needed to use the bathroom, and went into my room. It was nearly midnight.

Suzanne was in bed and had the sheet and lightweight summer comforter up to her neck. Her eyes fluttered, and she patted what was going to be my side. I turned the light off at the switch. I dropped my clothes on the floor down to my boxers. Suzanne watched.

"How long do you think those shorts are going to last, LT?" They went, too, and I climbed under the covers, glad I was a little drunk.

We met in the middle of the bed like a pair of lit fuses. It had been too long for us, and the first round didn't last. We laid still afterward, with her head nestled into my shoulder. The sea breeze pushed the curtain into the room. Soon we were inhaling and exhaling in unison.

"I don't know how much I can thank you for tonight," I said. "We would have been in trouble without you."

"You're welcome," she said, patting my thigh. "I've been in her position, on the receiving end, and I know how it can be. I guess it doesn't matter if you have all the money or none of it, or if you've gone to college or couldn't spell cat. To be treated like that, it's not right."

"I know."

"I'll tell you one thing, LT," she said. "I didn't know that you were such a man of principle, that you really cared."

"I made a commitment," I said, one that had been cemented by a high school kid reminding me of my own shortcomings.

"I mean, I liked you forever as a friend, and I knew you were okay and sometimes even funny. If you'd known what Derek was doing to me, nothing would have stopped you from ending it. That would have been easy for you. What you've been doing this last week is not easy."

"You didn't see her walk into the station that day."

"I didn't see her at all until today," she said. "You know what I mean?"

"I do."

She rolled over and kissed me. My hands went to her hips. If our first time had been an Instamatic photo, we were now making a movie, and every second seemed more urgent than the last. We fell asleep intertwined and interlocked, and that's how we were when I woke up.

Chapter Fifteen

I hadn't been sleeping since this thing started. The clock said six, and the sun had just started to trickle in through the east windows. I unwrapped myself from Suzanne as softly as I could and slipped out from under her arm. I wondered if there'd be a day when I'd be able to close my eyes and go back to sleep, where we would get up at noon and go out for breakfast and red-eyes. I slipped on a pair of jeans and a t-shirt and went down to the kitchen. I went straight to the Mr. Coffee. Another long day lay ahead. My television spot and the County Star were sure to produce results. I also had to figure out what to do with Rory. While she'd been okay here last night, this was not a long-term solution.

Suzanne came down in a pair of shorts and a flannel shirt she'd pilfered from my closet. Her hair was a sexy, disheveled mess. I felt like a very lucky man for someone with a shitload of trouble to sort out. I poured her a cup. She sat down and kissed me on the cheek.

"What a night," she said.

"What part?" I said, as that could have encompassed just about anything, and I had no idea which event she was referring to.

"You look worried," she said.

"I've got reason, no?"

"Stupid question. As long as you're not putting me on the worry list, it'll be okay. What's on your mind?"

I looked up in the direction of Rory's room. "I can't let Rory go home, and I can't keep her here."

"What about a women's shelter? There's one in Portland."

"That's not a bad idea, except to her, Portland might as well be Mars. I don't think she'll go."

"There's the convent at St. Mary's nursing home in Milltowne. Father Gregory took me there once after Derek had, well, you know. They hid me for a few days."

"I wish you'd told me that was going on," I said.

"I wish I had, too." She patted me on my arm and asked if I wanted her to make a call. I said, please.

Once she got the Mother Superior, a Sister Agnes, on the line, her voice quieted, and they talked for a bit. A few minutes later, she handed the phone to me, letting me know that she'd provided some background but not all of it. I explained Rory's missing daughters and that she'd been the victim of domestic violence, and that she had nowhere else to go. I was assured that housing and hiding her would not be a problem for the Sisters of St Mary's. I hadn't left the house and was already making progress, provided we could convince Rory to go there. I hoped this was an indication that things were turning around.

Suzanne and I shared a look when we heard Rory's bare feet on the stairs. If she had any idea of what had gone on down the hall from her, she didn't show it. She wore gray sweatpants that stopped above her ankle and a t-shirt that fit. She looked over at us and sighed. I asked her if she wanted some coffee, and she nodded.

"How did you sleep?" Suzanne asked.

"Good enough." I placed a coffee in front of her and slid over the cream and sugar. She dumped a healthy amount of each into her cup. I hoped a subtle negotiation might get us where we needed to be.

"Rory," I said, "I'd like to take you to the hospital today to get checked out."

"I'm not going to any hospital." This was stated with much less hostility than she'd used the previous night, but was nothing short of a fact. I had anticipated this.

"You know you can't go back to the Village, right?" I said, trying an inflection to relate that I thought this was a shame.

She didn't reply, but bit down on her lip and shook her head. I couldn't tell if it was agreement or dismissal.

"Unless, of course, you're willing to tell me who did this to you so I can bring them in."

"No." She had no fear of meeting me in the eye on that response.

"We have found a spot for you," I said. "Where you can stay, where you will be safe."

"I've stayed there before," Suzanne said. "When I had some trouble like I told you last night."

"I can't just cut you loose with nowhere to go," I said.

"I'm not going to any government place," she said.

"No," Suzanne said. "We wouldn't ask you to do that."

Rory's eyes went from Suzanne to me. "I'm not dumb. I know what happened and what this means. I can't go home. I don't care about that. But I want my girls. I'll go where you want if you can bring them back to me."

"Our plea on television and in the newspapers will make a difference. That's why I did them. I didn't think they'd have the results they did regarding you, or that Boomer would be parked in front of a television watching the news." We might have been better off if I'd let Suzanne handle this.

"I've been telling you that he isn't stupid. Just because he's big and doesn't dress nice or run around with those precious townspeople, that doesn't mean he doesn't know what's what. Maybe you should start listening to me."

I nodded. I was learning: I didn't remind her that Boomer hadn't done anything to find the girls and that he'd actually impeded our investigation. Instead, I made toast—a great breakfast—while Suzanne told her about the convent and the nursing home in Milltowne. We left thirty minutes later. I dropped Suzanne off at her house, and we waited while she went in and got some additional clothes for Rory. Even with bruising turning purple on her neck and an eye that was swollen, she looked better than I was used to seeing her.

I drove Rory up to the convent, taking backroads. The mill where the men from the Village worked was on Main Street by the river that ran through the city center. I wanted no chance of a Laurel police car sighting. I had some questions that Rory could help me with, but didn't want to come across as interrogating her. I turned down the radio and tried to act offhanded.

"I heard that Holly and Maisie were doing some work for Boomer every now and then," I said.

"I told you that. He had them on night crawlers and sea worms."

"When would they do this?"

"Not too often. Every other Friday and Saturday night. You know you get night crawlers at night? It's right there in the name."

"Are you sure that's what they did?"

"What else would they be doing?" She looked at me as if I'd asked another dumb question. At least the anger that marked her voice Tuesday at the station had dissipated.

"I don't know. Just double-checking, trying to keep the facts straight." I was guessing that in this case, Jimmy Goodwin's information, confirmed by Blink, was more accurate than Rory's. It would need investigating.

The nursing home of St Mary's was on the coastal side of town, situated on a tidal pool. The facility was a one-story building shaped like an L. The convent was behind it, a two-story brick building that looked like a prep school dorm. Before I could get Rory's clothes out of the back, Sister Agnes came out to greet her. Rory stiffened when Sister Agnes hugged her, then softened and hugged her back. When I started reiterating the importance of no one knowing that Rory was here, Sister Agnes stopped me short.

"I heard you this morning, Chief. We'll take good care of her."

Whether this was for my benefit or to not further embarrass or stress Rory, I wasn't sure. But I went along and told them to call me at the station if they needed anything. Then I went to work.

Chapter Sixteen

I reached the office later than usual, so skipped the sports and stayed on the front page article, *Twin Girls Missing in Laurel*. It featured a cut-up of the yearbook picture and a small insert of me. The sub-headline read *Town Police Asks for Help*. It could have easily said: *Chief Appears in Over His Head*. People were encouraged to contact us if they'd seen or had information about the Connolly twins. I was counting on this outreach working. If it didn't, I had nothing but the basics, and that approach had yet to find the girls. Still, I went through the nightly log. There was nothing much other than the incident with Rory, of which I already knew the details. Estelle told me that we had not yet received any calls on Holly and Masie. As it was already ten o'clock, that was a bad sign. A call came in a few minutes later from a Channel Eight reporter. They were interested in coming down and doing a story. That was a break. As soon as I got off the phone with her, Link Johnson showed up and planted himself across from my desk.

Link did not have information, but did have a concern—that I hadn't pointed out, either in the television interview or newspaper, that the girls were not from "real" Laurel but a throwback outpost that wasn't part of the town. I'd also failed to communicate the positive and safe nature of Laurel. As the Lead Selectman, Johnson also served as the Police Commissioner. Technically, that made him my boss. In this case, however, his concerns weren't based on my policing. What he feared was that people might now be less likely to visit and thus wouldn't be spending ninety-nine bucks to sleep in the crappy, wood-paneled rooms of his motel that sat just outside the square. When I pointed out that the important thing was to find two missing teenage girls, he retorted that if girls from the "normal" part of town were missing, the Woodman tribe would certainly not be helping us find them. By the time he shut up, I was ready to grab him by the collar and belt and bum-rush him out of the station.

"Have you seen *Jaws*?" I said after he'd killed too much of my time.

"Who hasn't?" he replied.

"Maybe you should watch it again and see if you can learn anything about resort town politics." Then I told him I was expecting a classified call from the FBI and that he'd have to leave.

"Jesus, we got the FBI in on this?" he said, even more distraught. It did get him out the door, however.

I was quick to answer the phone when it rang seconds later. Judy Woodroof was on the line. Her husband was a plumber, and they were both members of the volunteer fire department.

"I'm calling about those Woodman girls, LT," she said.

"Great." I slid the legal pad in front of me, stuck the phone on my shoulder, and grabbed a pen. "What do you have for me?"

"What the hell are you doing looking all over the place for them?"

"Why? Do you know where they are?" I hoped for the best—that she knew something that had been right in front of me, but I'd failed to grasp. While that could have explained the annoyance in her tone, I should have known better.

"Those people live like animals. Let them take care of their own."

"Judy, you're talking about teenage girls." I started counting to ten and concentrated on breathing deeply.

"They don't care about us, and we shouldn't be wasting town time and money looking for them. You've got enough to do with all these damn tourists running over us."

"Didn't your kids just graduate a few years ago?"

"Yeah, but my two take showers on a regular basis and don't date their own damn cousins."

I hung up on her. The phone kept ringing, and while most calls weren't as vile as Woodroof's, none were made to volunteer information. One resident after another questioned why the town was wasting time looking for *those people*. I tried not to get upset, as I'd had similar thoughts when Rory first sat in front of me. However, a number of law-abiding citizens were left with dial tones that afternoon. I couldn't let them distract me. I was having a hard enough time as it was.

I was about to ride out to Blink's to grab some lunch when Earl Goodwin showed up. I was hopeful. Between the rental properties he owned and managed and the houses he had for sale, he was all over town. If anyone had spotted them, it was likely him. His jeans were pressed, and his white dress shirt was open at the collar. His hair, perfectly combed, did not have a fleck of gray. I could feel mine turning every minute. I hoped we were finally going to get some help.

"What the hell are you doing, LT?" he said.

"Excuse me?" One can only count and breathe so many times before it's exhausted as an anger management technique.

"I understand that it's your job to find missing people and such, but this newspaper and television shit? It really paints the town in a bad light." This from a guy whose son was close to the girls, something he had no clue about.

"In what way?" I said.

"Well, people from away might think that it's not safe here, that we have some sort of deviant abducting women and girls, when it could be that those two just jumped on a Greyhound and got the hell out of Dodge."

"That hasn't been determined, Earl. Not that I have to answer to you, but we've questioned everyone at the stations in Milltowne and Kittery, and no one has seen them. Not the ticket people, not the regular drivers." He started to reply, but I plowed through him. "We've posted flyers all over town, and zero people have responded with anything helpful. So unless you have some useful information regarding the whereabouts of those girls, who are citizens of this town, this conversation is over."

"Look, I'm sorry, LT. But this summer has seven weeks left, and many of us can't afford to have business vanish because people are scared to come here. If you'd thought to mention these sisters were from a community that wasn't part of the town, then it might be different. Maybe you could have the papers and television do a follow-up, where you could put that out there, and it wouldn't be so bad for the rest of us."

"What about bad for them? Do you think that would motivate people to help or call in?"

"I know where you're coming from, and I'm sorry to be like an asshole. But they don't do anything for Laurel. Hell, I don't even know if they pay taxes, and that land they squat on is worth a goddamn bundle, being on the river like that. Banks in this state would fall all over themselves to finance a project down there. It's like a refugee camp."

"Yeah, who'd you hear that from?" I wasn't going to tell him that he was right.

"I've seen it for myself."

"When did this happen?" His mouth fell open, and his eyes got big. He ran a hand through his hair. He hadn't wanted that bit of information to slip out.

"You know real estate is my world, and that's a potentially sweet piece of land. I took a quick peek."

"Did you clear that trip with Boomer Woodman?" Maybe there was a reason Boomer hadn't kicked the shit out of Jimmy and his boys.

"I wasn't there for a cookout or anything, Chief." He shook his head and shifted in his chair.

"You ever seen those girls around?"

"No, of course not," Earl said, glancing at his watch. "I'm sorry to bother you. I'm just worried for the town. A lot of us depend on these eight weeks to make our year."

"I realize that, Earl." I remained calm and didn't ask how many rents it would take to make up for the loss of two teenage girls. Nor did I ask how his kid ended up with a better moral compass than he possessed. "You can go now."

He cocked his head, and his eyebrows came together over his nose. He started for the door, then paused with his hand on the knob.

"Jimmy was pretty upset when he saw the newspaper this morning," Earl said.

"It's my understanding that the Connolly sisters were actually part of the student body. Things have changed from when I was at Timbercoast, and it was probably worse when you were there."

"Wouldn't touch them with a ten-foot pole back then," he said, shaking his head. "Despite how this looks, and I know what you might have thought I sounded like, I'm glad we're making a little progress."

"Bye, Earl," I said. As far as I was concerned, if someone wasn't there to tell me they'd seen the girls, they were wasting my time. I'd blown through my lunch hour, but had lost my appetite anyway. Some small progress might have been taking place in the town, but it wasn't in this investigation.

* * *

I spent the rest of the day making queries to other departments, fielding no incoming calls of substance, and accomplishing nothing. At least my patrols reported no new disasters. I checked out at six-thirty and swung by Blink's to see Suzanne.

"If it isn't the big tv star," Blink said when I came through the door. "How's the manhunt going?"

"It's not, Blink. It's not going at all."

"That may not be a bad thing," he said. I looked over at Suzanne. She was cleaning up. She shook her head and shrugged. That was Blink.

"Those girls are still missing," I said.

"They're probably on a beach somewhere, laughing their asses off about all the fuss that's being made."

"I hope you're right, Blink, but I doubt it."

"What makes you say that?" His grin diminished.

"I'm not a fucking idiot," I said.

"Okay, okay," he said, putting up his hands. "Why don't you help yourself to one of those quarts back there? Schlitz rocks America, and you could use some rocking yourself by the looks of it."

I nodded and walked over to Suzanne's counter.

"Not a great day?" she said quietly. The longer she looked at me, the more her eyes seemed to focus. Her smile slowly disappeared.

"You might say that."

"Did you deliver the package okay?"

"I did, but it's been downhill since. What are you up to?"

"Oh, I'm sorry, LT. I'm supposed to go to Cape Elizabeth with Robin. Her sister Terry just had a baby. I can get out of it if you want."

"No, that's fine. You go have some fun. I imagine wine will be involved."

"At least let me make you a sandwich. I've seen the contents of your refrigerator."

"Sure," I said.

She stopped after slicing the roll. "I'm going to call Robin. You look like you could use a friend."

"Really, Suzy, you don't have to do that. I'd be lousy company tonight." She protested, but by the time she finished putting the sub together, I'd convinced her it was okay. I didn't need to bring her down to my level.

I took my roast beef and quart of Schlitz and went home. I got in my run and was actually starting to get fast again. I did weights for thirty minutes. I sat on the couch with my beer and thought about calling Trout to see if he wanted to come over and watch the Sox. I didn't have the energy to get up and walk to the phone. I fell asleep somewhere around the fourth inning and didn't wake up until morning.

Chapter Seventeen

The investigation had slowed to a crawl when I walked into the station Sunday morning. Based on the microscopic chance that Holly and Maisie had left early for California, I fired up the phone. I called every runaway hotline on the East Coast, and then contacted every metropolitan police department in a line from Boston to New York to Chicago and St Louis to Las Vegas to Los Angeles and San Francisco. None had any reports of twin teenage girls. My media outreach had also flopped, producing not one call of value. I couldn't ignore the possible connection between Holly and Maisie working for Boomer and their disappearance, but had no idea what they did for him. Nor could I imagine anyone disappearing over bait. None of my officers had seen Boomer anywhere on a Friday or Saturday night for the past two months. That left no path to finding out what the girls had been doing that didn't go through Boomer, and his answering questions wasn't going to happen. The acid building in my gut felt like it was gushing out of a hose.

If I'd stared at the walls in my office another minute, I would've snapped so I jumped in a cruiser and started driving. I went into the square and then down River Road to the Bluff and out past the Grime's estate. I cut back through town and passed Laurel Elementary. I'd gone there for eight years. There were two classes for each grade then, and Rory Connolly must have been in one of them. I cruised Gray Gull Beach, then went south all the way to Bishop's Beach. I passed the Captain's Galley, where I washed dishes as a teenager and bartended for eighteen months, the job I'd left to join the Department. Then I drove another circuit in the opposite direction. I didn't know what I was looking for, but whatever that was, I didn't see it—not among the families at the beaches, not with the tourists hitting the shops or the kids riding their bikes, and not with the old folks walking their dogs or the husbands mowing their lawns. I drove out to the Village and parked on Brown Street across from Woodman's Lane. I stared at the gravel road that disappeared into the green. Like a dope, I sat there for an hour. I considered driving in and asking Boomer all the questions that he wouldn't answer. Nothing good would have come of that. Trout was starting his shift at three o'clock, so I returned to the station.

"What've you been doing?" he asked.

"Failing," I said.

He rubbed his head and grinned. "In new ways, at least, or in the same old ways?"

"What do you mean by that?" I said, apparently missing the humor.

"You're being too hard on yourself," he said. "You haven't come across anything you couldn't handle, and now you got one. You can do everything right and still come up short. That's life, buddy."

"Thank you, Plato."

"Glad to help."

"You've been doing this a long time. What have I missed?"

"Unless you can tie Caleb down and slip him some truth serum, I don't know that we're ever going to hear what he did with them. I wouldn't bet on ever finding those girls. The world's too big."

"Do you remember that psychic up in Dayton, the one who found that lost prize Labrador retriever that was worth three grand? They had a big article about it in the Press Herald. Maybe we should take a ride up there."

"Are you serious?" Concern broke across his face.

"Why not?" I said.

"Jesus, LT," he said, taking a long look at me. "When's the last time you had a day off?"

"I don't know," I said. "I can't stop and do nothing in the middle of this."

"Sometimes that's what you need."

"You know me, right?"

"This isn't something you can put in a headlock and flip onto its back." He shrugged his eyebrows. "Why don't you call it a day and go to the Drydock? Clear your head."

"Is your boat in the water?" I said.

"Course. You want to go fishing?"

"No, I want to go to the Village."

"By the river?"

"That's the only angle we haven't looked at it from. Speaking of looking at the Village, do you know that Earl Goodwin has been out there?"

"Really?" His lips came together as he raised his eyebrows. "For what?"

"He's not the curious type unless it's something he can sell. You heard anything about that?"

"Nope. And I can't picture him and Boomer out on the ninth fairway at The Cascades talking over a deal."

"Where's the boat?" I said.

"You want me to go with you?"

"Who'll direct traffic in the square?"

"It's Sunday, LT. It's all going south."

We drove down to Billy O's Marina and climbed onto Trout's Whaler. Ten minutes later, we were skipping over the waves at the breakwater under the Bluff and coming out on the ocean. Laurel had three beaches, two town-run piers, and miles of rocky, crooked coastline. There were shoals everywhere. Rocks that jutted out like islands at low tide lurked under the waterline at high. If you didn't pay attention to the buoys and markers, you'd hit something. Not enough people paid attention. Our marinas were swamped with repairs. The bitterness in my throat came from having studied every detail of the Connolly sisters' disappearance and not having any idea of what had gone on under the surface.

We hooked south to Bishops Beach. Spray came in over the center console. Trout cut the throttle as we started up the Laurel River. We ran at half, and I broke out the binoculars. The tide was slack. Tommy cod ran in schools just under the surface as we trolled. Marsh ranged on both sides, channels cut into it for water flow, work done in the thirties by the WPA. Past the pale knee-high grass were unbroken stretches of trees and forest. Butterflies danced over the shore. Two snowy egrets paddled up one of the channels. A red-tailed hawk glided in circles. There was so much space and no sign of human life.

We came to the point where the Village lay inland. Two things marked the spot. The first was the two wooden boats tied to stakes on the marsh. They were twelve footers, painted the same gray as the shacks. They sported outboards, ten or fifteen horsepower, and were twenty years old. You'd think that they would have built themselves a dock and got their hands on something that could handle the ocean better than those relics. There was plenty of fish and lobster to be had. Apparently, it wasn't for them. The Village's other giveaway was the sickly trail of gray smoke that rose from behind the trees. The way the river widened into a pool made this one of the most beautiful spots in town. Out of sight behind it, the Great Depression lived on.

"What are you looking for, LT?" Trout asked, the engine now at idle.

"Two girls." I pointed to the boats. "Pull up over there."

I jumped out and took a look at the skiffs. I didn't expect to find the sisters there. I just hoped to find something. A crab trap was tied to the bow seat with a fraying coil of rope in one of them. The other had a couple of cheap department store fishing poles outfitted with mackerel jigs. They both had oars, which was wise, as well as an indication that the vintage motors weren't too trustworthy. There were no gas cans. They weren't going anywhere and probably hadn't moved all season. Of course, there were no shreds of clothing, clumps of hair, or even a speck of blood. They were just a couple of lousy boats tied out on a marsh. I'd been floundering since I'd stepped out of bed that morning.

I climbed back into the Whaler and made Trout bring me in a circuit by both banks of the river, forming the pool. It had been a fool's errand. If the tide were out, everything would be in the open, and not even the Woodman's were stupid enough to hide something in plain sight. It was eerily quiet. The mouth of the river north of Gray Gull wasn't nearly as wide, yet was full of boaters, water skiers, and tourists castling lines for stripers that had disappeared years earlier. I tapped Trout on the shoulder and called it a day.

We were headed back to the marina, but instead of pulling into his slip, Trout kept going. He looked over at me and grinned.

"No," I said.

"I can't hear you over the motor." Trout smiled as he pulled up at the pier below the Drydock.

"We're on duty, Nate," I said.

"I might be, but you're off for the day starting right now."

He led me up the gangway to the outdoor bar. It was two-deep with locals. The Adirondack chairs on the deck were filled with tourists. Nate waltzed into the service area, the crowd parting for him like he was some sort of celebrity. Chelsea Harrison was making drinks for the waitresses. She was a cute brunette who'd graduated from Timbercoast a few years earlier and was now at UMaine. She had the sense to stick it out longer than a semester, unlike some of us.

"Hey, Mr. Trout," she said. "Are you looking for Fred?" That was the owner.

"No, Chelsea. I was wondering if you could get us a couple of cold coffees?"

"You mean iced coffee?"

"No, I mean cold coffee, like from St, Louis." He looked at the beer taps, then slowly dropped his vision to the coffee mugs that were behind the bar. He raised his eyebrows to see if she got it. She gave him a nod, me a smile, and poured two Buds into ceramic coffee mugs. I couldn't deny that I could use a drink. I wondered if this was one of Dederian's old tricks. He ended a lot of his shifts here in the old days. Maybe I should have listened to Trout. It would have been a fine thing to sit in one of those chairs with Suzanne, a pint-sized gin and tonic in hand. Maybe that would have been enough to keep those girls out of my head for a few hours. I was trying to think of places we hadn't searched for them when Trout handed me my beer.

"How's the crime-fighting, boys?" Jamie Finn said. He was a local who spent his winters crab fishing in Alaska for some reason I couldn't fathom. It did provide him with his summers off and pockets full of money, however. His sidekick, Ed Pickey, a lobsterman, stood next to him. They were in jean shorts cut off just above the knees and t-shirts.

"It sucks," I said. Finn's eyes narrowed as he tried to determine if I was joking.

"In that case, maybe you should be drinking something better than coffee," Pickey said.

"What do you take us for, Pick?" Trout said. "We're on duty."

Pick was six-four. He took a look down into our mugs and nodded, then tilted his head, so Finn was inclined to look, too. They chuckled.

"I hope my money's safe in the Bank and Trust should someone hit it right now," Finn said.

"Rest easy, boys. We got it covered." I didn't see any reason not to mix business and pleasure, even if it were a Hail Mary. I couldn't stop. "You guys ever run into Boomer Woodman on weekends?"

"Boomer?" Pickey said, practically shouting. Finn shot a 'what the hell' look across to Trout. "What would we be doing with him?"

"I don't know. That's why I asked. You boys get around pretty good, and I heard he might be up to something."

"I can tell you, LT," Finn said. "We got enough of our own problems without messing with that bastard."

"Oh yeah, Chief," Trout said, elbowing me. "We got ourselves some Eagle Scouts right here."

They shuffled off after that not-exactly-an-interrogation. I felt like I kept walking into a patio door that I couldn't see, and I was getting tired of it. A few other folks came by and said hello, asked how we were doing, and commented on the weather, which was indeed terrific. No one offered any information about the Connolly sisters. None even asked how the search was going. More evidence of my failure.

I grabbed Trout's empty coffee mug and went back over to Chelsea. Her ponytail bounced as she hustled over.

"What can I get for you, Chief?"

"How about another one of those coffees for my associate, and I'd like a Tennessee version, maybe with some Coke?"

"I got you," she said, smiling. I watched her pour a stiff Jack and Coke for me. I guessed she did better than just passing grades at Orono. That drink started putting a dent in my frustration. Maybe skipping breakfast and lunch was going to work out, after all. Fred Princeton came over and told us that business was off a good twenty percent. Evidence indicated otherwise, as the deck had only gotten more crowded, except around us. Maybe it was the uniforms or maybe the guns. But I wasn't in the mood to argue with him. At least he didn't blame my media campaign. I went back to Chelsea for another round.

"Jesus, you guys are like the police force?" This came from the man next to me, who Chelsea had bypassed to grab my mug. He was wearing a white dress shirt over his pink I-Zod with the collar turned up. He had on khaki shorts and Topsiders. I was glad to see his blond hair was thinning. I put him at forty-five. Apparently, he'd watched our coffees being made.

"Keen insight," I said.

"And you're drinking?" He sounded put out about it. His accent said New York.

"What gave you that idea?" I reached out and handed Trout his mug. He was talking to Mary Worthington, a waitress at Allie's.

"You'd think there'd be regulations against that," he said.

I drained the mug Chelsea had just given me to prove a point, handed it back to her, and nodded for another.

"You don't feel safe up here?" I said.

"I do, but I'm not a teenage girl. Don't you have a couple of them missing?"

"What?" I could feel my chest tighten.

"It seems like you should be out looking for those girls instead of standing around tying one on."

"Damn, I should have thought of that." My voice had a bite to it.

"Take it easy." He adjusted his John Lennon glasses and backed up half a step into the person behind him. It was like I'd just sleepwalked for ten seconds. I'd put my drink down, the muscles in my neck and shoulders had tightened, and I was on my toes.

"Have you seen those girls?" I asked. "You have information for us?"

"No."

"Neither does anyone else. Why do you think that is?"

"Hey man, I just came up from Manhattan."

I was waiting for a trigger. My left foot was itching to shoot forward, and my shoulder was ready to drop. The right cross would fly to his jaw. I felt Trout's grip like pliers on my arm. With the other hand, he flipped a couple twenties to Chelsea.

"It's the Wild West here," I said, in forced retreat as Trout walked me back. "Watch your ass, or we'll fucking run you out of town." The guy fell back into his friends, who were watching us like we were in a movie scene you couldn't believe was happening. Trout dragged me to the boat.

"Maybe that wasn't such a good idea," Trout said, shaking his head and starting the engine.

"I told you." It was the only thing I'd gotten right all day.

Chapter Eighteen

I couldn't afford to suspend myself for stupidity, but I could torture myself, so that next morning I was back at work. A splitting headache barely registered on my list of problems, and I was used to feeling like I was running on empty. I planned on reviewing every log entry and report written by this department starting with the Thursday the girls disappeared and following up on anything that could even remotely be connected to the case. While we hadn't been able to tie anything in town in real-time to the Connolly girls, maybe hindsight would expose something. That particular Thursday, we had one bonfire extinguished, two bonfires verified with permits, and a few speeding tickets issued. That was it. Crime really picked up on Friday. There was a dispute over which cottage owned a right of way onto Gray Gull Beach, a fender bender at the Bluff, a good number of moving violations, and yet another call from the Glennons complaining about someone in their driveway. It had come in at seven-thirty that night, a tourist's wrong turn probably interrupting filet mignon and French wine. It would only take a minute to confirm that it was not a purple Galaxie 500 that had ruined dinner. I picked up the phone.

"Chief Nichols, here. How are you today, Henry?" I said when he answered.

"Well Chief, I hope you're either calling to apologize for hanging up on me last week, or you've found an acceptable solution for our Oak Ridge Road problem."

"Actually, Henry, I'm calling about a complaint you lodged on Friday, June twenty-seventh."

"You do realize that was ten days ago, and we've had several more incidents in the interim?"

"I do," I said, starting the calming counting in my head. "Thank you for clarifying that. Do you remember the reason for the call that day, Henry?"

"I certainly do. I'm getting tired of these people on my driveway."

"Could you please explain Friday the twenty-seventh?" All the call log had said was: "Car in the Glennon driveway. AGAIN!"

"We were having dinner, and Kate mentioned that she'd gotten up to get a drink in the middle of the previous night and actually saw someone parked in our driveway. She didn't bother to call it in because of the time, and she had neglected to mention it to me. Of course, I thought the department should know. I've scolded her for it. I don't want kids—"

"I'll be right over." I hung up on him again. Adrenaline vanquished my headache.

I was knocking on the estate door within fifteen minutes. A maid answered and led me through a beautiful entryway of floor-to-ceiling windows with cherry framework to the back of the house, where Henry and Kate Glennon were enjoying coffee on their kitchen deck. It looked out over a football field of a lawn that led down to their pond. A tennis court had been built off to the left. If one enjoyed peace, quiet, and solitude, I could see the argument for passing up the ocean.

"Chief Nichols," Henry said, rising from his chair. The Glennons were in their sixties. Kate was thin and athletic looking in a white and red tennis dress, and could have passed for forty. Her blond hair was held back by a pink headband. Henry was in tennis whites and wore a Yankees hat. He looked all of fifty. Their rackets leaned against the rail of the deck.

"I'm here about the car that Mrs. Glennon saw that Thursday."

"Why would that be of interest?"

"You've heard about the two girls who've gone missing?"

"Why yes," he said. "From what I understand, they're from that crazy village across town."

"That's the day they went missing, and anything that happened that night is of interest. We've had little luck so far, and those folks do have cars."

I hoped I hadn't come across as a wiseass, though my level of caring was somewhat low. "Your call came on Friday night, so we never followed up in regards to the girls."

"I see," Henry said, frowning. "Perhaps I could have been more specific when phoning it in. But it had occurred the previous day, and I hadn't expected you people to be able to do anything about it. I just wanted to reinforce an awareness of the unceasing nature of the problem."

"Please, sit down," Kate said. I joined them at the umbrella table, and the maid brought me a coffee without being asked.

"Mrs. Glennon, can you tell me what you saw?"

"Nothing much to tell. As you know, from our vantage point up here, we do tend to notice when someone enters our property. If we're not expecting anyone, it can be quite unsettling."

"I understand. Please, go on."

"I'd had trouble sleeping." She sat up in her chair and put her cup down on its saucer. "It was very late. Maybe two-two thirty? I'd gotten up to get a drink in the kitchen. As I was coming down the stairs, I saw some headlights near the end of the driveway."

"What did they do?"

"Nothing for a while. You know how it is around here with these kids. They're always out on Oak Ridge parking and whatever. I figured that maybe some young couple was having their way down there."

"My wife is a romantic," Glennon said, making a face.

"Do you notice anyone get out of the car?"

"No. Henry, who is a little more excited by this kind of thing, would have put the binoculars on them. I didn't bother. I just assumed they were getting busy, you know."

"How long were they there?"

"I'm not sure. I went into the kitchen to get some filtered water. Then I went back to bed. I do remember seeing the lights go off when I came back out to go upstairs."

"Did you see anything after that? Hear voices? A car door? Anything?"

I didn't want to ask about gunshots, but figured if there'd been one, she wouldn't have missed it. Sound traveled in the country. Even a conversation might have been audible.

"I'm sorry, no. If you recall, it was very hot that week, so we had the central air on. All the windows were closed, and I went right up to bed."

"They were still there when you went back upstairs?"

"I believe so. The lights didn't move, they just went out."

"Did you notice the color of the car?"

"I could see the lights but couldn't make out the car too well, so maybe it was black or just dark."

A description of the Galaxie's paint job.

"You don't suppose this has anything to do with those girls, do you?" Henry asked.

"I'm not sure," I said, though there was too much to let me believe there was not. Even in the middle of summer, there was rarely traffic in downtown Laurel at two-thirty, never mind on the outskirts. While I hated to think it, the Glennon's land was a good place to hide a body. It was a large parcel, at least a half mile square, and they'd posted No Trespassing and No Hunting signs as soon as they'd purchased it. So unlike other woodlands in town, there wouldn't be hikers, birdwatchers, or hunters traipsing through it. It was also as far away from the Village as one could get. And if one were there to dump bodies, they'd park in the driveway rather than out in the open on Route Nine. Only Kate Glennon's insomnia had given them away. There was also a secluded spot in the midst of it that few people would know unless they'd hunted every inch of it—like the Woodmans, Connollys, and Sampsons.

Anyone who'd attended Laurel Elementary was versed in the town's history. In the 1800's Laurel was known for two things, fishing, and shipbuilding. The shipbuilding was long gone, replaced by the cooking and serving of lobster, along with housing the people who came to eat them. But before all that, the Kents were the one family of ship owners who chose not to live on the river. Mr. Tobias Kent had diversified into a variety of enterprises, including farming, growing his own timber, and mining granite, which all took place on this property. The land between Route Nine and

Oak Ridge was peppered with outcroppings of the rock, which was used for foundations, among other things. The mining project hadn't lasted long as they found the ledge to be scattered in small pockets that were not profitable to harvest. One quarry remained on the land, however. We called it Elephant Rock, because the granite outcropping beside its pool resembled a black elephant lying on its side. Deacon and I had used it as a swimming hole when we were kids, and we only knew about it because of Blink. We'd ride our bikes up to the Route Nine side of the property, ditch them at the edge of the woods, and make our own trail. Even in the worst heat of the summer, it was cool, and we had it to ourselves. It was great for us at twelve, but once we discovered girls and their inclination to go to the beach, we forgot about it. If I were going to hide a body or two, that would be the place to do it.

"I might take a walk through the property just to check," I said.

"By all means," Mrs. Glennon said before her husband got a chance to answer, "march right out there if you have to."

I got her to explain where the car had been on the driveway. I could have started there, but the idea of that quarry picked at me. I'd look there first. If I found nothing, I'd go back to the station, get together some maps, and call everyone in for a proper search.

"Good luck," Glennon said as I headed out. "Or bad luck. I'm not sure which would be better."

I wasn't, either. If I was right and found Holly and Maisie, we'd be done picturing them on a California beach.

Chapter Nineteen

I left the estate. I was fairly certain I could find the quarry from Route Nine. We'd used trees as waypoints, starting with a Scotch pine that was off the road shoulder. If you went straight in from there, eventually you came to an elm, where we had to swing left. They were easy enough to find as I crashed through the thicket like a drunken moose, snapping twigs and pushing branches out of my way only to have them whip back. Slick alcohol sweat spilled from every pore. The sun flickered on and off under the canopy of leaves. I killed three deer flies on the back of my neck before coming out into the cluster of hemlocks that led to Elephant Rock.

I climbed the ridge of granite that formed the trunk. That rose up to the body, which on the land-side of the quarry was naturally curved like its back and head. The eyes, mouth, and ears that someone had spray-painted on it before we'd started going there had faded away. On the water side of him, there was a middle section cut out, so it looked like the elephant had two pairs of thick legs. You dove into the cold water from the feet. I held my breath and stepped onto the front legs, the black water of the quarry below.

For running a town this size, I'd seen my share of dead bodies, and not all had been the elderly passing peacefully in their sleep. A Lady J deckhand had mangled himself in a Datsun B210 he'd rolled after missing a turn. Sal Ragliano had shot himself in the chest with a deer slug while cleaning a vintage shotgun he should have known was loaded. We'd lost a few men at sea, and when they'd been pulled out of the Atlantic hours later, they weren't exactly pretty. They all had remained human, just broken in one way or another.

What was floating in the dark water of that quarry looked like rejects from a wax museum. Their arms and legs were pale, bloated sausages coming out of blue shorts and faded red and green t-shirts. Their trunks puffed like life preservers. Thankfully, they floated face down. I guessed that Rory would be lucky to recognize them after we pulled them out, though I'm not sure that lucky was the word for it. If they had belonged to someone who trusted me, I'd have done anything to make sure that person never saw them. The scent of decay and rot hit me like a fog. I sat down on the rock and tried not to heave. This was a crime scene.

As time went on, it had become more and more likely that the girls were not body surfing in Malibu or sun tanning in Acapulco. Though perhaps I should have, I had not expected this—Holly and Maisie Connolly no longer resembled people. It was hard to believe that someone from Laurel, Maine, could have put them here, even if that person was from Woodman's Village. The killer drove the same streets and had gone to the same schools as the rest of us. How was I supposed to protect my people from someone who could stand next to them in a checkout line and then do this?

I got Crowley on the radio and told him I'd found the bodies of the girls.

"Where?" he asked. He did not sound surprised they were dead. None of us should have been.

"Elephant Rock."

"Where the hell is that?" Rather than trying to explain, I told him to head up Route Nine and find the Bronco. I'd come get him. I told him before he came to call Pettibone, to get him here, too, and for him to bring his team from the crime lab. Even if I'd wanted to pull the girls out myself, I didn't know if doing so would tamper with evidence or rip them apart. I felt guilty leaving them and going to meet Crowley at the road. He said that the State crew would be there within an hour. He looked shaken when I took him in and showed him the bodies in the inky water.

"Jesus Christ," he said. The swarming flies emitted a sickening buzz. "We aren't going to have to jump in there to fish them out, are we?"

"We'll leave that to the Staties, who know what they're doing," I said. "You stay here. I'm going to get Cranky Fisher."

"Cranky?"

"He's the best hunter in town. They came in through the Glennons' driveway that Thursday night. It's the only time they haven't turned in a goddamn trespasser. I want him to track the path and see if we can find anything. I'll be right back."

I drove to Fisher's house. I caught him napping on the couch in his underwear. I told him we needed him to do some tracking. He balked until I told him if he wouldn't come, I'd have to call Shane Miller, who also claimed to be the best hunter in town. I didn't mention that this was about the dead bodies of the Connolly girls. He might have said to just go ahead and get Miller. He put on his camo pants and a t-shirt, and covered himself in bug spray. On the way back to Route Nine, I radioed Estelle and had her call the Glennons and tell them, "I found what I was looking for," and that they were likely going to see some public safety vehicles at the end of their driveway. I was back to Route Nine with Cranky in less than a half hour.

When we reached Elephant Rock, I told Fisher, a guy not much taller than me but twice as wide, to wait at the end of the trail. I sent Crowley back to the cruiser to wait for the lab crew, and I told him to keep it quiet. Then I brought Fisher up to the edge of the granite. The light had shifted behind us. Shadow had fallen over the quarry, but there wasn't any hiding what was in the water.

"What the hell is that?" Fisher said.

"Those are the Woodman's girls," I said.

"Holy shit." He wiped the sweat off his forehead.

"I'm pretty sure they got dumped in here two weeks ago. They were brought in through the driveway on the old Kent place. I'm guessing they came out on the other side of the quarry. I need to know what path they took, and we need to find anything—anything—that they may have left behind."

"Unless they got dropped out of the sky, there'll be something," Cranky said, his eyes following the edge of the rock around the edge to the other side. We climbed down the side of the elephant, and he started slowly, moving one step at a time, until his eyes fixed on something. "Right there," he said. "That's where they came in."

123

He was pointing to the edge of the rock directly across from the elephant's belly. Shoots of field grass were pushed over. Then he found marks that looked like two heels that had been dragged. I took out my jack-knife and cut part of one of my sleeves off, and tied it to a branch to mark the spot. I radioed Crowley and told him that if the Staties arrived to keep them on the rock, and that we'd come back and show them where they'd be able to take evidence. Fisher pushed forward, taking a step, studying what was in front of him, and then "aha-ing" or saying, "That's right." He had us trudging through the brush, sidestepping the path they'd taken instead of following it, and was able to point out just about every step they'd taken. Then he put up his hand.

"Look at this," he said, pointing to a foot-high sprout of a pine tree. It didn't look like anything but a plant getting not enough light. "See those specks over the needles. I bet that's blood."

Only when I bent down and stared exactly where he was pointing could I see what he was talking about. I took an evidence bag from my belt and pulled the plant. Another ribbon from my sleeve went there. We'd gone another twenty feet when he grabbed my arm and pointed to a broken twig on the ground.

"See that? See how the break is kind of pushed into the ground? That isn't from a goddamn squirrel stepping on it. Someone big, I bet."

We'd come far enough that I could see the break in the tree line over the driveway. It had taken us an hour to go a few hundred yards. Cranky brought us out of the woods just above where they'd entered. He pointed out two thin branches that were snapped and hanging.

"That's something that might be of interest to you," Cranky said.

"I can see where they went in," I said.

"Look a little closer."

There was a cigarette butt. With its yellow filter, it looked a Marlboro, and I knew at least two people from Woodman's who smoked them. That went in another evidence bag. We could see where the grass had been run down by the passenger side tires. I looked at the gravel of the driveway, but it was packed too hard to get a tread.

"That's the best I can do for you, LT," he said, looking up the driveway to the estate. "Those people don't even know about the quarry, I bet."

"Nope," I said. "Crowley didn't either."

"They don't hunt."

We had to walk down the Cape Road and then up Route Nine to reach the Bronco, which had been joined by Pettibone's patrol car and the van from the crime lab. We got there just in time to see the medical examiner's hearse pull up. I asked Cranky if he'd bring the state guys through where he'd just guided me. Maybe they'd come up with more evidence. Pettibone sent one of his men off with Cranky. Then he wanted to know how I'd found them.

I explained the call we'd received from the Glennons that Friday and how they hadn't reported that the incident had actually occurred Thursday. I knew of the quarry. He pointed out that, technically, I should have called the lab before I'd gone in so that evidence wasn't disturbed. That didn't strike me as logical, but the next minute he was giving me credit for excellent police work. I didn't feel great. It was only a matter of time before I'd be taking a ride to the convent in Milltowne.

I waited until they'd pulled the bodies from the quarry. Pettibone stopped them after they'd been placed on the stretchers so he could take a look. I tried to stay back, but he called me over. He said it was lucky they were in water because they'd been preserved, but I will be seeing those faces for the rest of my life—bloated caricatures of Halloween masks that only in the most sickly comic way looked like people. Eyes were engorged. Lips were parallel blue lines across their jaws. Black hair clung to their scalps, but strands were missing like they had mange. He said it looked like they'd been there for weeks and pointed out a few things as he examined them. One of them had a blackened bruise on her left cheek, and the back of her skull was loose as if it had been smashed. The other had two black marks on her t-shirt, bullet holes. Once the bodies had been loaded into the hearse and left for Portland, I handed over my evidence bags.

Before leaving for St. Mary's, I went to Crowley's cruiser and radioed my rookies. I told them that for the next twenty-four hours, everyone was working because we'd had some developments in the case and that Crowley,

Trout, and I would be busy. I asked Crowley and Pettibone to grab Caleb and notify Jacob Connolly, in that order. I wanted Caleb locked up. I sent Trout to the county seat in Alfred to get search warrants for the shack that the Connollys lived in and Ned's Service, and I wanted him searching that garage. Then I put the Bronco in gear and headed to the convent.

I tried to think of what I could say to Rory, but my mind wouldn't open that door. There would be no easy way to relate—not what happened—but what someone *had done* to her girls. The Boston Strangler and Charles Manson and Lee Harvey Oswald were household names in tiny, pristine Laurel. Every other television program showed someone getting killed. But seeing what became of faces and limbs and having the vapor of decomposition clog your nose while the buzzing of flies rang in your ears, that didn't translate from a screen or book.

Chapter Twenty

I t was just before five when I pulled into St. Mary's. Pettibone had radioed to let me know that Caleb was on his way to a cell and that they'd read him his rights. Boomer had watched them notify Jacob but had not said a word. He'd stood outside as Pettibone's men entered the Connolly shack to search it, then left in his truck. I would have liked to see what Boomer's face registered when we showed up. Though he'd been protecting Caleb from the start, I would have been surprised if he hadn't known his nephew was involved. My guess was that he'd rather have a killer go free than let us put one of his people in jail—even if his nieces were the victims. He might have had his own ideas about dispensing justice or, then again, he might not. But he'd surely bear watching.

I sat in the car and radioed Trout. He was about to impound Caleb's toolbox at Ned's, which held many implements that could crack a skull. I took a deep breath, walked to the convent door, and knocked. I still didn't know what I was going to say. I looked at myself in the reflection of the glass side panel and saw a puffy-eyed drunk with one cut-up sleeve. A nun answered, and I asked to see Rory Connolly.

"Mrs. Connolly isn't here right now," she said, pleasantly enough.

"You've got to be fucking kidding me," I said. "What happened? Where is she?"

"Oh, officer, I'm sorry," she said, frowning as if she'd been the one swearing at me. She pointed to the nursing home. "She's right over there, and doing quite well, considering."

"Thank you, Sister, and I'm sorry."

127

I crossed the parking lot.

The interior of the nursing home smelled of defecation and rot. If I hadn't just been in the presence of two bodies, I'd have said it stunk of death. I'd lost my parents in a car accident in Florida, and maybe it wasn't the worst thing that they hadn't had to face the long declines that could have put them here. I asked for Rory at the front desk. I was directed to the common room, where they were serving dinner.

I had been through things that had upended me. I'd learned of my parents' accident over the phone from a cop in West Palm Beach. My father had suffered a heart attack driving home from dinner, and the car that he took so much pride in—a '66 Thunderbird convertible—slammed into a guard rail and flipped on them. Not two months later, I'd returned from a day-long training in Waterville to notice that my wife's car was not in the garage. I found a note taped to the refrigerator and not a shred of her clothing in the closet. She sent a crew a few weeks later to get her furniture and bring it to St. Louis, where she'd shacked up with an old college boyfriend. Drunkenness was not a stranger then, and I was often in moods that I'd now be reluctant to revisit. Eventually, I'd come out of it. I didn't need to have children to know it would be worse for Rory, who'd already been through enough for anyone.

I walked down the hall. Rory had a cafeteria tray in each hand when she saw me. They crashed to the floor. My face told the story. The clatter silenced the room. An old man screamed for his pudding.

"No," she said, neither loud nor quiet. She slowly shook her head.

"I'm sorry," I said.

Sister Agnes came out of the kitchen and stood between us. She walked over to Rory, put her arm around her, and led her out of the room. Rory didn't even look when she passed. I followed them down the hall and into an office behind the front desk. Agnes placed her in a cushioned love seat, then sat down next to her, arm around her shoulder.

"Tell me," Rory said, tears pouring from her eyes. She sat rigidly, staring straight ahead.

"I found them today. They were not alive, and they'd most likely been passed since they'd gone missing."

"What happened to them?"

"I'm sorry to say—"

"You're always goddamn sorry. You're sorry, and you're responsible."

"We uncovered some information about an incident that happened two weeks ago. From that, I had an idea about where they could be. I'd hoped I was wrong, but I wasn't."

"Where were they?"

"Do you know where the Kent estate used to be? It's a rather large private home out on the Cape Road and Route Nine?"

She nodded and wiped her eyes with a tissue.

"They used to mine granite out of there, and there's a small quarry the size of a backyard pool. That's where I found them."

"They drowned? They can swim just fine, I can tell you."

"They didn't drown. They were put there with the hope that they wouldn't be found."

That snapped something in her. She began to break down, at first, with small tremors. They grew into something unhinged and convulsive. I was glad Sister Agnes was there, because I don't think she would have found comfort with me. She held Rory's hands in hers as she sobbed. I stood patiently for twenty minutes until she gathered herself as if she'd cried herself out.

"Where are they now?" she said, her voice cracking in mid-sentence.

"They're being brought to the Medical Examiner in Portland, to Southern Maine Medical."

"Take me," she said, standing up and wiping her eyes one last time with the sleeve of her Milltowne High Football sweatshirt. Sister Agnes handed her the box of Kleenex.

"Okay," I said.

"Would you like me to go, too?" Sister Agnes said.

Rory Connolly shook her head. "You've done so much for me already. I have to do this."

We left for Portland, and as I drove, I tried to think of what I could say to prepare her for what she was going to see. I had nothing but the truth.

"I don't like saying this, Rory, but I don't want you to walk in there cold. Your girls are not going to look like themselves. It's been ten days, and they've been in water. It affects the body."

"I can take it," she said, blowing her nose. She looked out the window and didn't speak again until Portland rose on the horizon. The largest building was, of course, the hospital where we were headed.

"Does my husband know?" she asked.

"He's been notified."

"Will he be here?" she asked as we pulled into the parking garage.

"I don't know."

She was out of the car and waiting for me before I could move. I hadn't been there often, but I knew the way to the morgue. Rory's eyes shot around the building, from the enormous reception area and atria to the wall of elevators. Who knew if she'd ever been in one, but she followed when I directed her in and hit the button for the sub-basement.

Pettibone was waiting for us in the hall outside the morgue. The walls were a pale industrial green, and antiseptic hung in the air. Pettibone caught my eye and nodded down the hall. He wanted to talk. I sat Rory on the bench outside the double doors of the examination room, and the trooper and I stepped fifteen feet away. She folded her hands in her lap and watched us. She looked dazed, not without reason.

The search of the Connolly shack had resulted in the confiscation of a .22 pistol and two old 30-30s, which were now being tested at the state crime lab. They'd found porn magazines in the loft that Caleb slept in. That loft was right over his sisters' bedroom, and they'd also discovered a quarter-sized hole in the floor hidden under the shabby rug next to the mattress that he slept on. It peered right into Holly and Masie's room. Pettibone said it looked like he'd drilled it rather than it being the result of a knot falling out of the pine plank. The hits would keep coming for Rory, but that wasn't something she needed to know now.

I'd had Caleb in custody and knew in my gut he was tied to his sisters' disappearance. But if not for a woman's insomnia, he might have skated on it. If the hospital walls weren't cement, I would have put my fist through one. I needed to be better.

"The Medical Examiner pretty much agrees with what I figured at the quarry," Pettibone said. "It's not pretty in there."

I nodded.

"You better be up for it." He started over to the door. "We'll be right out, ma'am. Sorry for your loss."

Pettibone introduced me to the coroner, a Dr. Bannon. He had the bodies side by side on a pair of raised stretchers, and he was between them. One was covered head to toe by a sheet, and the other, which he was in the midst of examining, had the sheet pulled down to just above the breast. A bruise covered the right side of her face. If they had once looked like their mother, they did no longer.

"Give him the full show, Doc," Pettibone said. Bannon cradled her head to show us the back of her skull. He pushed in the quarter behind her right ear with one finger as if it were Jello. I was barely able to stifle my gag reflex.

"This one, in technical terms, had her cranium caved in. I haven't performed the complete autopsy, as I've only had these young women for a few moments, but I think it's safe to say that a blow to the head was the cause of death. From the bruising across the face, it could have been that she'd been struck with force and, upon falling backward, hit something that did the damage. Or she could have just been beaten to hell from multiple angles. I should be able to determine that with more study."

He placed the sheet back over her head and then turned to her sister.

"Now, this young lady, her cause of death is quite obvious." He pulled down the sheet to her belly button. "Those black marks on her right breast and the middle of her stomach that look like bullet holes are indeed bullet holes. Could be from a .38. One obliterated what I believe was once a nice, perky tit. The other ripped through her stomach, and I would guess damaged other internal organs."

"Her mother's outside the door, asshole," I said. "So you might want to cool it on the bullshit." Pettibone looked over at me, eyes wide.

"My apologies, Sherriff. I wasn't aware." This guy must have gotten stuffed into a lot of lockers on his way to medical school.

"Do you think they were killed there or somewhere else and dumped?" I said.

"That's a question that Detective Pettibone asked earlier. Based on the way the bullet wounds have sealed and the way the skin has waxed over in places, I'd say they'd stopped bleeding before they hit the water. I can't be definitive on that yet, but it looks like they were killed, remained still, and were then moved."

"Can I bring in the mother now?" I said. Bannon nodded.

I went out into the hall.

"You can come in now," I said, standing in front of the door that I'd closed behind me. Rory stood and stepped forward. I noticed movement up the hall. Boomer Woodman was striding toward us, Jake Connolly behind him and off to the side like a dog at heel. Reynolds struggled to keep up. Rory didn't notice them until I softly said her name and put my hand on her elbow. Her expressionless face did not change.

"Jacob," she said. "Our girls are in there."

Boomer looked at her and shook his head. Then he settled his glare on me as if wanted to go at it. I would've been glad to oblige.

"That's why we're here," Jacob said, his voice high and squeaky. "You shouldn't be by your lonesome." He did not step to her but stayed off of Boomer.

"Were you about to go in?" Reynolds asked.

"That's right."

"We'll be joining you."

"That's your choice." I could have been a ballbuster and pulled out the immediate family protocol, but I didn't think Reynolds would handle those girls well. Yes, it was spiteful and petty. I opened the door and led them in.

Bannon had slid the stretchers next to each other, with sheets covering both bodies. He indicated where Rory should stand. I stood to the side behind her. Boomer crowded in next to her, with Jacob on the other side of him, not making an effort to get to his wife. Reynolds was behind them. Despite the chill in the room, he was dabbing his sweating forehead with a handkerchief. Pettibone nodded, and Bannon pulled back one sheet and then the other to the top of the girls' chests. Rory's hands reached for the stretcher to steady herself. Jake looked away as soon as the second sheet came up. Reynolds left the room. If they had once been identical, they were no longer. The faces, having started from the same point, had morphed grotesquely in different directions.

She turned to me, mouth open, eyes large. "These are my girls," she whispered. I couldn't tell if it was a statement or a question. She found her husband behind her. "Look at them."

Jake Connolly returned his gaze but couldn't hold it. His head dropped. Quiet moans escaped with every breath.

"Maisie," Rory said. She touched her daughter's forehead and tried to style what remained of her black hair so that it covered the hideous purple bruise marring her cheek. Then she said, "Holly," and moved around to the other stretcher. She began pulling her bangs down to cover eyes that were bulging out of their sockets.

"I've seen worse in Nam," Boomer said.

Rory looked up. "You're my brother," she said, whipping around to face him. Her voice rose and crackled like the death call of a fisher cat. "These are your blood. You should have done something."

"Rory," Boomer said. "That's just crazy talk."

"You said that he ran them out of town." She pointed a shaking finger at me. "Why weren't you looking out for them?"

"Rory," Jake said, his voice that of a mouse. "Please."

"I tried like hell," Boomer said. "I know you ain't going to like hearing it, sister, but those girls, they had some ideas of their own."

"They were nice girls, Boomer, and don't tell me different. They're gone, and I ain't ever going to be right with that."

They weren't anything to him.

Boomer folded his arms in front of him. "At least we can take them home and give them a proper burial."

"They won't be going anywhere for a while," I said. "We're going to need to do an autopsy on both of them."

"Haven't they been through enough?" Rory turned her anger on me. Tears escaped from the corner of her eyes. "You're going to cut them up into pieces, for what? They're already gone."

"Their deaths have been confirmed as homicides," Pettibone said. "One was killed with a blow to the head. The other was shot. There's no choice about the autopsy. It's mandated by the state."

Jake stopped moaning but had started shaking. He looked up at Boomer. "Who did this to them?" Jake Connolly said, barely audible.

"We're not quite sure yet," I said. Now was not the time to reveal how it looked for Caleb. "But we will find out, no matter what we have to do."

"We've heard enough bullshit from you clowns," Boomer said, the bass of his voice vibrating through the morgue. He looked at me like he wanted to swing. "We're leaving."

Jacob's head remained low, nearly at a right angle to his thin shoulders. Boomer started to the door.

"Rory, are you coming?" Jacob said. He hadn't moved.

"No."

"Jacob," Boomer said, sharply enough that he immediately followed. Boomer slammed the door behind him.

I was grateful that Rory'd seen it that way, because I couldn't have let her go with them. For her own safety, I would have put her in protective custody, something that could have turned the ugliest of hours even worse. Pettibone followed them out a few minutes later.

"Take your time, ma'am," Bannon said. "I'll be right over there when you've made your peace for today."

She stood at their heads, trying not to cry and failing, continuing to pat and fix their hair. I lost track of time. At a certain point, she gave up.

"Are you ready to go, Rory?" I asked. She nodded. She leaned over and kissed each of them on the forehead. I couldn't imagine what that felt like on her lips or what it did inside. I offered her my arm for support as I had the night she'd been beaten. She ignored it.

"I'm going to bring you back to St. Mary's," I said, once we were again on the highway.

She nodded, her eyes fixed out the window.

"You promised that you'd find them. And you didn't. You and Boomer both."

"I'm sorry," I said. It wouldn't have been right to point out that they'd been dead five days before I'd learned they were missing. In this job and in life, sometimes we are asked to carry things for the benefit of others. This was something I could do for her. I could live with it.

I put her in Sister Agnes' arms, and she was soon surrounded by the sisters of the convent. I asked Agnes to step outside, and I explained that Rory's daughters had been murdered, and that she remained estranged from her family. I told her I didn't know how long they'd need to keep her. Sister Agnes thankfully said that was one thing we didn't need to worry about. I didn't say goodbye to Rory. She'd seen enough of me.

I worked some things out on the way back to town. The killer had to be someone from Laurel, someone who knew the quarry was there, and as Cranky had pointed out, someone who hunted. Every man in Woodman's Village hunted, and none of them would heed a No Trespassing sign. I also could surmise, without the autopsy report, that there'd been an altercation. One girl had been physically assaulted, the other shot. We had a suspect with guns in his house. The suspect was a squirrelly kid who kept porn mags everywhere and drilled a hole in his floor to peep at his sisters. If you were from Laurel, you heard that norms on relationships between family members in the Village were different from the rest of the world. This was just fucked up. I made a note to have Bannon check for signs of sexual abuse. I didn't know if it was standard or not. But even I could see that everything pointed to Caleb.

Chapter Twenty-One

I arrived at the station hoping they had coffee on. I hadn't eaten since breakfast, and the fumes I was running on were dissipating. Arlene, an old friend of my mother's, was working the switchboard. She told me that they'd started the interrogation and that I didn't look well. I walked into the conference room. Caleb sat on the far side of the table. Crowley had him handcuffed to the arms of the wooden chair, a nice touch. Reynolds was on one side of him. Boomer sat on the other, leaning back in his chair against the wall, a smirk planted on his face. Trout was seated opposite Reynolds. Crowley leaned on the table with both hands, right in front of a cowering Caleb. His thin lips were clamped shut.

"Welcome, Chief." Crowley turned to me and smiled, then placed his stare back on Caleb. "This piece of garbage was just going to explain why we found a real sweet Colt Mustang in his tool kit at Ned's. Said firearm was wrapped up in a chamois and taped under one of the drawers. It looked to Trout as if it'd been fired, but I'm sure the state forensics lab will shed some light on that. Is there anything you'd like to tell us now, Connolly?"

"Before you answer that," I said. "What is Eugene doing in here?"

I'd had enough of his intimidation tactics. While I could handle him, his nephew could not, and I wasn't taking chances with anyone else, including my own men. Trout and Crowley turned to look at me, eyebrows raised.

"His nephew is facing a serious accusation," Reynolds said. "He's here to support him, and his guidance is clearly needed."

"Caleb's a legal adult," I said. "He's also a high school graduate. Eugene, you can leave now."

136

Boomer dropped the chair from its lean, slamming its legs on the linoleum. "The hell I will, little man."

"Counselor, you can advise Eugene Woodman that if he doesn't remove himself from this room and station, he will be your second client from this family, because we will lock his ass up."

Reynolds looked over at Boomer and nodded, and Reynolds's handkerchief went back to work on his forehead.

"I'd like to see you try," Boomer said, rising to his feet. Caleb looked from one of his protectors to the other.

"What do you say, Boomer?" Crowley said, hand on his nightstick. "Would you like to test out our accommodations?" He reached for the knob and opened the door.

Boomer pointed a meaty finger at Crowley. "You better keep clear of me out in the world, Beefy."

"Are you threatening a peace officer, Boomer?" Crowley's grip on his nightstick tightened.

"Is that what you call yourself? You look more like a fat cub scout."

"It'll be okay, Boomer," Reynolds said. "I'll be with him for the duration."

"Out, Boomer," I said.

Boomer shifted his stare to me. Then he looked at Trout and laughed. Trout rolled his eyes and shook his head. Boomer came around the table, which he needed to do to get out the door. I backed up so he'd have room to get by. If he came at me, I'd feint with my left, slide behind, and get his arm wrenched behind his back. That would give Crowley a clean shot at him, and Trout could slap on the cuffs. I hoped he tried us. I wanted to break that fucking arm. But he went past, not even giving me a brush. He stopped in the doorway and turned to his nephew.

"Whatever they say, Caleb, you shut the fuck up. They'll do anything to put you away. I don't care if they ask if you want a goddamn cheeseburger. You don't say shit. Got me?"

I shut the door in Boomer's face. Then I told Trout to go make sure he left the building. He nodded and went out. I slid a chair over so I was directly in front of Caleb.

137

"What did you do to your sisters, Caleb?"

"Nothing." He tried to shake his head, but it seemed more like a nervous tic. His eyes were on the desktop. Reynolds watched me closely from across the table.

"Do you know where your sisters were found?"

Again with the head twitch. He didn't say a word.

"They were in a quarry out by the Glennon place. You ever hunt out there?"

"I don't know."

"Did you know we've got a witness who saw your car out there at two in the morning on the day they disappeared?"

"Chief, what is this, really?" Reynolds said. "Are you trying to badger him into to admitting something he couldn't possibly know?"

"Where were you between two and three in the morning that night?"

"I don't know." He clasped his hands in his lap. His thin shoulders bunched in.

"So you weren't home?"

"He didn't say that," Reynolds said.

"Let him speak for himself," Crowley said.

"Do you have an understanding of the attorney's role here, officer?" Reynolds said. Crowley snorted.

"Did you like your sisters?"

Caleb raised his eyes, and his head tilted back. He didn't answer.

"Why'd you drill a hole in your floor? Did you like to look at them?"

"I don't know nothing about that," he said.

"Did you ever hit them?"

"I never laid a hand on those two," he said, raising his eyes and his voice. Apparently, this was a considerably more offensive charge than peeping. His eyes quickly returned to the desk top.

"Did you ever try anything with them, sexually?"

"Them two beanpoles?" he said, and snickered.

"Don't answer those questions, Caleb," Reynolds said. "They're preposterous."

CHAPTER TWENTY-ONE

"Okay. Are you a good shot with the Colt, Caleb?"

"I ain't saying nothing." He stared at the table as if it had been the one testing him.

The interrogation lasted for another two hours. While he didn't follow Boomer's instructions to the letter, he was able to blurt out "I don't know" another hundred times. When we reached the point where I got dizzy standing up to get a drink of water, I called it off.

We had our man. That was certain. His personality fit—a perverted, sexually frustrated brother who drilled a hole in his floor to peep at his naked sisters, who had an antagonistic relationship with him. He was in possession of the possible murder weapon. He'd been the last to see them. We'd found a butt of the cigarette brand he smoked near the bodies. He couldn't or wouldn't say anything in his own defense. All we needed was a few pieces of evidence from the crime lab to fall into place. A jury would hear what we knew and get one look at him, and Caleb Connolly would be going to jail for the rest of his life.

When I asked him what he wanted for breakfast, he stared as if I were speaking French.

Chapter Twenty-Two

I called Suzanne that next morning and told her that we'd found the bodies. I explained that I might not be seeing her for a few days. I couldn't risk losing focus now that I had a chance to close this case. What I didn't mention was that staying apart would also keep her out of the line of fire should Boomer snap and come after me, which was a distinct possibility. To her credit, she asked how Rory had taken the news. It seemed impossible that "as well as could be expected" made any kind of sense. But that's what I said.

I walked into the station at seven o'clock and brought Caleb breakfast sandwiches from Bartley's and a pack of Marlboros. I asked him if he wanted to talk. He looked confused, as if he'd just done a series of bong hits. When I left the cells, Russell from the County Star was waiting in the lobby, and I had phone messages from Channels Six, Eight, and Thirteen. If I wanted to do any actual investigating, I'd need to take care of the media requests. I typed up a press release, another thing I knew little about. I stated that the bodies of the missing Connolly sisters had been found, that they were considered homicides, and that all inquiries would be handled at a press conference at three o'clock. I had Estelle post a copy on the door of the station and call all the newspapers and television stations in the state to let them know the plan. The media had made an effort to help me, and even if nothing had come from it, I had little reason to complain about them trying to do their jobs now.

Pettibone arrived at nine in coordination with Charles Laurent, the county district attorney. We met in my office. Dederian hadn't thought much of

Laurent, but he'd arrived in his last year, and the chief was pretty set in his ways. With his tan and red-lined nose, Laurent looked like he was comfortable handling a golf club and gin and tonic, but I'd never had a problem with him. We'd also never experienced a case of this magnitude. Pettibone told us what the crime lab had learned—he'd made the techs work overnight. The Colt had been wiped, so they hadn't found fingerprints, which wasn't surprising. But it had been fired, and testing found the bullets matched those in Holly Connolly. It was the murder weapon. While an inspection of Caleb's tools hadn't turned up anything, the blood taken from the pine sapling in the woods matched that of Maisie. Laurent advised us to arrest Caleb, because we'd get through a grand jury fairly easily. In the meantime, we could work on a confession and gather evidence to seal the conviction.

We interrogated Caleb again after lunch, which he was afraid to order. He wouldn't speak until Reynolds arrived, Boomer's words apparently lodged in his brain. He wouldn't admit the Colt was his—despite us having found it with his tools. Nor would he say where he got it or why he'd hidden it, where he drove the girls that afternoon, what he did after work that Thursday, why he'd drilled a hole in his goddamn floor, why he had porn mags in his tool kit, or remark on the nature of his relationship with his sisters. Nothing.

I did my first press conference at three o'clock, standing in the sun in the parking lot of the station. Laurent, Crowley, Trout, and Pettibone stood behind me. Laurent had us outline what we were each going to cover so we'd come across professionally. I provided the details as best I could, so it became a human-interest story. The girls were from an "economically depressed" part of town, and yet popular at school. I stated how their mother had walked five miles to let us know of their disappearance, but that they'd been tragically killed the day they disappeared, and we'd never had a chance. Neither had they. No, the family would not be available, as they were private people and wished that to be respected. In addition to fifteen members of the press and assorted television cameras, Johnson, Goodwin, and a few others stood off to the side watching the proceedings. It was all I could do not to turn and ask if they were okay with how the town appeared now.

They'd be thrilled that the actors in this tragedy would not extend beyond the Village, and the satisfaction on their faces had me grinding my teeth. Those girls had wanted out as badly as our leading citizens wanted to keep them trapped there. And as Jimmy Goodwin said, no one had done shit to help them. We were supposed to be better than that.

I stepped back and let Pettibone answer the evidentiary questions, including our possession of the murder weapon. While I had not mentioned anything about the investigation, Pettibone called me out for doing some exemplary police work and a great service to the family by finding their missing daughters, even if the results were tragic. With his booming voice, he was made for this stuff. I was glad when it was over, though again my next scheduled stop was the convent.

Chapter Twenty-Three

Sister Agnes brought Rory to me in the foyer. She took a deep breath when she saw me and shrugged when I asked how she was doing. I wanted to tell her what we'd found out. I'd seen a bench outside, so I asked her to come sit with me.

She was wearing Calvin Klein jeans and a nice white blouse that must have been Suzanne's. Her hair was neatly pulled back. Her eyes were red. I'd seen her worse off.

"I helped out next door today," she said. "I pay my keep, but more so, I couldn't sit around and think about my girls. The old people are nice, and they don't know what's going on. The sisters are trying their best."

"We got some information from the crime lab, and some things have happened that you should know about. Do you think you're ready?"

"They weren't taken advantage of, were they?"

"No."

She let out a deep breath. "My Maisie and Holly aren't coming home. Words can't hurt me like that."

I told her that we found a gun in Caleb's toolbox. "Did you know if he had a Colt Mustang, a small silver semi-automatic pistol with a black handle? It's a nice gun."

"I don't. We got deer rifles, handguns, all over the place. I don't know who had what."

"It's the gun that shot Holly. Forensics confirmed that." A hand went to her face. "He's also the last one to be seen with them, having picked them up south of town. I hate to say this, but it looks like he may be the one

143

responsible for their deaths."

"No. They're his sisters." Her voice was certain and determined. "He would never do that."

"Can I ask you about their relationship?"

"What about it?"

"We searched your home the night we took you to see your daughters. I want you to know that this is standard procedure. It's not because you're from the Village. We found something in your son's sleeping area, the loft."

Her face went rigid. She held her breath.

"First, we found some Penthouse Magazines—you know, naked women in various poses—in his tool locker at work and in his room. That in itself wouldn't be concerning. A lot of guys have those hidden under mattresses. But under the rug was a half-inch round hole. It looked down into your daughters' room."

"It must have just been in the wood. We don't have the best building supplies, which I'm sure you noticed. There isn't anything wrong with how we live. We were happy until this."

"I didn't say there was anything wrong with how you choose to live. It was clear that the hole had been drilled. You can tell by the way the wood was grooved. That's an area of concern. So I have to ask again what the relationship was between your son and your daughters."

She put her head in her hands. Her body shuddered.

"They didn't get along as well as they could. Caleb is kind of a loner."

"Is that by choice?"

"What do you mean?"

"I talked to him prior to this, and he seemed bitter. Like no one would give him the time of day, everyone looked down on him. He didn't strike me as happy, but he did strike me as frustrated. That can lead to aggression."

"Do you remember reading *To Kill a Mockingbird* in high school?"

"I don't know. I wasn't much for English class. I could have."

"We all did," she said. "Do you remember Boo Radley, the kind of retarded guy who lived up the street from the Finches and saved the kids from Bob Ewell?"

I shrugged. "Maybe."

"The point was that Atticus, the father, told Scout that you never know what it's like to be someone until you walk in their shoes. Did you ever think what it's like when we go into Blink's or Bartley's and see the way you people look at us? Or maybe the way they looked at him when they went to Ned's? Do you think we don't know what you people say about us?"

"I'm sorry," I said. I started to count to ten and stopped. For once, I wasn't the one missing the point. A bit of reality needed to come out, even if it hurt her. I met her eyes. "But I'm always sorry, right?" My tone had taken an edge, and her eyes narrowed as she tried to determine where I was headed.

"I've done nothing but try to find your girls from the minute you walked into my office. No one from the Village has done anything to help me. But that doesn't mean anything to you, does it?"

"I guess it might mean something," she said, looking across the lawn.

"I told you from the start that I was going to see this through. If Caleb was the most picked-on kid in the history of Timbercoast, that doesn't make it right for him to do what he did. I'm not saying that he killed his sisters, but it looks that way. He did pick them up on Route Nine. He turned around and went back toward the Village. We have witnesses who saw that. He won't tell us where he took them. He won't talk now, but told us before that they thought they were special and made fun of him, which he didn't appreciate. He won't even tell us if the gun was his. He won't say anything. That's the defense a guilty man takes."

"He knows you want to put him away," she said, wiping tears from her face. "I know he wouldn't do this."

"I don't care who I put away as long as they're the one who killed your girls. If he did it, then yes, I want to put him away, and you should, too. There's other girls out there, from the Village and everywhere else. I don't want to see this happen to them, in Laurel, Portland, or the goddamn North Pole."

"What do you want from me?" she said, anger gone from her voice.

"I'd just like you to answer my questions. I know you've just learned your daughters are gone, and this is the worst time of your life. But I need answers to see that they get justice."

"Okay," she said.

"Did they fight, Caleb and your daughters?"

"He thought they got special treatment from their uncle. They got to go to town. Caleb didn't like that. All he got to do was work. Anytime he did go anywhere else, all he got was trouble because of where he was from. He didn't get to have any fun, other than those cars that he loved."

"Were you home the night your girls disappeared?"

"Yes."

"Did Caleb come home after work, and if so, what time did he get there?"

"He was late for supper. I'm not sure what time it was. But his dinner was cold."

"What did he do after that?"

"He sat out on the porch for a bit and talked to his dad. I cleaned up. By the time I went out, he wasn't there."

"He wasn't on the porch or wasn't in the Village?"

"He wasn't on the porch, but where he parks his car, you can't see it from there. So I don't know."

"Would he talk to his cousins?"

"Some of them. Boomer liked him to check in a few times a week. He could have been down there."

"You didn't see him come back?"

"I went to bed. I'm an early riser, and I used to sleep pretty good."

"And Jacob?"

"He went over with some of the boys and came in later."

"Would he talk to me, do you think?"

"Hell freezing over?"

"Even if it would help his son?"

"He don't believe you're trying to help, and you really aren't. I don't know that Boomer would allow that anyway. We take care of our own."

"I'm done listening to that, Rory," I said, getting up and pacing in front of her. "It doesn't ring true in this case, does it?"

She stared as if she were trying to determine from my face if there was

146

truth in what I'd said. Then she looked down, shook her head twice, and put her hands on her knees. She exhaled. Her head rose slowly, and she looked past me across the grounds.

"I guess not," she said.

I wasn't proud I'd exposed that falsehood to her. I wished I could've held back, but it had to be said. And she wasn't the only Woodman, Connolly, or Sampson who needed to hear it. I considered making up for it by telling her how well Holly and Maisie had been doing in school and in life. That Holly had a boyfriend, and he was a great kid who looked out for her. Maisie was witty and had friends, too. They had initiative and independence, and had seen a way out of the mire they'd grown up in, something that no Connolly or Sampson or Woodman had managed. But that just made this more tragic. I kept it to myself.

Rory's eyes glassed over, and I could see her fighting another breakdown. She looked away and cried softly. I hoped for a day when I could reveal her girls' accomplishments, and it could be celebrated. That seemed a long way off. I sat there, quietly watching a pair of robins hop across the lawn.

* * *

I was driving home, longing for my couch and the chance to mindlessly watch a Red Sox game. The radio broke into my trance. It was Regan.

"Chief, Boomer Woodman's here at the station."

"Oh, shit," I said, flipping on the blues and nailing the gas pedal.

"No, he's okay. Says he wants to talk to you. He's pretty calm."

"Tell him I'll be there in ten minutes." I eased off the gas and turned off the lights. Only a fool would consider an under-control Boomer Woodman any less dangerous than an enraged one.

Chapter Twenty-Four

I pulled into the parking lot at the station. Boomer leaned against his shiny truck and took a final drag from a Marlboro. He rubbed out the butt on his heel and flicked it, bouncing it off my six-year-old Bronco.

"How's a guy like you afford a rig like that, Eugene?" I said as I got out. It was probably worth more than any of the shacks in the Village. It was a question I should have asked weeks ago.

"I got a few business lines in the works, Little Timmy."

"I'm sure the IRS knows all about them," I said.

"Wouldn't have it any other way." He smiled, his teeth yellow in the spotlight.

"I hear you want to talk to me."

"That's right."

It was the first time he'd spoken to me without a threat, glare, or arched eyebrow. The change in course made me nervous.

"Let's go into the office," I said.

Boomer dwarfed the metal seat I placed him in. The red top of his Marlboro pack peaked out of his t-shirt pocket.

"What can I do for you?" I said.

"I want to talk to you about my nephew."

"You won't let him speak for himself, so it would be helpful if someone said something."

"That piece you found in his toolkit, was it a Colt Mustang?"

"That's right."

"Look, I don't like you. I don't like you going into our business. But—"

148

"You look, Eugene. I don't give a flying fuck about your 'we take care of our own' bullshit. It's gotten you two dead girls, a kid that's going to jail for the rest of his life, and a woman that you smacked around has lost almost her entire family. You're the problem, not the solution." That was another one I'd let go when it might have been wiser to sit back. Frustration, anger, hunger, lack of sleep, you name it, it was getting to me.

"Okay," he said, adjusting to his full height on the chair. "Are you done having your little hissy fit so that we can talk?"

"Speak."

"I gave him that piece a few years ago when he started at Ned's. In case anyone hassled him. I told him to keep it in his car."

"You'd testify to that in court?"

"If you made me. I mean, you got the gun that killed the girls. You shouldn't need anyone to say shit."

"That Colt is a new model and not cheap. Every other piece we confiscated is a relic. I'm surprised, is all."

"You don't know us," he said, shaking his head. "I wanted the kid to have something reliable."

"Why are you telling me this?"

"Those girls are my nieces. They didn't deserve that, for chrissakes."

"So you think Caleb did it?"

"That ain't for me to decide."

"Do you think there's a reason he'd be aggressive towards them?"

"Aggressive, that's a funny way to put it."

"You didn't answer the question. Was he jealous or frustrated?"

"What makes you think that?"

"They got plenty of cousins. I don't see them running all over town for ice cream."

Boomer cocked his head and shrugged his wide shoulders. "Yeah, they might have been my favorites. Might have got some special treatment."

"But not enough to let them have a real life with friends from school. I heard you put an end to that."

"I've got no fucking idea what you're talking about."

149

"I think you do. Are you a big Jimmy Goodwin fan?" That he hadn't gone after those boys still baffled me.

"Look, I come down here to help you for the sake of those girls. I'm with you on that, and you're here busting my balls."

"I find it interesting that after the way you've been telling Caleb to clam up, you're here giving us evidence we need."

He shifted in his chair, giving me a hard look. Then he stood up, walked to the door, and turned around.

"What was done to my nieces wasn't right. But I ain't stupid. When Reynolds came back and told me about the gun, I knew that was the piece I gave him. I can't win them all. That skinny little fucker. I heard about his peephole, too. His own sisters. You people are going to do me a favor for once by getting rid of him. If he came home and then started not showing up to that prick Ned's for work, which would be the right thing from where I'm standing, you'd just be back on my ass. I don't want to see you setting foot on my land again. Does that make sense now that I spelled it out for you?"

"You can sit back down, please. We aren't done."

"We'll be done when I decide," he said, but returned to his seat. He leaned back and crossed his legs.

"Did Caleb hunt with your people?"

"We all hunt."

"He knew about the quarry?"

"We hunt every inch of this town. Everyone knows that."

"Posted or not," I said.

"Who cares?"

"Where were you on the Thursday they disappeared, Boomer? Say from two in the afternoon to three in the morning."

"What you asking me for? You got your man. Now I got to be questioned?"

"I'm sure you can handle it. You visited Caleb at Ned's around twelve, talked to him for fifteen minutes. Then he left at two-thirty and picked up his sisters, and headed back in the direction of the Village. He returned to work before five. So he was gone for a bit. Of course, he won't say what he did. The girls were dumped in the quarry at two in the morning. So there's twelve hours that need to be accounted for."

"I was at the Village for some. I had a business meeting for some. Back to the Village for the night. Plenty of folks to testify to that."

"What kind of business meeting?"

"I got with Reynolds." He scratched at his chin and looked away, a sign of stress.

"About what?"

"That's what you call privileged information, I reckon."

"What did you talk to Caleb about?"

"Uh, the Pontiac that the boys take to work weren't running too smooth. I wanted him to take a look at it that night."

"Nothing about the girls? You didn't tell him to go pick them up?"

"I don't know what those two were up to every minute. I got my own business to look after. And I ain't their father."

"Do you think Jake Connolly would know what his daughters were up to?"

"He don't know shit, that one. Scared of his own shadow and probably his women, too."

"What work did Maisie and Holly do for you on weekends?"

"I got them digging worms."

"No, that was last year. I'm talking about this spring."

"I don't know what you've heard, but I'm telling you that was it."

I'd been certain that Caleb had killed his sisters. We had motive, opportunity, personality type, and the murder weapon. But Boomer sitting there trying to sew things up for us shook loose some doubt. If Jake or Rory didn't know everything their daughters did, that wasn't atypical. Boomer, however, had known everything. On a Friday night in May, he'd known what gravel pit they were drinking in and who they were with. He knew what they did for work and where they did it because he'd arranged it, and he'd just lied about it. It could be there was more to this than a perverted brother with an unhealthy obsession. But if I went right after Boomer as he sat there smiling, all I'd get was denial. The wall of bluster would rise. If I

151

let him think I was satisfied, that would give me room to work.

"Good enough," I said. "So you'll go talk to Caleb and tell him to stop this silent treatment?"

"I will not."

"I thought you wanted to help."

"This don't change anything between us. I can't let him get away with what he did, but I ain't letting us roll over for you, so the rest of us get fucked, too. That'd set a bad example for my people. I know what the domino theory is. I was there to see it. I took out plenty of them damn commies in my day."

"I'm sure you deserved a medal."

"You couldn't have hacked it over there, that's for sure."

"You can go now," I said.

"You're welcome."

He called me a pussy under his breath as he walked out the door. Of course, he wanted me to hear it, just as he wanted me to believe he was here to help. It was okay with me if he thought he'd succeeded.

Chapter Twenty-Five

I met with Trout and Crowley at eight in the morning to talk things over. I told them about Boomer's offer of help. That raised Crowley's eyebrows. "I don't trust that," he said. Trout scratched his head. He believed Boomer had come around and realized the kid was a lost cause. None of us could explain what Boomer might have had going with Reynolds before he'd hired him to represent Caleb or how he could afford the truck he'd been driving. Even with Earl Goodwin looking at the Village and Reynolds specializing in real estate, it was hard to imagine Boomer Woodman swinging some land deal. There had to be something else, though neither of my officers had caught anything about business interests that Boomer might have had a hand in. I stated that Holly and Maisie had been working for him on some Friday and Saturday nights, and that while he maintained it was bait, I'd heard something different. We couldn't tie any of this to the girls, though it was impossible not to think there was a connection. I asked for their opinions, because I didn't know what to believe at this point.

"It's got to be drugs or sex, Chief," Crowley said. "There ain't no goose laying the golden worm, if you know what I mean."

"Probably just the goddamn bait business again," Trout said. "If it was anything too bad, someone would have been in here bitching about it by now, right?"

That brought up another point. I had no idea what had happened in this town since the Fourth. I hadn't read the logs since Sunday. My desk was littered with papers. There were stacks of media requests and piles of phone messages, many from Link Johnson. The ones from Monday blamed me for low seat counts in restaurants and vacant hotel rooms. Tuesday's thanked me for solving the crime and heroically limiting this incident to "only a minor business disruption." The beauty of Laurel was that, often, nothing happened. I told my senior officers that I needed to wrap things up with Caleb, so I was putting them in charge of the town. Trout would take the day shift, and Crowley would run things at night. They were to get together and schedule the summer guys as best they could. If they needed state help, I told them to call Pettibone. That left me one less thing to worry about should I actually have time to worry. I would dig into Boomer Woodman. There were too many loose ends with him—the person who tied our knot with Caleb.

After the meeting, I took a ride over to Earl Goodwin's house. They had a place on the Abenaki River with a twenty-foot Mako tied to their own dock. Cindy Goodwin let me in and got me some coffee. While I wanted to talk to Jimmy, too, Cindy assumed I was there for her husband and brought me out to Earl. He was cleaning up the boat with his younger son, Nick, after an early morning run for stripers that came up empty. I didn't understand how no fish caught resulted in a messy boat, but whatever. He was okay with me asking questions as long as he could keep hosing down the deck. He had a showing at noon. I sent Nick up to the house.

"Do you do a lot of work with Dan Reynolds?"

"Sure." He flicked his wrist and sprayed his stern gunwale.

"What do you think of him?"

"If I were Caleb Connolly, I'm not sure that's who I'd want defending me if that's what you're asking. Not a lot of experience with criminal law. But when it comes to real estate, he knows it forward and backward, and he's a step ahead of all the other guys around here, probably the best from Kittery to Portland."

"Any idea how he and Boomer Woodman might have gotten together?"

"If you're talking about recently, I might be somewhat responsible for that," he said, letting up on the hose. The water stopped splashing. Gulls screeched.

"How so?"

"The land that Village is on is prime riverfront, which is why I went to take a look at it. I've had something percolating in my head for a while. You know Walt Harriman, the architect from Portland?"

"I've seen the signs."

"I had Harriman do some rough design work, on spec. That Woodman's land, we could put a multi-million dollar condo project in there if Reynolds' interpretation of the law they passed last fall in Augusta is correct, concerning density of housing with regard to zoning and wetlands. It lets you move square footage around to compensate for lot size. We could make a killing."

"Other than the fact that those people have been out there since Prohibition and, I'd guess, aren't too inclined to move." I had a hard time picturing Boomer across a table discussing a million-dollar deal with anyone.

"Don't be too sure about that, LT," Goodwin said. "I knew that Reynolds had done some work for Boomer a while back, so I went to him and asked if we could all sit down. You can't exactly drive in and talk to the guy."

"Tell me something I don't know. What was this work Reynolds did for Boomer?"

"When Chet Spanter got sick a few years ago, he had Boomer's name added to the deed, presumably to look out for his wife, who was a Sampson. I guess she somehow made it out of the Village. So they're related. They haven't operated it as a farm for years. It's a wasteland, but it could be used for other things. The old man died last year, and I think Boomer owns it outright now."

There wasn't anyone my age in Laurel who hadn't picked berries there as a kid. You got paid a nickel a basket. It was a couple miles past Cook's corner. I couldn't ever remember going to a call out there, and you had to go another five miles to get to the next house, which was in Brookville. I could think of some things Boomer could be growing out there if he wasn't interested in blueberries, and they weren't plants that were legal. Of course, there was always the possibility that Boomer wouldn't do the worst thing possible.

"Do you actually have some sort of deal in place with Boomer?"

"Let's just say we're working on it."

"You hear of any other businesses he's involved in?" I hoped to hit on the one that only Earl's son seemed to know existed.

"He's got the bait market cornered with Blink." Earl looked away and started up with the hose again. Then he stopped. "It might make sense for him to start up the berry farm again."

"Thanks," I said. "Is Jimmy around?"

"He was sleeping when we left. Why?" His eyes sharpened.

"I'd like to talk to him if I could."

"About those girls?"

"Yeah," I said. Father and son were both involved with Woodman's, on different levels and without the other knowing. That was something in itself. "Look, don't worry. He's a great kid, and he hasn't done anything wrong. When you're the quarterback, everyone wants to know you, and you have a good idea of what goes on in school. That's all."

"I heard the brother did it," Earl said, nodding.

"Sure looks that way."

"No problem," he said, stopping the hose again. "He needs to get up anyway. Just have Cindy wake him."

Jimmy followed his mother down the stairs rubbing his eyes. He walked into the kitchen, nodded at me, and grabbed a Coke out of the refrigerator.

"Am I in some kind of trouble?" he asked.

"No," I said. "Let's take that breakfast of champions outside where we can talk." We stood on the front lawn in the shade of a hemlock.

"You heard about the girls, I take it," I said.

He nodded, frowning.

"Are you doing okay?"

"It sucks bad," he said, pulling a handful of needles from the tree. "They were just getting started. They had everything against them, and they were going to beat it. Holly was just really cool. Their fucking brother, that creep. I'd like to get my hands on him." His arms came up and then fell to his sides.

"I bet you would." If this were the Wild West that Rory had envisioned for Laurel, Caleb might have been lynched by now.

"You said that they sometimes worked for Boomer. I need to learn more

156

about that."

"It was usually on Friday and Saturday nights, like every other week. I don't know how bad it could be, but they said it was almost worse than the worms, and that it was stupid. They'd be pretty depressed when one of those weekends was coming up. I guess they got treated bad and paid like shit. I tried to get them to tell me about it, but they wouldn't."

"They worked directly for Boomer?" I asked.

"Him and some other guy, I guess." He chuckled. "They really hated this other guy. Said he was an even bigger pig than their uncle. I guess Maisie would really go off on him."

"Jesus," I said.

"Right, hunh?" Jimmy said.

I now had another player to consider, provided I could find someone crazy enough to partner with Boomer Woodman.

"Just so you know," I said, "they died the day they disappeared. There wasn't anything you could have done."

"It makes me sick to think about it." He was beyond shock and into anger. I couldn't blame him.

"I get it. They didn't say anything at all about the work they were doing for Boomer?"

"Nope," he said, shaking his head. "Wouldn't talk about it."

"I need you to think, think hard, about anything they could have said that would describe the environment or atmosphere or people, anything at all would be helpful."

"Like I said, they hated going. They said for what they got out of it, it was way not worth it, that their uncle took a big cut, and they only got scraps." That told me money was coming in directly.

"What else?"

"I remember asking Holly on Tuesday if she could sneak out that Saturday because we were going to have a bonfire in the Oak Ridge pits. She said, 'No, we've got to go back up there.' So it's 'up there' somewhere. Maybe a second floor or a deer stand or somewhere north of here? Who knows what that asshole had them doing?" I couldn't tell if he was more dejected or disgusted.

"You've been a real help," I said, putting my hand on his shoulder. "If you think of something, give me a call." What those girls could be doing at night was beyond me, but it couldn't be anything good if Boomer was involved, that was for sure.

While we had the "who" nearly in our grasp, questions were left unanswered. We didn't know why the Connolly sisters had been killed. Forensics would only present us with the biological reasons for their deaths. I still couldn't explain how any of this had come to be in Laurel. But I could keep working. From the minute Rory Connolly had entered the station, information had come slowly, in small pieces and half-truths. There was more out there, and I'd need to unearth and decipher it to finish this.

My next stop was Blink's Store. I couldn't expect to keep on like this without eating and sleeping and had to get some food in the house. I also wanted to tap into Blink's all-encompassing knowledge of the town. And I found myself anxious to see Suzanne. It hadn't been long, but I'd almost gotten used to her being part of my days. I could practically feel her relief when I walked in.

"If it ain't Lieutenant Columbo, the crime solver," Blink said, showing his gap-toothed smile.

"Jesus, LT, you look like shit," Suzanne said.

"Thanks. I've got a new regimen of not eating and not sleeping. It's wonderful, and it's also why I'm here." I walked over to her counter. It seemed like her tan had darkened. Life went on for some people. I ordered roast beef, Italian, crab meat, and meatball subs, all large.

"Are you feeding the whole station?"

"No, I'm stocking my refrigerator. I haven't had time for eating, and I don't think it's a good thing."

"Can you stop by tonight? I'll make you dinner."

"I almost stopped by last night on my way home."

"You should have."

"It was after midnight, and the lights were off."

She raised her eyebrows and grinned like I should have anyway. If she had known the condition I was in, she wouldn't have been so inviting. Maybe we'd arrived at the place in a relationship where it was okay to be a mess, and I hadn't noticed. I told her I'd see her that night. Then I turned to Blink.

"I've got a question for you while I'm in the neighborhood."

"Yes," he said. "You can have a Coke, and no, I won't charge you for it. It's the least I can do to support our hard-working law enforcement."

"Thanks, I think I will." I went and grabbed a Coke, then walked back and flipped the cap into the wastebasket. I looked the old man right in the eye. If anyone knew what went on in this town, it was Blink. This store was a hub, and he talked to everyone.

"You hear of Boomer Woodman getting up to something on Friday and Saturday nights? Late night, maybe."

"Boomer?" he said. "I haven't heard of him doing anything."

"Does that mean you heard of something else going on?"

"I don't know, LT. Things are pretty sleepy around here, even this time of year." He shook his head and patted his thighs.

"Not so quiet that there aren't after-hours beer cases going out back doors."

Suzanne must have dropped something because metal clanked off the floor behind me.

"Jesus, Chief," he said, his mouth open. "I might take care of some friends once in a while. That ain't a hanging crime, is it?"

"I don't care about your beer, Blink. But I'm not fucking around about this other shit." I put my Coke down on the counter. The man had looked out for me since I was a kid and all through high school. He'd listened to me cry about losing my parents and moan about being deserted by my wife. Now I was giving him the hard stare. My neck tensed. "Something's going on around here, and I need to find out what it is."

"I might have heard something about a card game. Don't believe it has anything to do with Boomer, though."

"What kind of card game? Like at someone's house?"

"From what I got, it ain't like, 'Hey, let's go to Billy Bob's and play some poker.' Someone's running it. It's people from town playing, though, so I don't imagine Boomer's mixed up in it."

Blink's logic made sense. Boomer had no history of having anything to do with the rest of us. But we had a card game surfacing, some mysterious Woodman business venture, a possible land deal, and two girls disappearing all at the same time. Not to mention Boomer's new truck. Either we were the capital city of Coincidence or there were things going on that I had to start tying together. I needed to get my head out of my ass and start breaking them down one by one. Then I might be able to see how it all fit.

"Have you visited this game yourself, Blink?"

"As you said, I got on my own dealings on them nights. A man can't be two places at once."

"You know where it is?"

"I don't."

"You know anyone that's playing?"

"I ain't inclined to say, as I got a business to run here, and some of those folks might be my customers. But I wouldn't put it past you to take some educated guesses."

"Good enough." Several people I knew would attend such an event, and it would be easy enough to track them down. "Thank you for your help, and if you hear anything about Boomer, you let me know."

"You're asking a lot today, Chief." He looked at me like I'd slapped him. I chose not to remind him that we had two dead girls on our hands here in sleepy Laurel, Maine.

"Let me pay for my sandwiches, please." I handed him two twenties, and he gave me change. He didn't look at me, and we didn't speak. I walked over to Suzanne's counter and picked up my bag of takeout.

"Thanks, Suzanne," I said.

"See you later, LT," she said, looking uneasy.

I dropped them off at my place and went to see Rory at the convent. I'd already lost my appetite.

Chapter Twenty-Six

Rory and I sat next to each other on the loveseat. We had the office of the nursing home to ourselves. My eyes bounced from the photo of John F. Kennedy to the cross to the portrait of Jesus until they finally landed on Rory. I'd done nothing but tell this woman things she didn't want to hear for two weeks. That streak wouldn't be ending. I warned her there were some things that she didn't know about her daughters. While some of it was good, and she'd be proud, she would also hear things that would be upsetting. We were going to talk about her son, too, because I believed there was something that she could do for him. She took it all in. The scent of decay in the air around us seemed like a small thing now.

"Let's start with some of the good," I said, sliding a blown-up version of the yearbook picture from a folder and handing it to her. "You see that guy there, in front of your girls?"

"Yes."

"That's the quarterback for Timbercoast, a hell of an athlete and a great kid."

"So they got to look at him in the cafeteria? I saw you and your big friend plenty, and it didn't do much for me."

"The one smiling at him, that's Holly?" I said. She nodded. "That guy, the quarterback, that was her boyfriend."

She snorted. "What are you talking about?"

I repeated the story that I'd heard from Jimmy Goodwin, starting with their lab together in chemistry to the rendezvous they'd been having this spring on Brown Street. How she'd snuck out alone at first, but then Maisie

161

had started going with her. How they'd been fitting into the fabric of the school. Rory's eyes started tearing, and I got the box of Kleenex off the desk. I handed her the first one and placed the box between us. To me, the tragedy was made worse in that they'd been able to become part of the community beyond the Village, something our generation couldn't have accomplished even if we'd wanted it. But Rory was also the mother of girls living lives they hadn't fully shared with her. It was more weight for her to carry.

"I wasn't sure when would be the time to tell you this, but I thought you'd want to know."

She nodded. "I thank you for that." I tried not to project my own values and didn't tell her how happy I would have been about it if I were her. I didn't think it was right to ask for her thoughts, either.

"While they may have done it last year, your girls were not working worms and selling them to Blink's this year."

"Of course they were." The heightened strains of a soap opera argument bled into the room, then disappeared.

"There are two other sisters doing it. A thirteen and a ten-year-old."

"Those are Betsy Woodman's girls. They do it on weeknights, and my girls were doing it on Fridays and Saturdays. I know for a fact. Where else would they be getting their money?"

"They were working for Boomer, but doing something else."

"What would that be?" She clasped her hands in her lap.

"I haven't been able to figure that out yet. But I think it may be connected to what happened."

"Because Boomer's involved, it has to be something bad?" That it came out sounding somewhat like a question told me I had a chance to get through to her.

"He did just knock the hell out of you a few days ago," I said. I must have needed more training in domestic violence, because if we'd sat there for another month, I don't think I would have understood how she failed to see it.

"To discover the truth," I said, "I'm going to need your help. And for you to help me, you've got to be able to change the way you think. I need you

162

to step back and try not to see things through the lens of the Village, but as if we were talking about events that happened somewhere else, where you could look at them objectively. Do you think you can do that?"

"So, I just believe everything you say, and we'll all live happily ever after, except for my girls, who I could barely tell apart and didn't even make it to eighteen, as popular as they were? Come on, Nichols." She looked like she wouldn't have minded hitting me herself.

"I realize it's a lot to ask. There's probably a lot of good in that Village of yours, but there's something else there, too. It's what got you to walk five miles in the heat to get to my office. It's what put your girls in that quarry right as they were blossoming into young women. So no matter how difficult it may be, please just listen and think."

"All I know is the way I know," she said.

"You're smart, though. You've schooled me these last weeks on everyone from Sherlock Holmes to Atticus Finch."

She sighed, let out a sob, and pulled a new Kleenex to her eyes.

"Go ahead and say your piece," she said.

"You're aware that Caleb is our prime suspect?"

"He wouldn't do that to his sisters."

"All the evidence points to him. The thing is, he won't say a thing to us to prove otherwise."

"Because you'll use it against him."

"If he's innocent, there's no way for him to prove it unless he talks."

She bit down on her bottom lip. She looked at the bookshelf across from us and then back at me. "He doesn't think you'll believe him."

"I don't think it's that simple. The first time I brought him in, he sounded like he wasn't too happy with what went on in the Village. He seemed frustrated, and it seemed like he was going to tell us why. Then Boomer walked in with Dan Reynolds. Caleb hasn't said a word since. We can barely get him to tell us what he wants for lunch and dinner."

Her eyes blinked, her face blank.

"This idea you have of us wanting to hurt you and your people is wrong. I hope you can see that by now. When Caleb doesn't tell us where he brought the girls that afternoon, it makes him look guilty. So many things point to him, from the murder weapon to the dark car being seen near the quarry—and he won't refute any of it. The way it stands now, he's going to trial, and he's going to be found guilty. If he's innocent and he's not talking, he's not helping himself."

"But you think he did it."

"We need to be sure."

"So you want me to go in and get him to talk to you."

"That's right."

"And maybe get him to hang himself?"

"He only does that if he's guilty. Talking with us is the only way to help himself if he's not."

She nodded. "I see what you mean."

"There's another level to this, Rory. It's Boomer and Reynolds who are telling him not to say anything."

"They're just trying to protect him from saying something that's going to make it worse."

"That would be impossible."

She heaved another sigh.

"Boomer came to the station to talk to me last night. No threats, no screaming."

Her eyes widened.

"He wasn't there to help Caleb. He came to tell me that the gun we found he gave to Caleb when he started working at Ned's."

"No. Even if Boomer had given it to him, he wouldn't have told you."

"He sure did, and he significantly helped our case against Caleb." Her hand went to her mouth.

She shook her head. "On purpose, you think?"

"Which is my point."

"But this helps you. Why are you telling me?"

"Because I don't trust Boomer. I think there's more to this than what it seems. But I can't get to the bottom of it if Caleb won't tell me what he knows."

"And he'll go to jail even if he didn't do it, if he doesn't speak up?" Her face tightened with anger, lines coming out around her eyes and crossing her forehead.

"That's right."

"Take me to him." The view she'd held of the world for her entire life had finally shifted.

Chapter Twenty-Seven

"**G**et on your feet, Caleb." I opened the cell door.

"I ain't saying nothing. You better call Dan Reynolds if you're going to talk to me." His lips pulled back, and his eyes were jittery.

I walked him down the hall to my office. He looked over his shoulder as if he expected me to crack him. He waited at the door, and I moved past him to open it.

"Mama," he yelled and ran over to hug Rory. "What are you doing here?"

They sat down in the chairs opposite each other in front of my desk. I cleared a spot and sat on the corner. They leaned close, their faces barely a foot apart. Rory appeared on the edge of tears.

"I asked her to come," I said. "I'm hoping she can talk some sense into you."

"I'm not talking. I told you that." I looked at Rory and shrugged. She reached over and put her hands on his scraggly face and made him look at her.

"Did you do something to your sisters?" she said.

"I didn't kill them like they think."

"Then you need to start speaking up for yourself."

"I can't."

"If you don't," I said, "you'll be going to jail whether you did it or not."

"Why can't you tell us anything?" Rory said, removing her hands from his face and placing them in her lap.

"I can tell you, but I ain't saying anything in front of him." He pointed his needle-like chin at me.

"Do you trust me, Caleb?" Rory said. He nodded. "He's trying to help you."

"No, he ain't. You just heard him say I'm going to jail whether I did it or not."

I wondered if it was possible to hit the stupid out of someone. "We've got it all right now, Caleb," I said. "Possession of the murder weapon, motive, opportunity, witnesses, evidence. And you won't say anything to tell us otherwise. Why wouldn't we think you're guilty?"

I watched the second hand on the wall clock sweep from the twelve to the three to the six waiting for something—anything—to sink in.

"It's part of the plan," he said, nodding.

"What plan?" Rory said.

He went to speak, then stopped and glanced at me.

"Tell us, Callie."

"Boomer and that lawyer say it will be all right. They're looking out for me."

"That's funny because Boomer sat in that same chair last night and told me that he gave you that Colt, the murder weapon, two years ago."

"That ain't my gun." He shook his head and folded his arms across his chest.

"Whose gun is it?" I said.

"I don't know, but I never seen it before. I don't know how it got in my stuff."

"That's not what your uncle said."

"He did not." He punched his thigh to punctuate each word.

"I'm telling you he did." It would have been easy enough for someone to slip into the garage and plant it. The office door had only a simple keyed knob.

"Then it's okay because it's part of the plan."

"What is this plan, Caleb, honey?" Rory said. "Please tell me."

"I can't. Boomer wouldn't like it." I was tempted to step out of the office in the hopes that he'd tell her, and then she could tell me. But too much could go wrong with that.

"I won't let anything happen to you," she said. "I don't think your uncle is really helping you."

"So now you're with him?" Caleb said, looking at me like he wanted to spit.

"I'm with you," she said.

"No, you ain't."

Her hand shot across the space between them, and her palm hitting his cheek sounded like Rice cracking a line drive to left field. Even if I had been prepared to stop it, I wouldn't have been quick enough. He looked at her with tears in his eyes.

"Tell us," she said. It was not a question.

"They want me to be in jail for it, don't you see?" he said, stammering. "Because then it's our own fault, and the town won't care. It looks like I did it, when I really didn't. Reynolds says that the evidence against me doesn't mean shit because it's all circumstances."

"Circumstantial," I said. Laurent, Pettibone, and I all agreed there was quite enough of it to make a case.

"Yeah, that. He said that it would be enough for them to arrest me, and that's exactly what they did. But he said that once we went to a trial, there won't be enough to prove I did it, because I didn't do it. See? If I can sit tight for a month, I'll be a free man, and no one could ever bother me about it again. Boomer said that if I went through with this, it would take the eyes off of the Village. They'd forget about us, and everything would go back to normal. All our people would know what I did to keep these assholes out of our business. For that, I'd be in line to take over when Boomer got to be an old man and couldn't run things no more."

"Oh, Caleb," she said. "You didn't believe that, did you?"

Jesus H. Christ. I couldn't determine which was more absurd: the legal strategy itself or that Caleb believed it would ultimately result in a heroic ascension as Boomer's successor.

He shrugged. "Why not? Boomer said that if I didn't keep quiet that they might subscript him and make him tell them some things that he knew—like how those girls were bitchy at me all the time and how I didn't like it, and that I was jealous of them and then the jury would get the idea that I did kill them. And if everyone saw him have to talk, then they might, too. Because they," he said, nodding at me again, "didn't care what happened as long as they had one of us to blame. Makes sense, don't it?"

That explanation left Rory's head in her hands. What Caleb had told us was, in fact, a plan. The question was, to what end? Maybe what Caleb had told us was true. That they'd set him up, and when we got to trial, they'd come up with things that would drill holes into the narrative they'd provided us with. They'd pull something like Boomer telling us he was mistaken when he'd said the Colt was Caleb's. Or maybe a bunch of them would parade up there and say how much the brother and sisters loved each other. That seemed like a risky strategy, but not so much if they didn't care if it succeeded. It was easier to believe they were setting him up as the fall guy. If that were the case, they had done well, because he looked guilty as hell. He was stupid enough to be quieted by the promise that he'd emerge as a hero and succeed Boomer. By the time he realized he'd been tricked, he'd be sitting in prison for life. Of course, the third option was that Caleb had killed his sisters and dumped their bodies in a quarry in the middle of the woods. If Boomer hadn't come to me with the gun, I'd have believed it. Now I was leaning towards the fall guy scenario. Caleb was a perfect dupe. While that left us without our presumed killer, it did provide another more-than-plausible suspect, Boomer Woodman.

"Caleb," I said, now standing in front of him and talking with my hands like a politician trying to get a point across. "You're being set up to go to jail for the rest of your life for something you say you didn't do. Boomer just provided us with the evidence that will see to that. No matter what they've told you, if you don't start answering some questions, there's nothing that can prevent it." He looked to his mother.

"You understand that, right, honey?" Rory said.

"I guess," he said, shaking his head, resigned.

"What did Boomer tell you when he came by Ned's the Thursday that you picked up your sisters?"

"That they'd be going into town that afternoon at two-thirty, and I was supposed to go get them."

"And you did that?"

"Yeah."

"What were you supposed to do after you picked them up?"

"I had to bring them to West Laurel, but that was okay, because then I could go back to work."

"Where in West Laurel?" My arms were folded across my chest.

"The berry farm. Boomer's helping the old lady, Mrs. Spanter."

"Was he there?"

"Maybe. His truck was there." This didn't guarantee that Boomer was involved, but it did make him a person of interest. If I had known what I was doing, I would have made him a suspect from the start. Even if there hadn't been evidence, he was who he was.

"What did you do when you got to the farm?"

"I dropped them off and went back to work."

"Is that the only time Boomer had you driving them?" The question of Friday and Saturday nights remained unanswered.

"No, I was their chauffeur half the time. I barely had any time to myself between working at Ned's and driving those two around."

"Where else would you drive them?"

"Sometimes I took them into town, and I'd drop them at the bridge like I told you before. Them two were sweet on some boy, I think. They'd have me drive them to school every now and then, too. Then once in a while, on Fridays and Saturdays, I took them to the farm."

"What time?"

"Usually after dinner. I don't know."

"Do you know what they did there?"

"They wouldn't tell me. Big damn promotion from night crawlers, I guess."

"Did you ever pick them up after work?" I'd at least discovered the location of the shadow business, even if we still had no idea what it was.

"Nope."

"What did you do that night after you got out of work from Ned's?"

"I went home."

"You were late," Rory said. He shot a look at his mother.

"I had some cars to take care of. I like to get my work done."

"If only some of your relatives would talk to me and substantiate that," I said. "Who were you hanging out with back at the Village?"

"Davey Sampson, Matthew Sampson, my cousin Bootsie Connolly. Silas Connolly."

"But not Boomer?"

"He weren't there."

"Okay," I said. "Anything else I should know?"

He shook his head.

"What about Boomer and Mr. Reynolds?" he said. "They'll be mad if they knowed I talked to you." He had a point.

"Don't tell them a thing. You just go along with their plan. We'll keep this between us for now."

I had some things I needed to work out, and I didn't need Boomer and Reynolds on DefCon Four. I called Laurent at the courthouse and told him that we needed a search warrant. We had a new last location for the girls, and I was sure that the new owner wouldn't let us poke around. When I told him where and who the owner was, he dropped the phone. It would only take an hour, he said. That was okay. I called Pettibone and asked him to meet me there.

I drove Rory back to the convent and tried to assure her she'd done a great deal to help her son. I don't know if she believed that. She sat in the passenger seat, rocking and mumbling to herself the whole way to Milltowne. When I asked her if she was going to be okay, she nodded. I wasn't convinced.

Chapter Twenty-Eight

S panter's Berry farm looked deserted. The dirt driveway went in thirty yards and forked. To the left was a barn, painted red but faded to rust. An old farmhouse stood to the right, a white, two-story rectangle with peeling paint and stripped shutters. None of the windows had curtains. Fields of blueberry and blackberry plants flourished behind the buildings. While the coast was littered with trees so much that you couldn't see more than twenty feet off the road, the land here was flat and open like a plain. Gravel and grass paths led out to the back fields. In the distance were more outbuildings, built like miniature barns. They were faded to pink. If Boomer had somehow maneuvered his way into ownership, he'd done nothing with the place.

Pettibone arrived, and as we stood in the driveway, I updated him on what I'd learned from Boomer's visit, my stop at Blink's, and Caleb finally opening his mouth. Reynolds's legal strategy was the one that stoned him. All he could say was, "What the fuck?" He shook his head, and we walked up to the house. An old woman in gray corduroy pants and a torn green sweater opened the door. Her white hair was cut short.

"What do you want?" she said. It looked like she was chewing on something as she spoke. I told her who we were and that we had a search warrant to look around the buildings and grounds.

"George don't work here no more," she said.

"Okay," I said.

"Did you bring my groceries?"

"No, ma'am. Do you need help?" She shut the door in my face. We knocked again. She answered after another minute.

"Chet's out back," she said.

I explained again that we had a warrant to search her house. I could have been reading the phone book for all she cared. She left the door open and walked off to the living room on the left. *Let's Make a Deal* blared on a large black and white television.

We started in the kitchen. While the rusted yellow refrigerator wasn't full, there was more food in it than I had in mine. There were no dirty dishes in the sink. The tablecloth was clean. The living room was tidy. Pictures of her and her husband and the old farm stand in better days covered the walls. The bathroom was okay, other than discoloration from hard water in the toilet and sink. It looked like she slept in a bedroom on the first floor, as there was an unmade bed. As we walked upstairs, I thought of what the girls had told Jimmy. But the second floor held only four empty rooms and a thick coating of dust, so much so that you could barely see out the windows. Holly and Maisie weren't doing their work here. And unless Mrs. Spanter was putting on an award-winning performance, she wouldn't have noticed if there were a shootout in her own kitchen. We said goodbye and headed toward the barn.

A lawn separated the house from the drive, and then it was gravel in front of and beside the barn. The barn was perpendicular to the road, with wide doors with X-ed crossed panels facing the street. The old parking lot ran beside it. At the end was a dilapidated plywood kiosk where they'd lined up pints of berries for sale and handed out plastic quart buckets if you were picking your own. Unlike the house, there were fluffy white curtains on the windows that faced the lot. This was not an animal barn.

There was a regular door on the side. It was locked. I looked at Pettibone. He told me to wait and went to his car. He returned with a crowbar and popped it in seconds. We went in. The only light came in through the windows, but it was enough to see a switch inside the door. I flicked it on and found I'd been wrong about Boomer spending money.

Spotlights came down from the corners of the room, all aimed at its center. On a raised platform of gleaming white oak, varnished to the point that it shined, sat a poker table. I tried to catch my breath. This was not the folding card table that everyone had in their basement, but a real gaming table complete with green felt and leather edges. Leather-backed chairs surrounded it. A small bar had been built at the far end of the room near the street. It was the same gleaming oak as the platform. A brown refrigerator with a tap handle coming out of its center was behind it, along with a stereo system. Speakers hung from the rafters. All the place lacked was cages for go-go dancers.

"How long did you say this game had been going on?" Pettibone asked.

"A few months, maybe."

"When did Boomer Woodman take over here?"

"Sometime this spring."

"Maybe we aren't giving him enough credit."

The feeling of being one hundred percent wrong was even worse than being pinned, which had previously occupied zero on my scale of one to ten.

We inspected the room. A few feet in front of us and to the right was a large desk with a significant supply of poker chips organized on a custom rack—real ones with dollar values on them and not cheap red, white, and blue plastic. The bar had a galvanized steel wash tub for an ice bin, some empty kegs, and bottles of Seagrams, Cutty Sark, and Jack Daniels. There were shot and beer glasses, nice ones, thick and heavy. An empty cash box sat on a shelf. It had a fleck of rust on it, probably the only thing left over from the berry business. A foot-long two-by-four with wires going into it and a series of flashlight bulbs was screwed in under the bar top. Maybe they used it to remotely control the door.

"I don't think Boomer's been working the fields," I said.

"Not unless he's growing weed, too," Pettibone said.

"I'd like to know when he began thinking doing business with the rest of us was okay."

"Probably when the money started coming in," Pettibone said. "It could be that he's just the landlord. If anyone would be happy to look the other way, it would be him."

In the corner behind the desk was a door that had "Employees Only" written in red paint that the exterior could have used. Under that sign was another, a custom job on a piece of white vinyl. It read "Policy Strictly Enforced" with an outline of a Colt 45. This door was also locked. Pettibone looked over at me and smiled. The door soon swung open, and we were facing a staircase.

There was no light switch, so I ran out to the cruiser for my mag light. We followed its beam up the stairs. The loft looked to be more like the barn as it once was, unfinished and unpaneled. We found a switch at the top, and Pettibone flipped it. The light came on in random places and barely produced a shadow. There were vestiges of the farm life remaining. Stacks of wooden and cardboard bushel boxes were piled up in a corner. It was the rest of the room that gave us pause. Two mattresses lay across from each other in the middle of the floor, five feet from the side walls. Next to them were empty Pepsi bottles, the favored drink of the Connolly sisters. A black tube that looked like a relay baton sat on each mattress. I looked at Pettibone, and he shrugged.

"You don't suppose he's putting those girls out up here, do you?" he asked. My stomach roiled.

"I wouldn't put anything past Boomer, but the furniture doesn't match the downstairs business."

"Some guys don't care where, as long as there's a when." The yellowed and stained mattresses looked like they'd be best suited to hosting bed bugs and mice rather than frustrated men.

I trained the mag light and went to the mattresses. They were set up as mirror images. At the head of each was a thick four-inch square of black felt, a piece of wood with a slice of sheet metal, and a nail wrapped with a wire. Unhooked dry cells sat next to them. The wires then ran across the floor to the front of the barn. I picked up the black felt and found a hole in the floor. The black cylinder proved to be a collapsed telescope.

"I'm guessing this isn't an honest game," Pettibone said.

The telescope wouldn't have pulled in Mars or Venus but would read a card eight feet below just fine. I chanced infestation and got down on one of the mattresses. The hole in the floor was placed far enough out and beveled, narrowing as it went through the floorboard. While Caleb had drilled to satisfy some warped sexual proclivity, these holes were here to fleece rubes. By laying on the mattress, whoever was up here, and I was beginning to think I knew who that was, could see every hand on one side of the table. With a partner across the room, they'd have the game covered. Why I was surprised was beyond me.

"I guess this explains that pegboard with the lights behind the bar," Pettibone said, tapping the wire with his foot. "Smoke signals." Where the board was situated downstairs, none of the players could have possibly seen it, even if they were standing at the bar.

"You know who worked the telegraph, right?" I said.

"Had to be them," Pettibone said.

"So Boomer's involved," I said. He'd brought two teenage girls into a crooked poker game, and now they were dead. It didn't take Einstein to do the math. "Let's go get him."

Pettibone called the crime lab. I sent Crowley and Trout to Brown Street across from the Village and told them to wait for me, unless they saw Boomer. In that case, they could grab him. We put out an all-points bulletin for his Chevy truck. As soon as the lab arrived, Pettibone and I left, sirens blaring, for Woodman's.

My hopes sank when we raced into the Village and did not see Boomer's truck in front of his palace. Pettibone and I searched every shack, guns drawn. He wasn't there. I wondered if I'd been wrong, and the old woman had just enough of her mind left to somehow warn him. I drove all over town for hours, from Reynolds' office to Gray Gull Beach to Brookeville. That truck was nowhere to be found. So I went to a dive bar.

Chapter Twenty-Nine

Laurel was a small town that held folks from every walk of life. Even including the Village, we had few troublemakers. They could be classified into three categories. At the top of the list were the one or two like Vince Neely, petty thieves who were easy to keep an eye on. There were others who liked to make their own determinations on acceptable levels of fun. That was Shane Miller and his crew, who liked to pick up a few racks of High-life and take their rifles down to the dump to shoot rats at two in the morning. Most people, however, just needed to be redirected back within the lines every now and then. Those were the guys whose noses would lead them to a card game in the middle of a blueberry plain. They'd be able to tell me how big a hand Boomer had in what was going on, and they could be found at the Rusty Bullet, a hole in the wall at the pier on Cape Laurel.

Rusty's was the size of a mobile home that'd been chopped in half. The entrance was in the middle. A bar ran along its back side. The bathrooms were at one end, not that you'd want to use them. There were tables at the other. Picture windows were framed on each side of the door. I assumed that lobstermen weren't the only ones who sat out in West L gambling away their money, but I'd have bet the rent there were enough of them to make a stop at Rusty's worth my while. The place smelled like stale beer had been seeping into the woodwork for thirty years, which it had.

A few guys were scattered across the bar. To my right, Jamie Finn and Ed Pickey sat at one of the tables with half-full glasses in front of them. I got a pitcher of Bud from the bartender and pulled a chair over from the next table.

"Join us, LT," Jamie said. "You don't have to wait for an invitation if you got something to bring to the party."

"Thanks." Ed looked at me with a "what did we do now" expression.

"I'm in need of some help, boys." I poured a beer for each of them and a glass for myself.

"You putting a posse together to round up some rustlers?" Jamie said.

"No, not that. I just got a huge bonus from Augusta for keeping the most law-abiding town in the state, and I have a hankering to distribute it among some of our finest citizens." Their smiles diminished to grins, as they couldn't tell where I was headed. "The vehicle I would like to use to accomplish this is a poker game, preferably on a Friday or Saturday night. Would you gentlemen know where I can find one?"

"Why are you asking us?" Ed said.

"You're a couple of wild and crazy guys who I'd guess would be up for that kind of thing. Am I wrong?"

"Wouldn't admitting that put us into some kind of self-incriminating bullshit?" Jamie said.

"Maybe you might have just heard about it then?"

Their eyes met across the table. Their grins had fallen into straight lines and closed mouths.

"I don't think we know anything about it, LT," Ed said. "Sorry."

"Maybe you just need more time to think. I know, Jamie, that when I fished you out of the water on Memorial Day after you drove your Chevy into Batson Lagoon, you might have scrambled your eggs a bit. And you, Eddie, I broke up that little altercation between you and Chuck Lovely and then just sent you home. Maybe I should have taken you in because then I could've gotten you checked out in case you jostled something upstairs. So you both take a minute if you need to." I took a sip of my beer. It was nice and cold.

They looked at each other across the table. They were communicating with some sort of unwritten eye, eyebrow, and facial tic language.

"While we don't know much about it ourselves, LT, we do have someone

178

that you could ask about this," Jamie said. "But you can't tell him we sent him your way."

"Fair enough, provided Boomer Woodman isn't the name coming out of your mouth right now."

"It's not," Ed said. "Talk to your boy, Trout."

"Nate Trout?" I said, barely loud enough for them to hear it.

Jamie nodded.

"Well, look who it is, big swinging dick, Tim Nichols." Derek Anderson, Suzanne's ex, stood just inside the door with a wide smile on his flat-as-a-pie face, from which emerged the nose of a hawk. He wasn't slurring but he was loud, and I could see he wouldn't pass a field sobriety test.

"Derek," I said and turned back to Jamie and Ed. I hadn't finished my questioning.

Jamie's eyes, which had returned to me, shot left. Then I felt him. I picked up my glass and spun just in time to duck under a roundhouse right. I came up from my crouch and planted the glass, one of those cheap plastic pilsners, right on Derek's beak. He went sprawling backwards and fell to the floor. Blood poured from his nose. I snagged a rag from the bar top. It was soaked with beer. I threw it on his face. He screamed.

"You broke my fucking nose, asshole," he said.

"Consider yourself lucky," I said, stepping over him as I walked to the door. Laughter erupted as I went out into the fading light of sunset. There was no way I could have continued interrogating them, but they'd given me a name, Nate Trout. My most trusted officer and best friend in town.

I tried to imagine how his knowledge of this game, which he hadn't shared, could be a good thing. That was one indication I wasn't thinking straight. I had turned toward the station, but did a U-turn and headed for home. It was eight-thirty, and I hadn't eaten all day, and I needed my wits if I wanted to think this through. It wasn't until I passed Langford Road that I remembered I was supposed to have gone to Suzanne's. I banged another U-turn. The song on the radio proclaimed: "The shit had hit the fan." I turned it up until I couldn't hear my own thoughts.

There was a light on, so I stopped. I used Suzanne's phone to call Estelle and ask her to get my officers in at nine o'clock for a staff meeting. They were in need of another briefing. One would need questioning. I didn't think to apologize for being late until after I'd made the call. Great boyfriend.

"You smell like beer," Suzanne said. She was in the shorts and t-shirt she usually slept in. She'd been waiting up.

"I enjoyed one with your ex earlier," I said.

"You're kidding me?"

"I should have said that I was enjoying a beer when I ran into Derek. It would be safe to say that when I shared it with him, he enjoyed it much less than I did." She grinned and gave me a look, unsure to what level I was teasing.

"Just another day at the office," I said.

She made me a sandwich and a gin and tonic, and we went to the couch in the living room. I sucked down my drink and could barely speak. She placed me on the floor below her and had me take my shirt off. She started rubbing my shoulders. I drifted off. It was the closest I'd been to relaxed in days, even with Trout and that poker game creeping into my thoughts.

"Did you ever want to have kids, LT?" she said, taking a sip from her drink and placing it on the coffee table. She started back in on the shoulders.

"I wasn't married long enough to get to that discussion."

"I've always wanted them, but I wasn't going to bring one into a house with Derek in it."

I nodded. "That makes sense."

"If things had worked out with Analisa, do you think you would have had them?"

"Sure," I said. "I'd have loved to teach someone to ride a bike or throw a pitch. My backyard is perfect for wiffle ball. The elms on the left would be just like the green monster."

"I bet you'd be a great dad."

I rolled my shoulders as she walked her fingers up my neck. "I'd like to think so."

"What do you think about us having a kid?" She stopped and took a long sip of her drink. If I wasn't half asleep, I might have panicked. I took a deep breath. Over this past month, I'd come to appreciate honesty, especially concerning myself. And I'd learned that communication was the key to a good relationship from a Cosmo that sat five feet away in a magazine rack. I rolled out of my position and joined her on the couch so I could see her. Her eyes were bright, and her lips formed a hopeful smile.

"I'm still a little gun shy from my first marriage." I would have chanced a second drink to brace myself. "I mean, this is great, and I can see where it could go. It makes me wish I'd had the courage to ask you out before Deac. But getting married again isn't something I'm ready to think about."

"I understand all of that, LT," she said, continuing to smile. "I don't want to get married, either. That doesn't mean we can't have a child together."

"I'm not following," I said.

"It's like this. My clock's ticking. I'm thirty-five. You're not getting any younger, either. If this summer has shown us anything, it's that life is precious, and we never know what can happen. We've been friends practically our whole lives. I think you would make a great dad. I think I'd be a great mom. I hope you think that, too."

"I do," I said.

"Our gene pool is pretty good. I'm not too hard to look at. You were a state champion. We'd have a nice-looking, athletic kid who'd probably turn out to be a decent person, right?"

"Makes sense."

"So we keep seeing each other, and we, what do you guys call it, pull the goalie. We get me pregnant. We have the baby and raise the child together. It's not the 1950s. We don't need to be married to do this. We're good people, and we'd do well by a kid, married or not. I'm not going anywhere. Laurel's my home. I don't think you're headed elsewhere, either. If it works out that we want to get married or live together at some point, we do it."

"Wow," I said. If a possible Trout connection to the poker game had flummoxed me, this shut down my brain entirely. I didn't know what to think.

"I know," she said. "I've been working this out in my head for weeks. I wanted to be sure." She slurped the last of her cocktail. I couldn't speak.

"I'll give you some time to consider it," she said, still smiling. "I'll let you sleep on it. You can let me know in the morning."

"You're kidding, right?" I could barely get the words out.

"Yes, I am. You take your time and think it over as long as you want. Well, maybe not forever. That would defeat the purpose, right?"

"Right," I said. I'd never felt so light-headed in my life.

I woke early the next morning and left Suzanne sleeping soundly in her bed. I told myself it was because I had plenty to do and not an attempt to avoid the subject that had been introduced the previous night. I don't know that I believed that.

Chapter Thirty

Lawlessness could have engulfed the town—as if it hadn't already—because our entire force—myself, Crowley, Trout, and our three rookies—was jammed into the conference room with Laurent. It was the first time I'd ever used it for an actual conference. I updated the officers on what I'd found over the past two days, that Boomer had come in and stated that years earlier, he'd given the Colt to Caleb. They nodded, as it appeared that this was the nail in the coffin we'd been looking for—the murder weapon among the belongings of the presumed killer. Then they looked at me in disbelief as I told them that Caleb had finally spoken and denied it was his and revealed that his reluctance to speak had been part of a legal strategy that Reynolds told him would eventually result in acquittal as his case was built largely on circumstantial evidence. That produced a roomful of cocked and shaking heads, pursed lips, "god damns," and "son of a bitches." Then I told them there was more. That had them sitting up.

"Who knows anything about a poker game taking place out in West Laurel every other weekend?" I pretended to look around the room, but paid attention only to Trout. His face puckered as if he'd just bitten into an especially bitter lemon.

"What do you mean?" Crowley said. "Like guys getting together at someone's house?" None of the others said a word. That didn't surprise me. My rookies rarely left the square and the beaches and had probably only passed the farm when we'd done a circuit of the town during orientation.

"Nope. There's been a real game going on at Spanter's Berry farm. Anyone notice any late-night traffic headed out to Cook's Corner?"

Trout shook his head, eyes downcast. The rookies sat there, confused. I'm sure at least one of them wanted to ask where that was. Crowley put his hand on his chin.

"I've also learned that the owner of that farm is now Boomer Woodman."

"Are you shitting me?" Crowley said.

"To top it off, I believe that Holly and Maisie Connolly worked there during the game."

"So," Laurent said, doing the math for the room, "this means that we need to look into these deaths on a deeper level. There appears to be more to this than just a perverted creep of a brother. We don't know what Boomer Woodman's involvement could be, but these events are very possibly connected to this game. That's why we started looking for him yesterday."

The faces of Regan, Martin, and Griffin flipped back and forth between confusion and anger. It was as if they'd signed up for basic algebra and were now being asked to take a test on advanced trigonometry—a class I'd earned a D-plus in at Orono. Crowley was seething, and Trout let out a long series of sighs.

"You know," Crowley said, "Earl Goodwin was buying drinks for everyone a few Sundays ago at the Drydock. The bastard has more money than god anyway, but maybe he's been up there playing, and maybe he's been winning."

"Why don't you follow up with him?" I said. They'd seen enough of me at that house, and Crowley might have some luck. I let them know that our primary mission was finding Boomer Woodman, and that he should be considered armed and dangerous. If he was spotted, the orders were to stay on him until backup arrived. We hoped to know more as soon as Pettibone came in with lab results. I also told everyone to do drive-bys of Spanter's three times a shift, just to make sure he hadn't circled back. Then I stated Trout was tasked with investigating the game, and that we'd be heading to my office to discuss it.

"You sure you don't want me looking for Boomer right off?" he said, fingering his mustache.

"We've got everyone else on that," I said.

I dispersed the meeting, and Trout and I went into the office. I sat behind my desk. He pulled out his pack of Camels and put one in his mouth. His Zippo came out of his pocket.

"Nate," I said. "The no smoking policy in here hasn't changed."

"Oh, shit," he said, whipping the lighter away. The cigarette went behind his ear. He looked everywhere but at me. "Sorry about that."

"So, how's this game?" I said, like I was checking to see if he'd watched the Sox the previous night.

"I don't know, but I can sure find out."

"You do know, and I need answers."

"I'm not sure I like what you're saying, LT. You accusing me of something?" He wiped sweat from the back of his neck with his palm, then wiped his hands on his pants.

"Are you denying that you've been playing?" He looked to the side of the room, then at his feet. He made a whistling sound as he sucked in his breath, then met my eye. If I hadn't already known, his nerves would have given him away.

"Do I need to get a lawyer in here?"

"I don't care if you sat in on some damn card game. It's Boomer and what happened to those girls. You making some money out there, at least?"

"Haven't gone home a loser, yet," he said, trying to sound like he wasn't bragging.

"Good. We could all use a few extra bucks. What kind of stakes?" I needed to know the money being thrown around and figured I'd get further with a conversational approach.

"It ain't that big a game. Ten dollar ante, no limit on raising, though, and that can get interesting, let me tell you."

"What's the biggest pot you've taken?

"Just a few hundred. I saw Earl Goodwin scoop nearly a grand off the table with a straight flush. Beat Jamie Finn's aces over kings full house. Crazy shit. Crowley was right on it."

"Who's running the game?" I said.

"LT, you got to believe me. I didn't know Boomer had anything to do with it. Sure, he was there, but I thought he was just security, the bouncer. He sat in the corner behind the bar and watched everything with those black eyes of his. I figured old man Spanter rented the place out and made them put him on the payroll as part of the deal. You got to admit, the farm is out of the way and a good place for something like that."

"Old man Spanter died last year," I said. I could have been screaming, but kept my voice soft and casual. "Who's running the game?"

"A guy named Rico. Never seen him around town before. He does the money and the dealing. He wears one of those visors. Seems to know what he's doing."

"What was he like?" There was the other "pig" the girls had mentioned to Jimmy Goodwin. The dealer seemed like a fine candidate.

"Average size, maybe five-ten, one-seventy. Might have a little Boston accent. Seems like he's just there to do his job. Not much of a joker."

"So there's just him and Boomer there?"

He nodded. "From what I've seen."

"How's the house making any money?"

"They're taking ten percent of every pot."

"That must add up. How much you figure that runs on a nightly basis?"

"Could be a grand or two."

"That explains the new truck."

"I guess."

"How'd you hear about the game?"

"McNeely, the builder, mentioned it to me a while ago. At the Tavern one night. We grew up together, so."

I nodded. I hadn't realized until then that Trout didn't define himself as a police officer like Crowley or myself. He was a guy who worked a job. While sometimes that gave him insight that I lacked, in this case, it allowed him to cross a line he shouldn't have.

"You ever see those Connolly girls out there?" I asked.

"Jesus, no. You know me, LT. That's not something I would have ever sat on, no matter what. That shit and playing cards are two different things, like you said."

"You know Boomer came to my house. You know he's been trying to fuck up our investigation. You didn't think there might be some connection between the game and the girls?"

"LT, technically, the last game they had was the week before the girls went missing, and they haven't had one since. I never saw those girls there, not once. How was I supposed to know they were mixed up in it?"

I sat there staring at him with my mouth open. Was it so hard to do the right thing? Perhaps he wasn't aware of something called conflict of interest, or that with money coming in, maybe he chose not to think about it. There was a reason he'd been winning every week. He was a "Get out of Jail Free" card.

"I know," Trout said, showing a hint of a smile. "This caught all of us by surprise."

"We've been friends a long time, Nate. You've done a lot for me, and I appreciate it."

"I'm not done yet. You want me out there looking for Boomer? Or should I try to track down Rico, maybe?"

"No, Nate. I want you to put your badge and gun on my desk. Then you'll be leaving."

"What the hell?" he said. "You said you didn't care about a rinky-dink card game."

"I guess I can't be trusted, either."

* * *

By the time I called it quits that night, we'd spent more than twenty-four hours looking for Boomer and had been magnificently unsuccessful. This, despite the fact that he drove around in a truck the size of the Queen Mary. We'd been up every side street, dirt road, and dead-end in Laurel. We had a state trooper posted outside the entrance to the Village. It looked like Boomer had bolted, but running away wasn't in him. He was here, and I knew it. We just needed to find him.

Chapter Thirty-One

F riday morning, Regan and I set up in the Village and questioned every single resident, house by house, nearly sixty of them, including the kids. We started with the first one on the right, asking the family to step out on the porch, where we took their names and ages. It was a Woodman home, with Mark and Betsy as parents. That made the two girls Blink's worm suppliers. I couldn't interview everyone myself, so had scripted a series of questions for Regan. The initial queries would establish a rapport before we tried to pry some information out of them. I had to trust Regan to follow up if he had someone offer us something meaningful, or he could always bring me over. We positioned ourselves on opposite sides of each building, keeping the residents out of each other's earshot. After asking about workplace, names of relatives, education, and the basics, we would pivot to questions about Thursday, June twenty-sixth. Where had they been, did they remember seeing Caleb that night, did they see Boomer? Did they know and talk with Holly and Maisie Connolly? What was their relationship with Boomer? When was the last time they'd seen him? Did they know where he might be?

Mark Woodman came down the steps of his shack as if he'd been conscripted and was being sent to the front lines. He was thirty-nine and clean-shaven in that he wore only a five o'clock shadow. He was in charge of the crops in the gardens and received each basic question with a frown and all questions about Boomer with a grimace. He'd described their relationship as good and seemed grateful that he'd given his daughters the worm ranching job formerly held by Holly and Maisie. Not surprisingly, he couldn't remember a thing about that Thursday, nor did he have any idea where Boomer might be.

"Considering what happened to the Connolly sisters, do you have any concerns about the safety of your own daughters?"

'Nope."

"Why not?" I couldn't let it go.

He didn't flinch. "They know their place."

"And Holly and Maisie didn't?"

"I ain't speaking ill of the dead."

"Even if it can help them?"

"They didn't help themselves, and it's too late to help them now, ain't it?"

"Do you trust Boomer?"

"I got no reason not to."

I didn't have time to make him see the foolishness in that. It had taken me weeks to get through to Rory—and her daughters had been the victims.

Sissy Woodman, the older of the two girls, came next. She didn't know anything about the night her cousins went missing. Or what Boomer or Caleb might have been up to. She was as tough as her father. I asked her how the worm business was going.

"Good," she said. She pushed her black bangs out of her eyes. Her nose had less of a jump to it than Rory's and her mother's.

"You like it?" I asked.

"It's okay." She shrugged.

"You know Blink's a friend of mine. You could tell him I said to give you and your sister candy bars. He might just do it."

"We ain't working to make friends." She looked at me like I didn't get it.

"That doesn't mean you can't," I said. "Were you friends with Holly and Maisie?"

"They're my cousins," she said.

"I know that. That's not what I meant."

"They were okay."

"Did you hang out with them? Talk to them?"

"Not much." She was tight-lipped in her expressions as well as her answers.

"Even though you were at school together?"

"I stayed with my other cousins, mainly." Her eyes scanned the Village down to Boomer's house.

"And Holly and Maisie had other friends?"

"They thought they did." She looked right in my eyes, wanting to make sure this point got through.

"What do you mean?"

"Those people weren't really their friends. They're kids who wanted to use them, because they think we're trash."

I'd heard that before, from Rory Connolly. They'd all been well indoctrinated with the company line.

The interviews at the rest of the shacks did not go any better. The only information that got entered in our notebooks were names and ages. The Thursday the girls had been killed didn't exist in memories. Nor did anyone have the slightest idea where Boomer might be. None of them had a bad thing to say about him. That he was on the loose in town or could have been hiding in the woods a few hundred yards away might have had something to do with that. Whether his people respected him, believed in him, or were terrified of him—all of which could be true—they weren't giving us anything.

We drove up to the textile factory in Milltowne and pulled the Villagers off the production line one by one. The don't-say-a-fucking-word stares they gave each other when we'd bring one into the office would have cut steel. Jake Connolly was back at work, and we questioned him, too. He looked me in the eye and evaded answering with the same determination as the others, putting as much bite and steadfastness into his squeak of a voice as he could. I wanted to ask him if the sky were blue just to see if he could answer a question honestly. I couldn't tell if they didn't know anything or refused to tell us. Connolly didn't ask about his wife or son or the state of his daughters' case. He was another one I wanted to put through the wall.

When I got back to the station, I brought Caleb into the office. Since his mother's visit, he would at least walk down the hall without whining for Reynolds. I asked him what he knew about the poker games. Not surprisingly, "Nothing" was his first answer. "Though I knew about it," he added, puffing out what he had for a chest.

"Did Boomer have your sisters working them?"

"They was up there for it, so I think they did." He nodded.

"Why didn't you say anything about it yesterday?"

"You didn't ask, and Boomer said you didn't know nothing about it and to keep it that way."

"Do you know what they were doing?"

"They was all secret about it like it was some big deal. Boomer made me drive them up there, and he'd bring them home. At least it got them out of the house, so I didn't have to listen to them. You think they could have thrown me some gas money. They never thought of shit like that. Any of them."

"Boomer really hasn't helped you out much," I said, and sat back, hoping for a response.

"Always somebody being the fucking boss." He spat that out like a bad oyster.

"We're looking for him. If he wanted to get away, where'd you think he'd go?"

"That poker room is pretty sweet."

"Yeah, we looked there."

"Then I don't know."

I locked him back up.

Biggest guy in the smallest town, and we couldn't find him. I was still in the office at three o'clock, when Estelle came sprinting through the door.

"There's another one out here," she said, ready to pop.

Chapter Thirty-Two

J ake Connolly was shaking when I brought him in. He was in the same work clothes he'd been wearing when I'd talked to him earlier. He smelled of sweat. I sat him in the chair. His eyes shot around the room, from me to the floor to the typewriter to the file cabinets. He couldn't keep his hands still. They jumped back and forth from his lap to his knees. He was a different man than I'd left at the mill.

"You don't look too well, Mr. Connolly."

"I think I did something really bad." I was glad I was sitting down.

"Tell me, and we'll see what we can do about it." Maybe there was an aspect to the girls' case that I'd missed completely. Jacob hadn't figured in it, even in the most remote way. He'd been less than a pawn with Boomer running the board.

"I told Boomer where Rory is."

"You couldn't have. You don't know where she is."

"I do. She's with the nuns at St. Mary's."

"How the fuck did you find out?"

"She called me at the mill. She wanted me to talk to Caleb, so he don't go up for this. You see, we already lost our girls. We don't want to lose our boy, too."

"And she told you where she was?"

"Yup."

"Why would you tell Boomer? You saw what he did to her."

He looked down and wiped his eyes. "I didn't mean to say nothing. He come by the mill after you left. He was worried, and I said that his sister was trying to help. I let that slip, and then he got the rest out of me, that she talked to Caleb. I guess he didn't know about that. He said she might think she was trying to help but didn't know what she was doing, being a woman and all, and was fixing to get us all kicked out, the whole Village. She was really screwing up, and he needed to stop her." He balled his hands into fists and punched his thighs. "I didn't think enough about what he meant by that. I was just stupid."

"You think he wants to hurt her?"

He nodded. "Boomer said, 'All the fucking bitches in your house are trying to ruin me.' He was pretty hot."

I called the convent and got no answer, so I tried the nursing home. I told one of the attendants to get Rory and hide her, because there might be a developing situation. Then I ran out to the cruiser. Boomer's truck was in the parking lot, and that stopped me. I ran back in. Jake was walking out. He looked drunk.

"Do you have Boomer's truck?" I asked.

"Yeah."

"Where'd you get it?"

"He had it in the woods near the Village. We got some spots out there."

"What's he driving?"

"He's got the Pinto, a red one. I think he figures you won't be looking for him in that."

I was tempted to put Jake in protective custody in the cell next to his son. I'm sure that would have been a touching reunion, but I was wasting time instead of getting to St. Mary's.

"You better come with me," I said, and threw him in the back of the cruiser. We took off with my foot on the floor. I drove with one hand on the wheel and one on the radio. I contacted my men and let them know that Boomer was now driving a red Pinto and that his truck was at the station. I raised the Milltowne PD next and asked them to get a car to the convent and to lock down Rory until I got there. I contacted Pettibone and asked him to impound the truck and have the lab techs look at it. Those girls had crossed town to get to the quarry, and if it wasn't in Caleb's Galaxie they could have been in Boomer's truck. Corners came too fast, and I rode the shoulder, bouncing Connolly around pretty well. He'd spilled his guts to Boomer at two o'clock, so if Boomer hadn't gone straight to St. Mary's, we still had a chance.

The officers from Milltowne were talking to Sister Agnes in the driveway when I came to a halt. I popped out and left Jake in the back. They introduced themselves, identified me, and then informed me that Sister Agnes had told them that Rory had been picked up by her brother. Sister Agnes confirmed that and felt the need to apologize before I could say anything, apparently based on my expression. She explained that Rory didn't look like she was being forced and that the brother had said they were going to see her son. That I knew was a lie.

Pettibone radioed as we were driving back to Laurel. They'd found blood on the corner of the bar in the game room. It matched that of Maisie Connolly. They'd found other droplets on the floor. Those matched Holly. And there were three empty gallons of bleach in the trash behind the barn. One of them had a fingerprint that didn't match that of either Caleb or Boomer. It was something, but nothing that felt like a victory. We had a manhunt on now, full force, looking for Boomer and his sister. Jake Connolly was curled up in the back seat, continuing to punch his thighs. I asked for an update from Laurel. No one had spotted the Pinto, and Crowley hadn't been able to track down McNeely. Apparently, he'd gone to Rangeley for some fishing.

"Okay, Jake," I said. "If you're Boomer and you're hiding out, where do you go?"

He buried his head in his hands and didn't answer. I pulled the car over.

"Jacob," I said. He didn't move. I said it again, only this time I screamed. He looked up like a kid who'd wet his pants. "Do you want to see your wife again?"

He nodded.

"How about your daughters? You want to find out what happened to them? Because I'd bet my ass that Boomer had something to do with it." He stared at me blankly as he tried to stop sobbing.

194

"What am I supposed to do?" he said.

"Where is he going to go?"

"The Village," Jacob said. "They'll hide him."

"We've got someone stationed there."

"That ain't nothing. We got some other ways in, off'en the river and Brown street. We got some spots we can hide a car and walk in. There's a root cellar in the woods. You got to know where it is. He could go there."

"Where else, Jacob?"

"We got a farm now, that berry farm. Not too many know that."

"We got people there, too. It's locked down as a crime scene."

"You got the whole place covered? There's well buildings all over the map. I went out and looked at some water pumps."

"What the hell are you pumping water for?" Maybe they had a growing operation, too.

"Ain't no creeks out in the back, and they was talking about growing cranberries. You need a bog for that."

Jesus. H. Christ.

"Anywhere else? Any treehouses out in the woods around town? Any other property?"

"Don't think so."

I headed for Woodman's Village. All quiet, the state trooper stationed at the entrance claimed. Martin was parked at the head of the oval. He leaned against the cruiser. I pulled up next to him.

"We got a place to check out," I said. "Get the shotgun." He nodded and grabbed it.

"Okay, Jacob," I said. "Where is this root cellar?"

"You want me to show you?" he said.

"How else are we going to find it?" I turned to look at him.

"They'll think I'm a snitch."

"Your daughters are dead, your son is going to jail, and your wife is with someone who just kicked the shit out of her." He looked at me like he was thinking it over. "If you don't open your mouth right now, I'm going to kick the shit out of you."

195

"It's this way." He pointed to the fields and woods east of the Village. We started walking. He led us fifty yards through a field sandwiched between two half-acre vegetable gardens. We came to a small group of trees that marked the beginning of the woods that ran from the gardens to Brown Street. We went up a path to a rock outcropping the size of a car. He nodded to the right of it. There was a wood building that looked like an outhouse.

"That's it?" Martin took a circuit around the building and rock. He shook his head. Nothing.

"That's just the door," Jacob said. "There's stairs. You go down, and there's a room dug in. It's pretty big. We keep our preparations there."

I put my flashlight in my left hand and my pistol in my right, then stacked one wrist on top of the other. I stepped to the door. Jacob started backing up, one foot at a time.

"Where the fuck do you think you're going?" I said. That Boomer was a veteran and might know booby-trapping techniques crossed my mind. Jacob was stupid enough to go along with something like that, but too thick to have gotten us here if that's what Boomer wanted.

"No...nowhere," he said, stopping.

"Martin, if you hear gunshots, you stay up here, call for backup, and don't go down without Pettibone or the trooper he's got stationed out at the entrance. Got me?"

He nodded. His face looked tight, losing its childlike pudginess. I'm sure this wasn't something he'd envisioned when he'd signed on for the summer. This was not tearing up a ticket for a co-ed in a bikini out at Gray Gull or stepping between Cranky Fisher and Shane Miller in the parking lot of the Port Tavern. It wasn't much different for me. I'd never pulled my service revolver until this case. Murder and death and kidnapping were something from television. Right and wrong had been a matter of reasonableness or what was best for the community. I'd never considered the concepts of truth and justice. They hadn't entered my vocabulary.

Martin slowly opened the door, and I shined the light down the staircase. I counted ten steps to the earthen floor. They were covered with dirt, but I couldn't tell if they'd been used. There was no way not to expose myself as I went down.

I took a deep breath and relaxed my grip on the flashlight and gun. I placed my left foot on the first step. Then I put my right on the second. I listened and heard nothing. The flashlight reached a few feet into the space. The wall was granite, and I could see that the room ran backward instead of forward. That was a worst-case scenario. Everything would be behind me. I took two more steps, expecting to get a knee shot off. Nothing. With four steps to go, I jumped down and sideways into the room, spinning in the air and landing in a crouch. The flashlight's beam swung onto shelves and jars. That was it. I took my first breath in what seemed like ten minutes. My shirt was soaked.

"Clear," I yelled.

Chapter Thirty-Three

I went back to the office and changed my shirt. Then I pulled out a topo
map of Laurel to identify places where Boomer could be hiding. With
the exception of the square and the beaches, woodland carpeted the
rest of the town. We'd need an army to cover it. An empty house would
make sense for him, too. Those would be the few currently for sale. I had
Regan call Earl Goodwin and ask for a list, and told him to go check them
out. An area that Boomer did know was West Laurel. I found an updated
copy of the town tax map to see if there were any other parcels Boomer
might have purchased. There weren't. What I did notice was that the land
across the street from Boomer's farm was owned by Dan Reynolds. I called
and caught him at his office just before five o'clock. I asked him to stay.

Hunger struck on my way there. I had four sandwiches in my refrigerator
that were starting to go bad.

Reynolds was on the third story of the professional building. The only
door on the landing had his name in etched glass. I walked in. The reception
area was pleasant, with windows that overlooked Brown Street and plants
the size of televisions. His secretary was typing away, but stopped and said
hello. She was a knockout in her early twenties, with auburn hair that fell
about her face. It was impossible to miss the curves revealed by her tight
red blouse. I told her that I was there to see Reynolds.

"So, you're the police chief," she said.

"Is it the haircut that gave it away?" I said. She laughed.

"Well, it's great to meet you. I just moved to town, and I'm a bit of a lead
foot. To be honest, it's only a matter of time before I'm going to need a ticket

fixed."

"I'll take care of it," I said, laughing. "How do you like it so far?"

"It's great. I'm at the SeaScape. It's lovely there, and the town is so fun."

"Best time of the year," I said.

The mahogany door to the inner office opened, and Reynolds filled it fully. "That will be enough, Charlotte. Come in, Nichols."

He went behind his desk and waved me into one of the leather chairs he provided for his clients. It was more comfortable than my own office chair. Reynolds's desk was also mahogany, and massive. It was sparsely covered despite having several stacks of manila folders lined in rows on top of it. The door opened again, but before Charlotte could say a word, he barked at her that no, we didn't want any damn coffee. She rolled her eyes at me as she closed it.

"What brings you my way, Chief?" He drummed his fingers on the desk.

"One of your clients, as a matter of fact," I said. Funny that he was more respectful when he didn't have an audience.

"I believe I only have one that you may be concerned with."

"I'm talking about Boomer Woodman."

"Why would you consider him a client? I'm representing his nephew, as you know. I am also aware that you brought his mother in to try to get him to talk without my knowledge. You're playing it loose there, Chief."

"I'm trying to get the truth, and his clamming up doesn't help."

"While you might have been within the law to ask him, I wouldn't say that was an ethical approach."

"That's rich," I said. "A lecture on ethics from you."

"Now look here," he said, coming to his full seated height. "I'm trying to cooperate, and you're insulting me. I certainly don't need to justify the legal defense of a young man who has limited understanding of the process. So why don't you get to the point? I'm hoping to get in nine holes at The Cascades."

"Let me correct myself," I said. "I'm here about a potential future client. Boomer has abducted his sister Rory, who, I might add, he beat the shit out of last week."

"Neither of those assertions have been or could be proven. Do you know for a fact that she didn't go with him of her own free will? Are there witnesses to attest to this? Because that's not my understanding of the events."

While the wall of leather-bound books behind him provided him with the foundation to make such an argument, it shouldn't have allowed him—objectively or morally—to ignore the obvious: Boomer Woodman was a threat to everyone around him. Holly and Maisie Connolly could attest to that.

"You've talked to Boomer?" I said.

"I have."

"Where is he?"

"I don't know." He shifted in his chair.

"We have an APB out on him."

He shrugged. "That puzzles me. From what I understand, Rory Connolly was glad to see her brother, and they wanted to have a conversation without her being watched and monitored every second."

"That's bullshit, and you know it."

"Actually, I don't."

"You're aware we've determined that Holly and Maisie Connolly were murdered in the barn on the Spanter property, which Boomer owns?"

"I am, as Mr. Laurent has shared that information with me." He motioned to the phone on his desk with an open palm.

"As the owner of a property where a murder has been committed, we'd like to question him. That he's also a suspect shouldn't surprise you. Where is he?"

"As I just told you, I have no idea. If I did have knowledge, as an officer of the court, I'd be required to tell you. Now, are you done wasting my time?" He pursed his lips, and then tapped a pen against the folder closest to him.

"How did you come to represent him?"

"When you brought in his nephew, Boomer asked me to take the case."

"I'm not talking about Caleb. I'm referring to the purchase of Spanter's Berry Farm from his senile aunt."

"You can understand why such a purchase would necessitate legal representation."

"Of course, but how did he come to you?"

"Chet Spanter had Boomer's name added to the deed a few years ago, so naturally, Mr. Woodman had to sign the paperwork." At least that checked out with what I'd heard.

"Where did the money come from to purchase the farm?"

"That would be a good question for him. From what I understand, they live very frugally in his outpost."

"You own the land across the road from the farm."

"I do." He glanced at the map of Civil War-era Laurel that he had framed on his wall.

"Do you have a house up there?"

"There's nothing on it, which I'm sure you know. I imagine you also know that I live on Wellport Beach."

"Do you like to play cards, Reynolds?"

"What kind of question is that, Nichols?"

"In addition to everything else, your new neighbor ran an illegal poker game on his property."

"I'm shocked. Shocked to hear gambling is going on in this town of yours." He laughed at his own joke, slapping the desk top.

We still didn't know why the girls had ended up dead. With Boomer as psychotic as he was, something as simple as not following orders or some perceived slight could have triggered him. But it was impossible not to believe the girls' role in a crooked poker game had something to do with it.

"I'm wondering if you've ever sat in on that game," I said.

The snarky grin left Reynolds's face.

"I might place a bet on the golf course, but poker, no. For the record, I am unaware of any activity, gambling or otherwise, going on at the Farm. You do realize that my role is to facilitate a purchase or sale. We attorneys do not have it in our purview to monitor what happens after that transaction is completed." Another of the monogrammed handkerchiefs came out from his pocket to dab his forehead.

"You do not know where Boomer Woodman is?"

201

"I do not, for the last time."

"Right."

"Just because those people don't live according to your standards doesn't mean that they don't have their own hopes and dreams, as well as disappointments. If you don't think Boomer isn't torn up by what happened to his nieces and his nephew's alleged involvement in it, then you don't know people, and you may be in the wrong job."

"Did you just tell me that you think Caleb is involved in the murder of his sisters?"

"My job is to do the best I can for him. It's the function of the legal system to pass judgment."

"Murder, gambling, and beating up women doesn't illicit my sympathy, no matter what kind of language you dress it in."

I got up and left the office. He was reaching for the phone when I shut the door behind me. I assumed he wasn't calling to push back his tee time.

Chapter Thirty-Four

Jake Connolly had only come to me out of fear for Rory's life. He didn't know shit about Boomer's whereabouts, but at this point, neither did I. I took ten minutes and drove over to the berry farm. It was worth taking a look. I wasn't buying that Boomer only wanted to talk to his dear sister in private. Nor was I considering something that Pettibone had mentioned, that Rory may have become the Patty Hearst of Woodman's Village. Questions remained. Why had Boomer grabbed her, and what exactly was he planning to do?

The parking lot was empty. A ribbon of yellow police tape stretched across the entrance. I stopped, took it down, drove in, and replaced it. The lab techs must have moved on to Boomer's truck, conveniently parked at our station. Without them here, he could have easily snuck in as I had. I went to the poker barn and looked over the crime scene. The cleanup had fallen short. Markers at the corner of the bar showed where spots of blood had been found. More tape outlined the floor halfway between the table and the bar. In my mind, Maisie is struck and careens into the bar, where she cracks her head on the corner, a sharp right angle of hard wood. She'd have been moving with substantial force, but we had someone who could generate it. Holly sees this and either runs at him or screams, and she is shot. Whether it was Boomer or Caleb, or someone else, it must have happened quickly. I hoped that the fingerprints on the bleach jug would tell us more.

The sun was starting to set as I went to the house. The old woman answered the door. I showed her the warrant and walked in past her. It was as if nothing had moved in forty-eight hours. Mrs. Spanter sat down in front of her television and watched *Three's Company*. I checked the rooms and the basement. No signs of intelligent life. On my way out, I stepped in front of the television and asked if she'd seen her nephew.

"That fool?" she said.

"When's the last time you saw him?"

"He's running around with my Nanabelle down to the creek to fetch some water." There was no creek.

"Doesn't your plumbing work?"

"What are you talking about?"

I went over to the kitchen sink and turned the faucet. Cold water came gushing out.

I went back outside and decided to walk the property. I'd check out the pump buildings Jake had spoken of. At worst, I'd get some exercise, and if I didn't find Rory and Boomer, there was the chance I'd come across marijuana. I wasn't convinced that cranberries were a money crop.

Past the barn, the path turned from gravel to grass, with fields of blueberry bushes on either side. The grass was a few inches high, and there were visible tire tracks. Maybe Cranky Fisher could have told me when they'd come through and if they were from a tractor, mower, or car, but I had no idea. Quite an empire Boomer was building with seasonal berries and gambling. Perhaps the gambling was to fund the resurrection of the farm. That was a narrative Reynolds would spin.

I came to the first outbuilding, a five-minute walk behind the barn. It was the size of a closet, and there was nothing in it, not even a rusted rake. I kept on and noticed something else: three-foot high surveyor's stakes with hunter-orange plastic strips being pushed gently by the breeze. They were planted throughout the fields.

The next outbuilding, an eight by ten shed, was another fifteen minutes back. That was crammed with pumps, piping, and spider webs. The path then took a ninety-degree left and ran parallel to the road. I was now close to a mile behind the house and barn. After two hundred yards, there was another shed, this one the size of a single-car garage. Even as the light faded, I could see the grass that led to it looked run down, too.

Like the poker barn, there was a garage door in front and a regular side door. I opened it and went in. Out of the corner of my eye, I caught movement to my right and turned. My hand reached for my gun. Then fireworks. The starbursts were yellow and gold.

My face rested on the cool dirt floor. It smelled of the black fill my dad used for his tomato garden. I didn't know how long I'd been out. When I tried to lift my head, a burning knot at the base of my skull sent shockwaves north. I blinked my eyes into working. A wooden chair came into focus. I tried moving my hands so I could get up and was blanketed by pain. They were tied behind me. Trying to move my legs didn't hurt, but the attempt informed me they were bound at my feet. I reached for my gun belt. It was gone. I exhaled long and slow and tried to relax my muscles so I could think. The pain wasn't quite as horrible. I stared at the forty-pound bags of fertilizer across from me.

A car drove past and pulled around behind the shed. Two doors opened and closed. I heard the bass of Boomer's voice. The room brightened with moonlight when the door opened. "Get your ass over there," he said, and Rory scrambled to the wooden chair. He put a boot to my ribs. I'd anticipated it and braced myself. The fissure of hurt it sent through me was a fraction of what it could have been, a small victory. Boomer picked some rope up off the floor and tied Rory's hands behind her. He grabbed a propane lamp off a shelf. My eyes adjusted to the light.

I wasn't about to give up, but if Boomer produced another shiny .38 and put a bullet in my head, there was nothing I could do about it. That I now knew he'd killed the girls was no consolation. Like Pettibone said, I should have shot him when I had the chance. If it was true that you'd see your life play out before you when you died, the show was going to suck.

I'd gotten a nickname for accidentally breaking a kid's nose in fifth grade, then found the one thing I'd been good at, wrestling. I'd put everything I had into it and succeeded. Everywhere else, I'd come up short. Maybe I'd had it backwards with the concept of applied effort and result. In high school, I'd been happy to tag along with Deacon and Suzanne, only occasionally getting dates of my own. I could have asked out plenty of girls who would have been happy to go with me—I was a nice person—but I was chicken. I'd lasted one semester at college. I'd passed my classes, but was too simple to see the value in it. I might have learned things that would have kept me off of this dirt floor or Holly and Maisie Connolly alive. Instead, I'd let things in Laurel go on the way they always had. It was easy, requiring no thought and minimal effort. That credo defined me. I'd married a gorgeous summer waitress who I'd romanced in a matter of months. Analisa hadn't realized a town that was so alive for three months a year could become Sleepy Hollow for the other nine. Newlyweds could make it through that first fall on their own, but then reality strikes. When she talked about moving somewhere where restaurants stayed open past eight o'clock in December, I wasn't willing to do it. I'd warned her Laurel was like that. Suzanne was right when she said Analisa was a bitch, and it probably wouldn't have worked out anyway, but I never gave it a chance. Coward. Now in my thirties, it had taken me months to get with Suzanne, even with Deac in the distant past and her flashing the green light as soon as we'd reconnected. The opportunity she'd put in front us would vanish before I had the chance to consider it. My policing philosophy of "you get along, I'll go along" had worked well enough until a few weeks ago. It was easy until it wasn't. One of my men, who was also a friend, saw fit to sit in on an illegal card game that he should have been shutting down. Where did he learn that from? I let Blink sell beer out his back door. The question I'd always asked was, "Who was it hurting?" The answer was: Two girls were dead, and their mother and I would be joining them. Sure, Pettibone would figure it out. But Boomer had bested me, and the only good thing he'd ever done in his life was kill people on the other side of the world who'd done nothing to him.

He sat on a crate halfway between Rory and me. He got up, and I braced for another kick. Instead, he pulled me up by the arm and flung me into a sitting position, my legs out in front of me. My eyes shifted to Rory. She sat straight-backed, her feet below her knees, as if patiently waiting for class to start.

"Let me ask you something, Little Timmy. Did my sister here suck your dick? Cause if she's any good, then I'll have her do mine." He went over and stood in front of her, fooling with his zipper. "Would you like that, bitch, with your boyfriend watching?"

"What the fuck are you talking about?" I said, surprised that the words came out crisp and clear, because my brain was shrouded in fog.

"She's quite fond of you, the slut." He turned to me, and I could see his fly was open. "Sells out her own family."

"I will admit," I said, "I'd enjoy watching her bite it off."

He hadn't considered that possible outcome and zipped up. He walked over and grabbed me by the hair and yanked me left and right, then dropped me and laughed. He returned to his crate.

"Do you want to tell me that I'm not going to get away with this, or you want to save it until I send you two off'n the Arundel bridge in Brookeville in that fine cruiser of yours? It does drive mighty nice. Pity to ruin a rig like that."

"You are too stupid to get away with this," I said.

"There you go," he said.

"The girls, the card game, kidnapping, killing us. You don't have a prayer."

"If I were you, I might want to be the one praying," He kicked out his foot to nudge mine.

"I've been out of contact for three hours. My department will be looking with the State Police. They'll be back here." That was a lie.

"So, are you telling me to hurry up and get it over with?"

"Do what you have to do. You'll pay for it, all of it. Caleb didn't kill those girls. You did."

"Jesus, you're dumb."

"Sure I am. They were murdered in the poker room, beaten and shot. Caleb wasn't there. He only dropped them off. So that leaves you."

"That's what you'd like to think, isn't it?" He laughed.

"Spare me the bullshit," I said.

"You think that dope Caleb is so innocent? Too bad you ain't going to get the chance to ask him what he did for work Thursday night, and if he don't know where that quarry is." Boomer shrugged. "I'll give you half credit on that one, Little Timmy. You did find them bodies."

Rory choked, and Boomer looked over at her. "Caleb didn't like them two much. I can't says that I blame him. They thought they were something special. The mouths on them two. Turned out to be a couple of real pain the asses."

"You had them rigging that game for you, and that got them killed."

"Not quite." He lit a cigarette and leaned back. "Everyone around here thinks they're so fucking smart. Let a jackass win a big pot, and they know they're going to cash in every goddamn week. Jesus, is that funny. I learned some shit over there in Saigon. Didn't spend all my days in the jungle. Your Deputy Dawg sure liked to play. He's going to be a real help to us when you're gone."

"I fired him yesterday."

"Did you? What a hard ass. He's still got a future as an errand boy for me, don't you worry."

"So why you'd kill the girls?" I said.

"I don't recall saying I did. But they had their noses in places that they didn't belong, and their mouths weren't far behind. That was a problem."

"Such as?"

"You think I need to explain this shit to you, you got another thing coming."

"You're not too good at explaining anyway. You told their mother that we ran them out of town. How'd that work out for you?"

"Sister turned out to be as big a snatch as them two. The apples and the tree."

"They were your blood," Rory said, with the venom she'd unleashed on me the day she'd walked into my office.

"Christ," he said, his voice filling the garage. "I busted my ass for all of us. You don't know what I had up my sleeve."

"You should've been looking out for them," Rory said.

"You don't think I wasn't? They was fucking around with those boys from the high school, and I put an end to that. I took them off digging worms and gave them a nice job on Fridays and Saturdays. They could have made some decent money if they kept out of my other business."

"They had a chance to lead normal lives, and you took that from them," I said.

"Normal? Is that what you just said?" He stood and ground out the Marlboro with his boot, then backhanded me. The yellow and gold starbursts flashed, and I went over. "That's the problem with you folks. You think we're the losers. Well, let me tell you, we was turning that shit upside down."

"Yeah, you got a nice truck," I said, righting myself. "The rest of them drive pieces of shit that Caleb kept on the road. Is that how you take care of everyone?"

"Patience, Tiny Timmy. These things take time."

"Where'd you get the money to buy into this place, your new truck? What's your grand plan?"

"Wouldn't you like to know? I'm working on some six-figure shit. You probably wouldn't understand it if I told you. People won't be spitting on us no more."

"That's what my girls are worth?" Rory said. "A fucking truck?"

"They shouldn't a been shaking us down, sister. They wanted in on something they had no part of. I warned them plenty. They weren't much for listening, and they got what was coming to them."

"Who's us?" I said.

"I could tell you, but then I'd have to kill you," he said, slapping his thighs, laughing. "Shit, I'm going to do that anyway."

"You killed your nieces." Rory hung her head and started sobbing.

"I had about enough of you two." He got up. "Let's go for a little ride. You two are star-crossed lovers, just like in the movies. We're going to see to that. Plenty of people know how you're sweet on her, hiding her off how you did."

If he were going to send us off that bridge, he'd have to get us into the cruiser. That would be my chance. I'd use what I had available, which wasn't much. I'd have to hope for an opening where I could drive my shoulder into him or take him down with a leg whip. If I could get him on the ground and remain on my feet, I might have a snowball's chance. But I'd need to be conscious. If he capped us and tossed us in there like I'm sure he was planning, being the dope he was, we'd have no chance.

"You know the coroner will do an investigation," I said. "He'll see that we were tied. If you knock us out, he'll see that, too, and no one will believe the story you're trying to concoct. There's something called science that will put a big fucking hole in it."

"Shut the fuck up." He backhanded me again. This time I didn't go over. Rory mouthed 'keep going.'

"You're too dumb to have thought of this by yourself, Eugene. Who's your partner?"

He socked me the other way. My jaw ached.

"I'm guessing whoever told you to do this isn't any smarter than you are. Maybe you can get a cell together."

Another crack. He stood back and looked at the blood on the back of his hand. He wiped it on his pants.

"Jesus, you can't shut up, and I'm the idiot. How'd you get to be Chief anyway? That Crowley must be one dumb bastard if you got it over him."

"He's going to enjoy putting you away for this."

That brought another one, this time open-palmed across the left cheek. I saw Rory bend at the waist and then come up and whip around like someone throwing the discus. The chair swung through the garage and connected with Boomer's head. He went down on top of me. I bucked my legs and rolled him off. She swung again and caught him on the shoulder. He tried to get up, and she smashed him in the head. She raised the chair again and brought it down on his back. He went flat.

"There's a jackknife on my gun belt. Where is it?"

"The car," she said, dropping the chair and running out the door. Boomer moaned and started to move. I heard the car open. He put his hands out in front of him. I'd spent years doing core work. I slid down on my back and brought my knees to my chest, then drove my feet into his head. That pancaked him. Rory came through the door. She had my gun in one hand and the knife in the other.

"Hands first," I said, sitting up and turning to offer my wrists. It hurt to even raise my arms. The knife snapped open, and she sawed through the rope. My hands came free, and I turned in time to see Boomer rising to his hands and knees.

"Quick, the gun," I said. Just as she was handing it over, Boomer dove and took her down. The .38 fell next to me. I picked it up.

"All right, Boomer, freeze," I yelled, aiming at his broad back.

He spun, pulling Rory in front of him. He had one forearm under her chin and the other wrapped over her head.

"Drop it, or I snap her fucking neck," he said.

I was seated on the dirt, pointing the gun at them. Her head was directly below his. The room was poorly lit, and my vision was hazy. The angle was poor. I tried to calm myself by controlling my breathing, like I used to before going for a pin. Channel the adrenaline. It was something I'd learned on my own, something I never used writing tickets or driving drunks home on icy roads.

"Drop it," he yelled. The muscles in his arms flexed. Rory gagged.

My hand stopped shaking. I pulled the trigger. The room exploded in white light.

We waited outside. Rory was draped over me, convulsing with tears, her thin body pressed into mine. Blood and brain matted her hair. I'd turned on the lights to the cruiser so they could find us. We stood between the shed and car, the blue swirling. Once a second, it illuminated the dent in the front fender where I'd planted Boomer's head. That body part was now splattered across the back of the garage. I tried not to shake.

Chapter Thirty-Five

I t was a Saturday in the middle of July. The sun was out, and the
humidity had lifted. Birds were singing, and families were driving to
the beach. I should have been picking up sandwiches from Blink's and
packing a cooler for Suzanne and me. Instead, I was back at the station on
two hours of sleep that I wouldn't have termed sound. I'd been answering
questions until four in the morning for Pettibone and the State Police's
incident investigator. I got to tell the story again to Laurent at seven o'clock
when I walked through the door. There was still work to do, and I was
anxious to finish it. Too many people had suffered for too long.

I called Reynolds at home and let him know what had happened and that
he needed to come meet with his remaining client. He did not sound happy.
I'd probably endangered a tee time. I contacted Sister Agnes and arranged
for Martin to pick up Rory. Then I left for the Village with Regan to talk to
Jake Connolly. I assumed Woodman's would be quiet, either because they
hadn't heard or were in shock.

We pulled up in front of the Connollys' shack, and Jake came out with two
of his relations. They watched us, shifting on their feet and whispering to
each other. Maybe they thought we were going to take them all down.

"Good morning, boys," I said.

"We heard what you did," Jake said. "You feeling like a big man today,
Chief? Come to gloat?"

"I could've done nothing and let him kill your wife," I said. I let that hang
there like a punch to the gut.

"I didn't know that," he said. The taller one patted him on the back.

"We have reason to believe that he's responsible for your daughters' deaths, too."

"Shit," the third man said, stroking his beard. "That can't be right."

"We do not make things up," I said. I was too tired for another lecture. "We're talking to your son in a few hours to get this sorted out. If you want to be in on that, you should be at the station at noon."

"Okay," he said. "I can come."

"Your wife will be there, too."

We ran back to the station, and I found Laurent and Reynolds talking in the conference room. Reynolds asked if he could speak to me in my office before we questioned Caleb. I granted the request. He was in weekend casual, having forgone his tie but wearing a navy blazer. He sat down in our noticeably uncomfortable chairs and wiped his glasses with his handkerchief, taking his time. Then he looked over at me and cocked his head.

"Mr. Laurent just shared the knowledge that you gained last night regarding my client. It appears that he was not the killer, after all."

"Something that we could have established last week if you'd allowed him to talk to us. Maybe with different results for everyone involved."

He brushed that off without even a blink.

"You've come to the conclusion that Boomer Woodman killed his nieces?"

"It looks that way." Boomer may have dealt the blow to Maisie and put the bullets into Holly, but he wasn't the only one behind it. The words he'd used were "us" and "we." It seemed that the poker game, farm purchase, and Boomer's "six-figure" deal all fit into the narrative, and Boomer just did not have the wherewithal to put these in motion or navigate them by himself. There was another party who was also responsible in some way. Maybe this was the "pig" of a partner that the girls had described to Jimmy Goodwin. I wasn't stopping until I discovered who that was and exactly where they fit into this mess. Reynolds himself touched the case in two of those three areas, and I wouldn't have put it past him to know more about that poker game than he'd let on. If I found that I was wrong and this was indeed a deeply twisted family squabble gone awry, I could walk away having done as much as I could and as much as I'd promised.

"From what I understand," Reynolds said, "Boomer confessed before you blew his head clear off his body." Laurent had a big mouth. That description went beyond what he was due in discovery evidence. They probably both hoped to get to the golf course by noon.

"I didn't say that."

"As far as Mr. Laurent is concerned, the case is closed." Reynolds's lips pressed into a tight, closed-mouth smile.

"He's the district attorney," I said, giving him a fake smile of my own.

"Well then," Reynolds said. "Should we proceed to the matter at hand?"

We went into the conference room with Caleb and Laurent. We hoped that Caleb could fill in some missing details. If we could get Caleb to realize his current position, Reynolds and Laurent could then work out their deal. I was glad that Pettibone had taken my gun because if Reynolds didn't change his legal strategy, I'd have been tempted.

I explained that Boomer had abducted his mother, held her hostage, and that in the process, he'd been shot and killed. I didn't tell him that I was the one who'd done it, and he didn't ask. Maybe Reynolds had told him. Whatever he'd heard, he was more jumpy than usual. His hands bounced from the table to his skimpy moustache to his hair in an endless circuit. I told him that we knew he'd disposed of the bodies, and that there was no use denying it. He nodded as if I'd mentioned that we were having chicken for dinner. I also let him know that answering our questions honestly could help him. Caleb looked to Reynolds for reassurance and was told it was important to do so. Without Boomer to strongarm the process, it looked like we might have a normal interrogation.

"I get it," he said. "I told you I didn't kill my sisters." This added as if a great accomplishment.

"When Boomer came out to Ned's that Thursday, what did you talk about?"

He looked over at Reynolds, who nodded. He glanced at Laurent as if he expected him to reach over and slap him, and then turned to me.

"He wanted me to go pick up Holly and Maisie at the Village, because they go to town on Thursdays. But I had a carburetor on a crummy K-car apart, and I couldn't leave it, so I was late getting out, and they'd already left. I had to catch up to them. Then they didn't want to get in the car when I told them that Boomer wanted to see them, and I had to promise to take them back to town so they could get their goddamn ice cream." I thought of Jimmy Goodwin and smiled.

"Where did you take them?" I asked.

"Out to the farm," he said.

"And this was at three o'clock?"

"About."

"What happened when you got there?"

"I don't know. We went into the barn."

"Who was there?"

"Me, Holly, Maisie, and Boomer."

"That's it?" We were getting more of the truth. "You didn't mention that last time we talked."

"You didn't ask me." He grinned, as if that was a reasonable answer. "Besides, I wasn't going to rat out Boomer."

I held back from asking where that had gotten him.

"Then what happened?"

"He told me to beat it."

"So what did you do?"

"I went back to work."

"Is that the last time you saw the girls?"

"Then."

"What do you mean?"

"Boomer came over to the house wicked late and told me to get my car and drive him."

Laurent kicked me under the table.

"Where'd you go?"

"Back to the farm."

"To do what?"

"He had the girls all wrapped up in tarps. Me and him carried them out to the car, and then we drove them to the quarry. He had me shine the light, and we went through the woods and dumped them in the water."

"Wait a minute," I said. "When did you find out they were dead?"

"On the way over to the farm, Boomer said that they'd got out of hand and they had to do something about it, that some shit went down. He said they were going to ruin everything for us, that if he hadn't done anything, I wouldn't have even been able to keep working at Ned's."

I sat back and ran my hands through my hair, trying to massage the hurt out of my temples.

"You thought that was all right?" I said.

"They was dead when I got there. I couldn't do nothing about it. They were my sisters, but I knew how they could be, all for themselves, and didn't give no crap about the rest of us. I took Boomer at his word. You don't cross him."

If I hadn't been so worn down, I might have gone over the table.

"What did you do after you ditched the bodies?"

"We went back to the Village. Boomer put some gas on the tarps and put them in the fire pit. He gave me two hundred bucks cash."

"That much?" I said.

"Yup, and he said if I kept my mouth shut, he might get me a job out at this poker game, and I could make as much in two days as I could for a week at Ned's, maybe open my own garage, even."

My hands covered my face, stifling a scream.

"You said Boomer said, 'They had to do something about it.' Who was the 'they'?" Reynolds's posture stiffened, and the handkerchief that had cleaned his glasses was now working on his forehead. I didn't play poker, but I knew what a tell was. It struck me how often I'd seen this when things got tough for him. He knew something.

"I don't know. I didn't see no one else there but us. I might have just said that, the way I talk." Caleb had a point. Making sense wasn't one of his strengths. The handkerchief was folded and returned to its place in Reynolds' jacket.

"Anything else you want to tell us?" I said.

"Nope," he said. He stood up. "Am I free now?"

Laurent motioned for him to sit back down. He'd started out by drilling a hole in his floor to peep at his sisters and wound up dumping them in a quarry where he and his uncle had hoped no one would find them. Freedom was not going to be a consideration of his for a long time.

"Caleb," Laurent said. "You transported dead bodies and knew about a murder. You're an accessory."

"But I didn't kill them or nothing." His mouth hung open, and his eyes welled.

"Unfortunately, Caleb," Reynolds said, looking more comfortable than he had a few moments earlier, "what you did still constitutes a crime. We'll get you the best deal that we can. Can we talk, Laurent?"

I called the county jail to have him transferred out that afternoon.

* * *

Rory was waiting for me when I got off the phone. She looked better than when I'd last seen her, in that her hair wasn't peppered with brain matter and coated with blood. Her eyes were back to the red they were when she was upset. She wore Suzanne's jeans and a denim shirt that the nuns must have provided. I hoped she'd thrown out the blood-covered clothes. She was paler than ever and couldn't have slept even a fraction of what I had.

"How are you doing?" I asked, a stupid question.

"I don't know," she said. We looked at each other. She breathed softly, the lines at the corner of her eyes barely evident. If she didn't appear to have stepped off the beach for a strawberry daiquiri, at least she looked settled.

"It's an understatement to say that you've been through a lot. If you hadn't been able to get your hands loose, it could be neither of us is here."

"He never gave anyone credit that they could do something better than him. He took my girls from me. I couldn't let that rest."

"I'll always be grateful."

"If you had to put a bullet through me to get to him, I would have been okay with that."

"If we're lucky, we'll be able to put some of this behind us one day."

"I know you only wanted to help. I didn't see that. I'm sorry."

217

"You've got nothing to apologize for. I could have been a lot smarter about some things."

She tilted her head and showed me a hint of a smile, a first. I saw her girls in her, and how Jimmy Goodwin could have been drawn to them.

"I want things to be different now," I said. "Between you and me, between this town and Woodman's. How it's been isn't right. I could have tried to change things so something like this could have never happened. I'm as responsible as anyone."

She nodded. I wasn't sure whether she was agreeing to the first statement, the second, or both.

"What do you want to do now?" I said. "About yourself, I mean. I've talked to Sister Agnes, and she said that you can stay with the sisters as long as you want. You can keep working in the nursing home, too."

"I want to go home," she said.

"To the Village? Will it be safe?"

"I don't know that it will be friendly." She looked down, then exhaled and raised her eyes. "Some of them won't come around right away, but I don't think anyone will get after me once they hear what happened."

"Are you sure they'll believe it? I talked to some of those people this week. They didn't exactly have open minds."

"Maybe I can help them see. It took me a while myself."

"Any problems, you call me and get the hell out of there." We'd come this far together, and I wouldn't handle it well if something happened to her.

"We aren't all like Boomer."

"If you're sure you'll be okay," I said.

"It's where I belong," she said with a smile. "I do want to keep on at the nursing home, though. They could use my help."

"That's great," I said. "If you ever need a ride, you let me know. We can arrange that. If you need to talk to someone about what you've been through, like a psychologist, we can arrange that at no cost, too."

"No." She exhaled and looked me in the eye. "What about my son? What's going to happen to him?"

"The DA and Reynolds are talking that over now. He's going to have to go to jail. He and Boomer, you know what they did. Jacob is coming in at twelve to meet with them. You'll all be able to talk."

"If anyone had given poor Caleb a break," she said. "He could have been happy with his head stuck in an engine."

I nodded. It was a disgraceful rationalization. But if anyone deserved leeway, it was the woman sitting in front of me. Estelle buzzed to say that Jake Connolly had arrived and that Reynolds and Laurent were waiting with Caleb in the conference room. I stopped before I opened the door for Rory.

"If you ever need anything, you let me know, okay?" I said.

"Wait," she said. "Do you know why he killed my girls? What was he talking about?"

"Not for sure, no. But I'm going to find out."

"Good." Her instincts had been right on from the start. It was a question that needed answering.

Chapter Thirty-Six

"Time to take the victory lap, Chief," Crowley said, poking his big head into my office.

"Sure," I said.

That started the second parade of the summer. Laurent followed and patted me on the back for cracking the case, saving him from prosecuting the wrong man and eliminating the need for a contested trial that would have been largely predicated on circumstantial evidence. Johnson barged in to congratulate me on creating positive PR for the town. There hadn't been a lunatic menacing all of Laurel, but a random nut with family problems. With our new law and order image, he thought we'd be known as one of the safest vacation spots in New England. Pettibone looked at me differently, too. He no longer offered advice every time he opened his mouth. Even though Boomer had danced around admitting it, we knew he killed his nieces. I'd graduated from hick to hero. Everyone was satisfied—except me.

Reynolds's behavior ate at me, and not just because he was a pompous ass. He'd shown his tell when I'd asked Caleb about the "they," and when Boomer had talked about the girls shaking them down, he'd said "us" and "we." He'd also said the girls "had their noses in places that they didn't belong" and that "they could have made some decent money if they kept out of my other business." I wasn't ruling out the poker game as a factor, but that "other business" had to be his "six-figure" deal, and that meant real estate, which meant Reynolds. Maybe the girls had seen it as the ticket to their college money. If that's what they got mixed up in, Reynolds was involved. How and how much were the questions.

After Laurent finished with Reynolds and Caleb, I brought him and Pettibone back into my office. I went behind the desk and asked them to sit down.

"We've got this wrapped up rather nicely," Laurent said. "Kudos."

"You should take some time off," Pettibone said. "Especially after last night. That's pretty much mandatory."

"We've got a problem," I said and stated that while we knew Boomer had in all likelihood killed his nieces, I believed there was another person enmeshed in what happened. I explained my reasoning. What I didn't know was this party's degree of agency in the murders. Laurent and Pettibone looked at each other.

"LT," Laurent said, shaking his head. "It would have been hard enough to prove that Boomer was the killer and look at all the evidence we had. You have a lot of work to do if you expect me to go to court with another accessory. Someone would have to be as thick as Caleb Connolly to get tangled up in this."

"I'm guessing you have someone in mind," Pettibone said. He seemed interested.

"There's two candidates. The mystery man dealer from the poker game, Rico, and Dan Reynolds."

"Whoa," Laurent said, a hand coming up as if he were stopping traffic. "Reynolds? Do you think he'd have been inclined to get caught up in intrigue with high school girls? Especially in some secret real estate deal that no one seems to know anything about? Pettibone's right. You need to take some time off."

"Don't put a halo over him," I said. "Did you find his defense strategy for Caleb to be ethical?"

"Look what he had to work with," Laurent said.

"It could be as simple as this revolves around that damn poker game," Pettibone said. "We know the girls were there."

Laurent stood up. "I'm satisfied with what we have right now. We've closed the biggest case in the state in years. If you want to keep on, good luck to you. You're going to need some real evidence. I'm not fucking around with theories and 'might have.' If you get something ironclad, let me know. Otherwise, I'll be out on Square Pond with my fly rod." Pettibone and I sat there while he got up and left.

Pettibone shook his head. "What can I do?"

"If you can find this Rico, I'll see what I can kick up about the game around here."

"I'm on it," he said, patting me on the shoulder.

"Thanks." I handed him a copy of the file.

"If I were you, I'd give Crowley some marching orders and take a few days off. That's some shit you saw last night."

"I'll be okay," I said.

He nodded, curled his moustache, and wished me luck. That left me with a real estate deal to uncover and a poker game to investigate. I went straight to Earl Goodwin's office.

Chapter Thirty-Seven

Goodwin Real Estate's office on Main Street looked like it belonged to a mariner instead of a salesman. Interspersed with the pictures of a few homes were those of 1800-era schooners, Boston Whalers, lobster boats, and cabin cruisers. If you came to buy from Goodwin, you were going to be reminded that the ocean was why you were here, and you'd better be ready to dig a little deeper in your pocket. His secretary buzzed me right through to him, a perk of being a local hero. It was only a matter of time before that wore off, maybe sooner with some than others.

"So, Boomer," he said, shaking my hand and inviting me to sit down. He looked grim.

"Yeah," I said. "I'll get right to the point. What was the deal on the table that you and Reynolds had with Boomer Woodman?"

"Why are you interested now?"

"That's my business. Can you just answer the question?"

He picked up a gold pen from his desk and began to twist it open and closed. "This isn't anything new that we've been working on, LT. I believe I mentioned it to you before."

Apparently, he was going to make me break it down bit by bit.

"So let's start by talking about the 'we.' Who is that?"

"Dan Reynolds and I put this together."

"You'd been working with Boomer on it since when?"

"This spring. There's a lot of moving parts, and we'd just nailed them down. This is quite a setback. We were signing in a few weeks."

"Are you going to make me pull this out of you, or can you just tell me what the fuck was supposed to happen?"

"Take it easy, LT. You're not the only one put out by this shit." He slapped the pen back into its holder. "We were buying the land that the Village was on. We were going to put in a considerable condominium complex there, everything first class. Reynolds started things in motion by having Boomer buy Spanter's. That's where we were going to move the Villagers. Of course, they could also operate the farm again, too. It was a real development opportunity for them."

"So they were trading out that riverfront to move to the middle of nowhere?"

"More or less. We were getting them all brand new mobile homes, nice places instead of those shacks they live in now. And they were getting money. Everyone benefitted."

"Boomer was for this?" That explained the stakes out on the farm. They had house plots marked off.

"Sure. As bent as he was, he liked the idea of a nice place to live and money going into his pocket."

"How did he come to buy that farm? And a brand-new truck, too? I don't believe they found buried treasure in the river behind the Village. Did you front him some money?"

"Not as part of this deal. He and Reynolds had some joint business enterprises going. I assumed they were talking about the farm, maybe something about cranberries. I'm not sure. I only came in on the land development side concerning the condominium and relocation project, meaning design, the selling of the properties, and the exclusive real estate rights."

"When did you decide it was going to be viable?"

"Mid-May." Now I knew why Boomer didn't kick the shit out of Jimmy Goodwin and his friends when he found them with his nieces, something clearly out of character. He didn't want any personal shit getting in the way of his deal.

"How many condos were you getting in down there?"

"I'd have to look at the plans."

"Ballpark it." I didn't believe that.

"A couple hundred."

"That many?"

"Give or take, like I said." He spoke softly, as if it weren't an important detail. I wasn't buying that, either.

"Okay. You got a builder lined up? Anyone from town? McNeely perhaps?"

"We're bringing in Larry Grant from Portland. This is too big for a local outfit."

"How many trailers are you going to put out on the farm?"

"Mobile homes, LT. They're different. We'd probably have a local do the site work."

"How many was that?"

"Fifteen or so, and we'd fix up the main house to the current century."

"How much money was going to Boomer and his people?"

"Boomer is the one who actually owns the land. He was getting a hundred thousand cash on top of everything else." There was his six-figure deal, though it seemed to me that two hundred condos were worth a hell of a lot more than fifteen mobile homes and a hundred grand.

"I guess you were making out a little better than that," I said, tired of his dancing.

"I'm missing out on every cent if whoever takes over for Boomer doesn't happen to think our proposal is a good deal."

"Who else have you talked to from the Village?" It was always possible that Boomer had another lackey besides Caleb.

"Not a soul. Boomer wasn't running a democracy there, LT." Now that I'd gotten that out of him, there was still the poker game to dissect. I couldn't believe that was a one-man operation, either.

"Have you been in the barn that they fixed up?"

"Sure." He frowned as he thought better of that answer.

"You know about the poker game?"

"I'm not going to answer that one."

"Believe me, I'm not bringing in anyone for playing cards. Go have a drink at the Rusty Bullet if you want that verified."

He threw up his hands. "I knew about it, but I haven't played. Had nothing to do with it. I've got enough vices, Chief." He laughed to make sure I realized he was joking. Another one of those things I knew around town was that his secretary qualified as one.

"Stop bullshitting me, Earl. I know you played, and I know you won big. I haven't slept, and my patience is thin. Who was running that game?"

"That's not my area of expertise. All I know is I'm out a lot of money if Boomer's replacement doesn't like the deal, provided they even have one."

"You can tell me who ran that game, or I can stop by River Road and ask Cindy if she knows the nature of your evening property showings with Sally Grobek." I nodded back at the outer office.

He ran his hands through his hair and groaned, then looked up. "I don't know for sure. Boomer was there. Reynolds wasn't, but he must have known about it. We'd meet in that barn and use the table to lay out the site map. I'd be surprised if he had anything to do with it, though."

"Why is that?"

"He's a lawyer. I think he does pretty well, and we were going to clean up when this deal went through. What does he need with a poker game?"

That was another good question. But with zero contacts in town, Boomer couldn't have put it together himself, and I was finding Reynolds' fingers in every piece of the pie.

* * *

My next stop was Trout's house. We hadn't seen each other since I'd let him go, which we were officially calling a resignation. He didn't say anything when he answered my knocking but stepped back and let me in.

"You took out Boomer, I heard," he said.

"I did."

"Good. Now, what do you want?" We stood in the hall inside the door. Past him, I could see breakfast plates still on the kitchen table. I guess I wasn't getting invited in for coffee.

"You got anything lined up?" I said.

226

"In forty-eight hours?" He was alone in the house. His wife ran the desk at the Maine Inn. His two kids were grown and lived in Massachusetts.

"Something will come up," I said. "You're a good man."

"But not good enough for you."

"You could have really compromised us, not to mention there's plenty of folks around town who knew and could have—"

"I know. I know. I'm an idiot."

"We all make mistakes," I said. The television played on in the living room across from us.

"I don't imagine you're here so I can cry on your shoulder."

"I need to know about that card game."

"Why? You got your man."

"I got the man who pulled the trigger."

"That ain't enough?" He leaned back against the wall. High school graduation pictures of his son and daughter were on the wall behind him.

"We still don't know the why, and we both know Boomer didn't have it in him to put it together and get the word out. I think there's more to it. I don't think, 'Their uncle was dumb as a stump and bat shit crazy' is a good enough explanation for killing those girls."

"What do you want to know?" I'd convinced him that I might have a point.

"Who ran it? Who played?"

"I appreciate how you handled this, keeping it between us."

I nodded.

"There was the dealer, Rico, who ran the table and handled the money."

"You know his last name?" He shook his head. Hopefully, Pettibone would be able to make some progress. "Not from around here?"

"The only time I've ever seen him is in the barn."

"You think it was his game?"

Trout shook his head. "He didn't talk too much. He did his job, but wasn't selling it, you know what I mean? I'd say he's hired help."

"What was it like between him and Boomer?"

"They didn't seem like buddies, but he's not known for having friends."

"What did Boomer do there?"

"He ran the bar, sat on a stool, watched everything like a hawk with that stare of his. Probably didn't help beer sales much."

"Whose game do you think it was?" I leaned back against the opposite wall to give him some room. His and Marilyn's wedding picture was next to my head.

"No idea, but hard to think of him planning it out like you said."

"You ever see Reynolds there?"

"No."

"His name ever come up at the table?"

"Nope. What's he got to do with this?"

"The two of them had a few real estate deals going."

"Are you shitting me?" He stepped into the hall and widened his stance.

I shook my head. "How about the twins? Did you see them?"

"Jesus, LT, I told you that if I had, I couldn't have sat on it, no matter what. They were just kids."

"You know it was a crooked game?"

"What do you mean?" He tugged on the tuft of hair over his right ear.

"They had those girls upstairs, with telescopes and holes in the floor, and a signal system with lights that ran to behind the bar."

"They must not be very sharp, then. I won every time I played. Never lost."

"You ever think that they might have been playing a long game with you? With you there, they're not getting busted." That was a possibility he—or any officer—should have considered, especially with Boomer Woodman in the room.

"Fucking shit," he said, stamping his feet.

"How many times you go up there?"

"Three or four."

"Do you remember who was there? Anyone not local?" There had to be an inside man at the table.

"Nope. One time Earl Goodwin had a guy up from Portland, who was working a job with him."

"Grant something?" I asked.

CHAPTER THIRTY-SEVEN

"Sounds right." There was the tie to real estate, which was a tie to Reynolds.

"Anyone there every time you were?" If the plant wasn't from out of town, that meant he was from Laurel, and Boomer wasn't close to anyone here besides Reynolds. That was a fact. So the plant had to be recruited and brought in by Boomer's partner. The partner probably brought in the dealer, too. Reynolds was involved in every other enterprise, so why not this? "What about McNeely or Goodwin?"

"Nope, neither of them. Jamie Finn was there, Hilly Kranepool, Pickey, and Derek Anderson. Jesus Christ, did he win big one night."

Of course, Derek would pop up. I didn't like the odds of a loser like him taking a big chunk of money. I had plenty of puzzle pieces, but couldn't get a grip on how they fit together. With Crowley and the kids running the town, I was alone chasing this. I needed help.

"You want to do some work for me?" I said.

"Does this mean I'm back?" he said. A slight, hopeful smile snuck onto his face.

"It doesn't. It means I'll think about it, but to be honest, I'd say it's a long shot."

"Maybe I'll pass then." His lips became a flat line.

"You like people responsible for two dead girls running around Laurel?"

"Boomer is out of the picture, isn't he?"

"He's not a solo project on this."

"You think?" He scratched the back of his neck.

"I have some thoughts."

"Feels like we should be on your porch talking this through." The smile reappeared. I realized that for Trout, the time on my porch was more about the friendship and beer than the casework. That didn't mean he wasn't helpful, just limited in what he could be counted on for.

"I can promise you all the Bud you can drink there if you want to give this a go."

"Okay, then." He offered me his hand, and we shook.

I told him he could swing by the station and I'd let Estelle know to give him his badge and a radio. I sent him to the town hall to review every real estate transaction in West Laurel and the areas surrounding the village. Then I told him to go up to Scarborough to Coastal Chevrolet and find out who sold Boomer the truck and how he'd paid for it. The cliché of following the money might clarify things.

Chapter Thirty-Eight

I had to go to Blink's. I was sure Suzanne had heard by now, and I hadn't called. She'd either be worried or pissed off or both. I hoped she wasn't too angry to answer a few questions. When I walked in, a group of customers was crowding her sandwich counter. It was lunchtime, not that I ate anymore. When she spotted me, she left them to Bev Keene, who worked with her on summer weekends. She had me wrapped up before I could get three steps into the store.

"Is it the uniform?" I said, hugging her back.

"Shut up, LT," she said, pulling me over to the wall and getting us out of the entryway, both her hands grasping mine. Blink grinned and made the pistol sign with his hand and fingers. The people waiting for sandwiches were all looking.

"Not a goddamn word, LT?" she said, the smile vanishing.

"I don't know anyone who likes a four-in-the-morning 'guess what' call, and then I started working this morning and got sidetracked."

"You shot him," she said. "Isn't that the end of it?"

"Not quite."

"Aren't you going to take some time off, for chrissakes? I can get Bev to cover me tomorrow."

"Let's see how it goes," I said.

"You look even worse than the last time I saw you. You're going to crash."

"I know. I just need to wrap some things up."

"It wouldn't hurt to be a little smarter about it."

"That's not the first time I've heard that." She nearly broke into a grin. "I

231

have a question for you. Who was Derek's divorce lawyer?"

"Dan Reynolds. Why?"

"Do you know when he picked up the Camaro he's driving?"

"Beginning of June," she said. I nodded, and that was a mistake. "He's not involved in any of this, is he?" Her voice was a mongrel of anger and horror. Her white teeth dug into her bottom lip.

"I don't think so, but he might have had a part in this crooked card game that Boomer was running out at Spanter's Farm."

"You've got to be kidding me?" Her face twisted. "With Boomer fucking Woodman?"

"They had a mutual acquaintance."

"I didn't know there was such a thing."

"No one did."

Her eyes started to well up, and I hugged her. "I'm sure it's nothing to worry about." I hoped for her sake that I was right.

"Will you come over when you're done tonight?" she said. "Whenever that is?"

"Sure," I said. A 'no' would have brought tears.

"Please be safe today," she said.

"Hey, I'm not even carrying," I said, pointing down to where my gun belt would have been. "How much trouble can I get into?"

She latched onto me one more time, then kissed me on the cheek and walked back over behind the counter.

"You're never too old for boyfriend troubles," Bev told their customers, eliciting laughter and at least a brief smile from Suzanne. I went over and said hello to Blink. He asked if I were okay because he, too, thought I looked like shit. He told me to come by on my way to Suzanne's, he'd have something for me. I thanked him and left.

I took a minute in the parking lot and leaned back into the headrest. I didn't know where I stood with Suzanne. Since I'd woken up on the floor in that shed, she'd only briefly entered my thoughts. Maybe under the circumstances, that was normal. I'd gone into survival mode and then had been riding a hyper-focused panic and adrenaline wave. If I hadn't wanted to learn about a possible Derek-Reynolds connection, I don't know that I'd have thought to come here as soon as I did.

Days earlier, I'd believed we were heading to a place where I'd be able to share certain things with her. That would seem normal for someone you would consider having a child with, a proposition I'd nearly managed to table for twenty-four hours until I saw her racing to me. Suzanne had intelligence and plenty of common sense, and I could trust her. Without her, we would have never gotten Rory settled. If I presented Suzanne with a problem or theory, I was confident she could come up with her own take on it, objectively and with insight. She'd deserved to hear about Derek because she'd always be tied to him, then I watched her nearly lose it over the chance he was connected to any of this. I hadn't realized the power of those ties or the heaviness that piece of knowledge could bring. Some things could float in the wind, like your boss selling cases of beer after hours on weekends. Others would not. If I off-handedly mentioned the real nature of Earl Goodwin's late showings with his secretary, what would that mean for Suzanne when she ran into Cindy in the produce aisle of Bartley's? I hadn't considered what it—and her association with me—could cost her. She didn't need to walk down the street and question the faces looking back. I was paid to do it and deal with what that wrought. She hadn't asked to carry that weight. It would be wrong to put it on her. If that meant I had to pace a mile back and forth alone across my living room to work things out, that's what I'd be doing.

Chapter Thirty-Nine

I went straight to the Rusty Bullet. Derek wasn't there, but Jamie said he was working with Sarofian's crew out at Bishop's Beach. The houses on Bishop's ran twice the size of those at Gray Gull. The lawns were like putting greens. Hedges were artfully trimmed, and flower beds glowed. Some even had their own tennis courts.

I pulled up at three o'clock. Charlie Sarofian, a young guy who'd moved up from New Hampshire, was on the ground directing sheets of plywood going up a rope to what was going to be a second story. They were guided by Chad Wrenn on a ladder and being passed off to Derek. I asked Sarofian if I could talk to Derek for a few minutes, and he nodded and called for him to come down. He was a hard worker, I'd give him that. When he saw me and didn't move, Sarofian had to yell at him a second time. He came swearing down the aluminum rungs. Sarofian walked off so we could have some privacy.

"What the hell do you want?" Derek's nose didn't look bad other than a red line across the bridge. He wasn't exactly a handsome devil to begin with, and maybe that was a good thing for me.

"I heard you're pretty lucky with cards."

He took a breath and exhaled, giving me half a glare as his mind tried to figure out where I was going.

"Is that a crime?"

"It is if you're playing in an illegal game."

"I don't know what you're talking about," he said.

"I had a man undercover at Spanter's. You know Nate Trout. You shouldn't be surprised."

"I heard you were the one surprised when you found out he was there." He laughed.

"That's a good one, Derek. I'm guessing that you don't quite get how undercover works."

"What the hell are you talking about?"

"I'm not looking to bust anyone for the card game, that is, if I can get some cooperation. Be straight with me, and I'll let you get right back to work."

"I'm supposed to trust you after what you pulled on me?" He jerked his pointing finger to his beak. I was glad he was talking about that and not his ex-wife.

"You tried to sucker me, Derek. If you'd succeeded, you'd be sitting in the county jail right now." He would have liked to swing right then, and the strain to suppress the impulse showed on his reddening face.

"Yeah, well, what about you and Suzanne?"

"You blew that one yourself."

He kicked at the grass with his work boot.

"What are you talking about, this undercover crap?" he said. I guess he saw my point.

"I know that the game was rigged, and I know you were working with the house."

"You don't know that."

"I heard it from Boomer's lips," I said. Derek was too angry and not scared enough to talk. "That was before I put a bullet in him."

"Dirty fucking Harry," he said.

"Don't you forget it," I said, smiling. "I know Reynolds is the one who put you up to it. The cheating, I mean. Did you make some good money taking advantage of your friends?"

"They're big boys." I'd been correct.

"Let's hear it. How'd you work it?"

"You think I'm telling you?" He grinned like he had me.

"What do you think would happen if I went over to Rusty's and let slip that the card game up at the farm wasn't on the level and that one of their drinking buddies was in on it?"

"I don't think it would go over too well." He looked over at his crew sending plywood up without him.

"No, it wouldn't. How'd it work?"

"Boomer had some signals. He was always flipping a chip around, touching his hair. It was kind of like reading signs from a third-base coach. Sometimes I'd play to win, and sometimes I just pushed the pots. Those weeks I didn't get as much. To make it look good, I'd leave with the boys and circle back for my cut."

"Did you know the Connolly girls were working there?"

"Yeah, I seen them after they come downstairs."

"Did anyone else know about them?"

"Just Boomer and Reynolds."

"I thought Reynolds was only the brains behind the operation." I tried not to look excited.

"That's right," he said, putting a hand on his forehead. "Fucking Boomer couldn't count to eleven without taking his shoes off, so Reynolds would come in to settle up after it cleared out. But I do think those girls were pretty sharp."

"Not sharp enough, I guess," I said, going along. "They ever fight with Reynolds and Boomer?"

"They were pretty mouthy about a lot of shit. Boomer would laugh, threaten to backhand them. That'd crack them up because if there was a screw-up, he'd usually been the one to make it."

"What about Reynolds?"

"He didn't like them much," he said, cocking his head. "They laughed at him, too, only he didn't think it was funny. Called him a fat pig who probably couldn't find his pecker. Told him that he should get a drool bucket, the way he looked at them. Shit like that. I thought it was funny."

"You didn't think this information might have been helpful when we were looking for them?"

He stepped back and put his hands up.

"You take that back. It didn't come out that they was missing until after.

236

We didn't even have a game the week before that. That was a family problem, wasn't it, with all those inbreds?"

I told him that if I found out that he talked to Reynolds about this, I'd let loose at Rusty's. That would keep him quiet.

Chapter Forty

I f Earl Goodwin was the king of Laurel's realtors, then Glen Cabot was the serf. He sold one or two houses a year, usually for friends. While Goodwin's signs littered the town, it was an occasion if you saw one of Cabot's. That didn't mean he didn't know what was going on, though running his business out of his landscaping garage could give one that impression. The Cabot real estate empire was located in an outbuilding of the Great Woods Resort property on the road from town to Gray Gull Beach. Great Woods had been built early in the sixties, and had one main motel building and a set of scattered mini-cottages. It was due for an update. But the grounds, kept by Cabot, were worthy of Bishop's or the Grimes compound, one of the other jewels in Cabot's landscaping crown. He was pushing fifty, but often went out with his crew. Saturdays were when he did his paperwork, and I was hoping to catch him at his desk. I found him crammed into one side of his space, the other taken up by riding and push mowers, and a vast assortment of rakes, spades, and hedge clippers arranged on pegboards.

"What can I do for you, LT?" he said when I walked in. He took off his ball cap, and his mop of gray hair spilled out. "You finally ready to do something about that travesty you call a yard?"

"Not quite, Glen." When I was, I wouldn't be able to afford it anyway. "Have you heard about this deal going around with Woodman's Village and a condo development?"

"Course I have. Damn shame what happened to those girls this summer. I always said that Boomer was crazier than a tick in heat on a weasel's ass.

But no one's worrying about him anymore. I guess you've seen to that."

"Was there real money to be made there?"

"Plenty. Have you seen the plans?"

"I haven't."

"I do some work for Larry Grant up in Portland, who they were getting to do the build-out. It's called On the River. Nice place, close to two hundred spots, and I had the grounds." He reached into his desk and pulled out some blueprints and renderings. They showed a grand-hotel-style edifice with three wings, two pools, a small marina, tennis courts, and various gazebos and clubhouses. The landscape drawings looked like they'd keep Cabot busy for the rest of his life.

"How much do you think they would've cleared?"

"The math is pretty simple. Those condos on the river will go for forty or fifty grand each, maybe more. Say two-hundred times forty-five, that's six-point-three, coming in. Now the upfront costs would figure to be half that, so three-point-one-five."

"How much to move out the Woodmans, Connolly's, and Sampson's?"

"A mobile home might run fifteen grand tops with site work, and they're probably not going top of the line for those people. So they're looking to clear a couple million, easy, counting what they'd pay out in finance and marketing and whatever they're throwing in the way of cash to the Woodman's folks. That's, of course, provided they sell all those units, which might not happen in a day. Could take a year or two."

"They offered Boomer a hundred grand plus the move and the trailers. That's a little short, right?"

"What's a lot of money to some people sure isn't to others."

"You wouldn't take that deal."

"If I were them, I'd want to get out of the shit show they live in. That land's worth more to anyone else than it is to them. They'd be getting an upgrade, but there's no reason to give it away. If they were really smart, they'd push for some sort of limited partnership stake and then settle for what they can get up front. I don't know what those people would do with that kind of money and wouldn't want to hazard a guess." He sat back and folded his arms across his chest.

"What do you think of Reynolds?" I said.

"He's got some ideas, and he's not afraid to follow through. You know he's got big plans for West Laurel?"

"You just told me."

"No, beyond that. He's got the land all along Route One across from the farm and down toward Wellport. He's going to put a shopping center in there across from Cook's Corner."

"Why would he do that?"

"You like driving twenty-five minutes for groceries? It's thirty-five to King's Department Store or Sears. Might as well drive to goddamn Portland. That bastard is dialed in. Laurel is growing."

"So he's got a lot at stake."

"Sure does. All he had to do was not fuck up, and he was going to be a mighty rich man. Make a lot more than he does writing up those house closings. Don't know how things will shake out now, considering. Maybe he can keep it together. But what's your angle, Chief? Why are you turning over these rocks? I thought it was decided last night."Cabot's eyes narrowed.

"There's always something," I said.

"Ain't that the truth," he said, shaking his head. He advised me to take a ride up to see Larry Grant and talk to him. I had a better idea.

Chapter Forty-One

I t was five o'clock, and I still hadn't eaten when Trout called in with his report. Over the past three years, Reynolds had purchased every parcel for a mile on Route One south, starting from Cook's Corner. Boomer Woodman had paid his great aunt five thousand dollars for the berry farm. Even though it was across town and away from everything, that didn't seem like a lot. He'd also found Boomer had handed over another five grand in cash for his truck. That poker game must have been gold, and I hadn't known it existed. Boomer couldn't have accomplished any of this without Reynolds' help.

I asked Trout to do one more thing for me. I sent him the Trading Post in Kittery to see if he could find sales information on our Colt Mustang. The Post wasn't far off, and they sold more guns than anyone in the state, including those beyond the basics like that Colt. Maybe tracking its ownership was something we should have done as soon as we possessed it, but there it was, right in our lap. Easy. It had never struck me as a gun Boomer would carry or spend money on for his nephew, not when he could have given him a .22 that had been in the Village forever. A shady lawyer who ran a poker game and established fall guys was someone who would carry a flashy little automatic, however. I was still on his tail as I crossed town.

I stopped at the Café Seine and got two coffees. Everyone said it was the best in Laurel. I also got a bear claw, hoping the sugar rush and caffeine would carry me for another hour. I now had more than two million reasons why Reynolds and Boomer would get rid of the girls if they threatened their plans. "A bigger pig than even their uncle," Jimmy had said. That described Reynolds, according to Derek Anderson. The third set of prints on the bleach gallon hadn't been identified. They could simply belong to some stock boy—or they could be those of a party with something to gain by erasing evidence of the killings.

I drove to the SeaScape apartments outside Bishop's Beach. Charlotte Emery's yellow Charger sat in the parking lot of what used to be a hotel in the thirties and forties. After checking the mailboxes, I rang the buzzer for Apartment Three. She came to the door in a long t-shirt and bare feet. A bikini strap reached around her neck. She smelled of suntan lotion.

"Chief Nichols, what are you doing here?" she said. Her face scrunched in thought, probably trying to recall doing something worse than forty in a twenty-five. I handed her one of the coffees. She smiled and thanked me.

"I need to ask you a few questions," I said. "Not about you, of course, but your office. Would you mind?"

"I guess not."

We went in. It was a nice place, bright and airy, with a little deck that looked out over the woods. We sat at the breakfast bar. I explained that Boomer Woodman had been killed resisting arrest and that we believed he was responsible for the deaths of his nieces. I added that there were some loose ends we needed to clear up and that I'd already spoken to Mr. Reynolds that morning.

"Do you remember Thursday, June twenty-sixth? Would you know if Mr. Reynolds left early that day?"

"Is he under suspicion for something?" This brought a furrowing of her brow.

"I'm just trying to corroborate some testimony."

"That's so long ago. I know he occasionally leaves early to play golf, but I can't remember the exact dates." The contentment on her face told me the coffee was excellent. I could barely taste mine. "I'd have to check the appointment book to be sure."

"You don't happen to have a key to the office, do you?"

"Of course."

"Could you spare a few minutes to take a ride up there?"

"I do have a date tonight, but if it won't take too much time, I can do it."

"I'll drive. No ticket."

"You've cleared this with Mr. Reynolds?"

"I don't think we'll need to bother him."

"I don't know if I'm comfortable with this if he's not aware."

"This is a capital case, Miss Emery. It's critical that I verify his office hours for that day." I didn't have to explain everything. "If things work out, he won't even know that we've been there."

"This better be worth several tickets," she said.

Fifteen minutes later, we were standing in Reynolds' office. She retrieved the appointment book from her desk and handed it to me. On Thursday, June twenty-sixth, he had names down for three o'clock and four-fifteen. They'd been scratched out. The poker barn was ten minutes up the road.

"Does this mean that he left early for sure? He has names crossed off in the book here." I showed her.

Charlotte nodded. "I had to reschedule those appointments. I think if you look into the following week, you'll find them. Of course, I had to stay until five. I don't get any breaks around here."

"When did he have you cancel them?"

"Now I remember. Mr. Woodman came by that morning," she said, making a face as if the cream in her coffee had curdled. "Unannounced, which had me shuffling around some of the earlier appointments that day. I really should have remembered. After he left, Mr. Reynolds told me to clear his afternoon starting at three o'clock."

"How was he on Friday? Did he seem like himself?"

Charlotte smiled. "I do remember him snapping about having clients first thing that morning as if it were my fault. But he's not exactly happy-go-lucky. Him being an asshole is just him being him."

"Does he ever hit on you? Make inappropriate comments?"

"Are you kidding? Yeah, he's a bit forward. When I deflect him, he acts like he's joking. That's how it is these days. He pays just enough to make it worth it, too."

"Do you know if he has a gun?"

"You're joking."

"I am not."

"Jesus Christ, what's going on?" she said. Her eyebrows came in low over her eyes. She held her hands together in front of her. "I did see a check go out to a club that might have to do with something like that. Hold on." She sat at her desk and pulled the checkbook out of a locked drawer. She flipped back to April. Here it is. A $150 check had been made out to the York County Sportsmen's Club. 'Membership' was scrawled on the memo line.

"Charlotte, is there something that he touches on a regular basis that I could take with me?"

"Like for fingerprints?"

"I'm afraid so."

"What is he suspected of?"

"It's really so I can rule something out. Our DA is a bit of a crackpot. You know these lawyers."

"I sure do, as I hope to be one myself. But I don't think you're giving me the straight dope here, Chief."

"Does that mean you won't point out something for me?"

She cocked her head and raised her eyebrows, then put a finger to her lips. She went into the inner office and came out holding a manila folder by its edges. I took out an evidence bag, and she placed it inside. When I dropped her off, I assured her she'd never be paying for a speeding ticket in the town of Laurel, Maine.

Chapter Forty-Two

After weeks of frustration, I finally had a picture of how all these pieces may have fit together. That Boomer had acted alone was as likely as my becoming Director of the FBI. He may have been the muscle, but Reynolds must have been pulling the strings. If he thought that Maisie and Holly Connolly were going to torpedo all he'd put in motion, he had millions of reasons to get them out of the way. And it looked like neither he nor Boomer had lost any sleep doing so. If I could prove Reynolds's knowledge of these events or put him in that barn, our gone-fishing DA would be forced to act. All I needed was to match the fingerprints on the manila folder to the bleach jug or prove that he was the owner of the Colt, and we'd have him. Maybe he could become Caleb's cellmate.

I stopped at the station and handed off the evidence bag with the folder to Griffin. I sent him straight to the State Police Crime Lab in Portland. I called Reynolds in Wellport Beach. No answer. I then contacted Chief Franklin there and asked if his department could keep an eye on the house and let me know if Reynolds came home. It was six-thirty. I could've gone straight to Suzanne's, but I had enough juice left for one stop, so I took the long way past The Cascade Country Club. I knew how he liked to spend his afternoons. Sure enough, Reynolds's Coupe de Ville was in the parking lot. I pulled in behind it so he couldn't leave if he wanted to.

"It's a little late for you to get out there, LT, the way you slice," Bob Callahan, the sandy-haired club pro, said when he saw me enter his shop. "You'll be in the dark by the third hole."

"If I ran into less wise guys around here, I might have the time to work on that."

I asked if Reynolds were still out on the course. He'd been in for an hour, and Callahan directed me to the clubhouse. Before I went, I asked him for his course log for June to check out a certain Thursday afternoon. Reynolds's name did not appear on the sheet. My legs felt like concrete as I slogged my way to The Cascade House. It was tucked into a pocket of pines overlooking the eighteenth green. A patio spread out beside it, a danger zone when I played. The tables were full, but Reynolds wasn't there. I went through the sliding doors into the dining room and found him at the bar. He wore a pink golf shirt and tan slacks. His Titleist visor was still on his head. He looked pretty comfortable with a martini in hand. He caught me headed his way and put down his drink. He pulled the cocktail sword and slid off an olive with his teeth.

"Nichols," he said. "You look a bit underdressed. Doesn't Wyatt Earp wear a cowboy hat and a low-slung gun belt?" The two gentlemen he was drinking with appeared slightly amused, but one look from me erased their developing smiles.

"I need a word," I said.

"If it's about my client, this is my third Beefeater, and I've punched out for the day. You know nothing can happen before Monday anyway."

"Outside, please."

"Or what, you'll blow my head off?" He laughed.

"I just have a couple questions. Your martini won't even get warm."

"Very well then. Lead the way."

We went back out through the patio, and as we were going to need some privacy, I led him to the cart lot. It was full of vehicles, but empty of people.

"Is this really necessary?"

"We can go down to the station, if you like. I have some questions about your involvement with the Woodman's folks that I'd like answered."

"The only one that matters, who killed Holly and Maisie Connolly, seems to have been emphatically answered. Your associate Mr. Laurent is very satisfied."

"Let's start by you telling me how this real estate deal for Woodman's

Village came together."

"How does that have any legal bearing?"

"I'm hoping your answers will clarify that." I could feel my pulse starting to race and tried to calm myself down. Reynolds was fairly certain I wasn't much brighter than Boomer. Let him hang himself with that security blanket. "Could you please explain?"

He sighed like an algebra teacher about to go over basic arithmetic with one of his more simple students.

"After Mr. Spanter died last year, Boomer purchased the farm from his Aunt. A little while after that, I approached him about buying it. He was not interested in selling to me."

"But you do have the land across the street?"

"I do."

"Why all the interest in West Laurel? There's nothing there."

"Land speculation is not a crime. Unless I'm magnificently wrong, Laurel will soon be a very desirable location. The population of this state is growing. It's close enough to Boston and Portland, but retains a country charm, not to mention miles of coastline. People will soon be looking for affordable options that don't come with the price of waterfront. Right now, land in West L is relatively cheap."

"How did you come to develop this plan of moving the Woodman's folk out to West Laurel and putting condominiums on the river?"

"As you can imagine, Mr. Goodwin is also interested in real estate opportunities. We talk frequently. Do you have a point? I'm sure my drink is approaching room temperature by now." He leaned against a cart and drummed his fingers on its roof.

"How did Boomer Woodman come up with the money to buy the farm and then do some very nice renovations?"

"That would be a question for him. Good luck asking it."

"I live in the house that I grew up in," I said, gladly acting like a dope. If I gave Reynolds the chance to lord his knowledge over me, with him being three martinis in, there might be no stopping him once he got talking. "I don't have a lot of experience in real estate. I'm just trying to understand how this could come together. The only commerce Boomer Woodman ever did in Laurel was buying cigarettes and beer."

"Nichols, you're asking about things that have no or little relevance to Caleb, who is my client and only connection to these events. We know what he did, and he will be pleading guilty. As for further questions, I simply don't have the inclination to continue."

I ignored him. "Boomer thought moving the Village was a good idea?"

"The man was not a saint, obviously. I think he was tired of being looked down on, and as low as he was, I believe he wanted to do better for his people. There was money to be made, too, and like many of us, that motivated him."

"Is money a motivating factor for you?"

"Do you work for free? Of course, it is."

"Enough for you to get involved in running an illegal poker game with Boomer so you could set up this other deal?"

"Please. I've had enough of this." He turned and took a step toward the clubhouse.

"We both know that Boomer didn't have the connections in town or the brains to put together a game like that. Someone else had to have a hand in it."

He stopped and turned. "Was I also in Dealey Plaza in November of 1963?"

"I have witnesses that put you with Boomer Woodman at the poker barn every night after the games."

"That's ridiculous." Now he looked pissed. He reached into his pocket, presumably for his handkerchief, and came up empty. Derek Anderson was not going to be happy with me if he wound up on a witness stand and these details came out. Too bad.

"I also know that you had a problem with Maisie and Holly Connolly."

"I've had enough of this. I never even heard of those girls until Mr. Woodman hired me to represent his nephew. That you could imply such a thing after all I've done for those people is not only insulting but unprofessional. If you weren't wearing a badge, I'd kick your ass. This conversation is over."

He pivoted and stepped toward the clubhouse. I put one hand on his

248

shoulder and another on his arm and tossed him into the back of a cart. He knocked over the golf bag someone had left there, but somehow stayed on his feet.

"That was a mistake," he said, up on his toes. "You don't know who you're dealing with."

"I just have one more question. Where were you on the afternoon of Thursday, June twenty-sixth, between the hours of three and five o'clock?"

"At my office. Some of us work for a living."

"No. You canceled your appointments and left early."

"You're mistaken."

"I've seen your appointment book, and that's been verified by your secretary."

"That girl's IQ is lower than her bust size. I don't know where you're getting your information, but if you intend to pursue this, you will find it impossible. The principal offender is dead, and what you're spouting here is fanciful conjecture. You may be good with a gun, but the train of thought that has brought you here seems to have left the station without you."

"Don't tell me you were here that afternoon, either, because I've checked. You were in the barn at Spanter's."

"What witness has told you that?" He laughed and was back on the flats of his feet.

I'd already rattled him with that shove. If I could continue to nudge him out to the edge, he'd eventually leap. All I had to do was keep him correcting me and explaining things he believed I was too simple to understand.

"I know from several sources that you and the twins did not get along. That they got under your skin. That you'd be spitting mad and carrying on when they'd blow you off and make fun of you. That you'd been aggressive toward them. So what was it, Reynolds, that bothered you about them? That they wanted a bigger cut of the poker action or maybe a piece of that real estate deal? Or was it that a couple of gutter snipes clearly identified you as a loser? A big, rich respectable man like yourself. That's the same problem Caleb had. They frustrated him, sexually and otherwise."

"They were high school girls, Nichols."

"You've been divorced three times. You pay a shitload of alimony. You aren't getting anywhere with your secretary. You're the perfect type to try to take advantage of a high school girl. Who else would be impressed with your beach house and Cadillac and willing to overlook that dyed hair and Dough Boy body? I've got a feeling that you don't like women very much after what they've done to you."

"So now I'm a predator? You spin quite a yarn, but wrong again. I have no trouble with women. As you've noted, I've been married three times."

"Maybe they wanted more than whatever pittance you allowed Boomer to throw at them. Maybe you were afraid they'd walk around Laurel and strike up conversations with some of your customers, who they'd be sure to recognize. That could have thrown a real monkey wrench into that money-making machine that you, Goodwin, and Boomer had lined up with On the River."

"That's enough. Mr. Woodman and I did have quite a plan in place. I have no need to deny it. We were going to take those people out of that shithole and move them into respectable housing on a road that borders civilization, and put a little money in their pockets. I don't believe that's a crime."

"Holly and Maisie Connolly came to pose a threat to that. And you snapped."

He shook his head and laughed, resting his hands on his thighs. "Could you be more obvious? Poking at me with nothing and trying to get a response. Laurent must have laughed his ass off at you."

"Funny, you said earlier that you never even heard of those girls until Boomer hired you for Caleb."

"Irrelevant, my friend. You were right about one thing, however. Those two were connivers. But you're having a hard time understanding. Let me use my imagination and guess as to what happened in that barn. Then maybe you can go back to writing speeding tickets or whatever it is you know how to do. Of course, as I wasn't there and never heard a word about it, this is strictly conjecture on my part. Not to mention I'll sue your ass from here to China should you ever repeat it. Are you following me?"

"Proceed." He could not resist.

"Let's say someone helped educate Boomer in real estate and fronted him some money to facilitate a more substantial deal that would benefit many. Perhaps some of that seed money could have gone toward buying a much-needed property for his people. Maybe that someone could also assist him with this crazy idea he had about running a card game in that barn, but only in the way of some general advice."

"Come on, Reynolds. Boomer couldn't even count the money at the end of the night." He shook his head and waved that response away.

"Maybe these teenage sluts who didn't know any better saw money being made and wanted more than they were worth."

"How much was that?"

"Perhaps someone like Boomer, with his obvious limitations, may have thrown them a twenty. Each."

"Big money," I said, shaking my head. That wasn't going to get them to California.

"For those two? That's plenty. But maybe they couldn't be happy with that. Maybe they heard us talking about moving them out of Woodman's. Maybe those bitches might have heard the word 'million' and got some ideas. Perhaps those two didn't think it was such a great deal because, as dumb as Boomer was, he might not have been inclined to share any of the proceeds with his people, other than to get them their trailers. So maybe these girls didn't see enough coming their way. With a role model like Boomer, they may have overlooked that they were given a ticket out of that shanty town, which is no small thing. Maybe they demanded their own cut, a substantial cut, or they threatened to exercise their mouths. That is not something that would have gone over well with Boomer. Could be they had too much balls for their own good, as I think their uncle admitted in front of us at one time."

"So you had them brought to the poker room and killed them."

"That would make zero sense. If that were the case, one could have anticipated the exact type of trouble that arose. But maybe Boomer did feel those girls needed to be straightened out. He might not have appreciated those two possibly fucking up his payday and the betterment of his people."

"Boomer doesn't strike me as the 'call a meeting' type. But I know he met with you that morning, unannounced, then you cleared your calendar, and he went to talk to Caleb. That resulted in them being brought to the barn. That strikes me as your idea, not that of an oaf who could have walked up to them and cuffed them whenever he wanted."

"Maybe he offered them something decent to quell their unrest."

"What did you two come up with, fifty bucks?" Holly and Maisie had seen their tickets out of the Village dangling in front of them.

"Let's say that snatch Maisie may just have had the temerity to tell him to stick that offer up his bulbous ass."

'Bulbous ass' was a detail that sounded like a sore point and a valid descriptor for Reynolds—a detail that indicated this was not speculation.

"Maybe the counter to that offense was a very stiff backhand that had unforeseen, accidental consequences. The small snowball off the top of the mountain that starts the avalanche."

"Who hit her? You or Boomer?"

"Boomer, of course. I wasn't there, and there is no one on the planet who can prove otherwise. I thought I made it clear this was conjecture. Were you not following that?"

"And then you shot Holly?"

"I guess that would be Boomer, too."

"Two sloppy shots aren't Boomer's work. He's bragged about his marksmanship on two continents, and he doesn't strike me as a guy who'd carry a small personal protection piece. Boomer's more of a .44 magnum, and he wouldn't need a gun for a teenage girl. But for a partner who's a bit of a dandy and sometimes found himself in questionable spots, the Colt Mustang is the perfect piece."

"It doesn't matter what you believe, Nichols. You are as impotent as can be. You can get the FBI, the CIA, Scotland Yard, and Commissioner Gordon of Gotham City down here, and they'd never be able to substantiate any of this. Nor could you ever place me in that barn on that day, because I wasn't there."

"You just told me what happened. I think you were."

He chuckled and shook his head. "That's unfortunate. All I've done is guessed as to what may have occurred between Boomer and his nieces. Any attempt to prove what I just produced from my imagination would only discredit yourself. You're impotent, which is strange for the hero who shut down a gambling operation and brought a killer to justice with a silver bullet. I hope you realize that."

"Except for two things. There's a set of your prints on one of the bottles of bleach we found out behind the barn." Because I didn't have information confirmed didn't mean that I couldn't use it.

"I doubt it." He again reached for his missing handkerchief. His weight shifted from foot to foot. "That would only suggest that I like to clean, and I believe I've already admitted to being at the barn for real estate purposes."

"Forensics has confirmed that bleach was used to clean blood from the crime scene. That places you there."

"You've got to be joking. That means no such thing."

"Boomer would have never spent two hundred dollars on a pop gun, either, not for himself and especially not for his idiot nephew. But the great thing about that Colt is its serial number is clear as day. The Colt factory traced it to Maine and Kittery Trading Post. The Post has—"

He took a step back and leaned into the cart he'd spilled into earlier. Even as tired as I was, I could see the telegraphing as if it were in slow motion. I ducked the club coming at my head and came up, landing a body shot with my left. The right cross that I'd been waiting weeks to throw landed on his jaw and dropped him like a sandbag.

A woman screamed. I looked up to see a couple walking toward us from the clubhouse.

"God damn," the man said. "I just bought that MacGregor. It's a fucking Nicklaus."

He stormed past me. He went to grab it where it remained wedged in the roof's side post. I stopped him with a hand on his chest.

"Don't touch that, please. It's evidence." I finally had some witnesses.

Epilogue

The rest of the summer of '86 seemed almost normal. We patrolled beaches and extinguished unpermitted fires. We wrote parking tickets and pulled over speeders. Late-night altercations in our town's drinking establishments were few. Maybe our partiers feared the long arm of Laurel's now ultra-experienced peace officers. The town was as it should have been, with green and blue backdrops bookending a ribbon of brown sand. In the aftermath of the chaos, the Little League Tigers made the state tournament, and we gave their convoy of station wagons a lights and sirens escort from the bandstand to the turnpike. Before my seasonal guys had to return to school, I took the entire force out to dinner at the Sea Squall, including Nate Trout. We spent a lot of money, got drunk, had some laughs, and no one got hurt.

From not eating for weeks while continuing my workouts, I was again in peak shape. Ironically, I now had little reason to be but kept up with the running and lifting. If anyone had been charting my blood pressure, they would have seen it fall off a cliff. Without redlined stress, I was sleeping again, too. Sometimes I'd be waking up across town at Suzanne's. Other mornings I'd be in my own bed with her arm resting across my chest. She'd had me invite Rory and Jake to have dinner with us, a beautiful gesture. Rory, who I called at the nursing home every Wednesday to check in, had declined with a pleasant, "I don't think so." I didn't blame her for wanting to ditch the rearview mirror.

I believed that Reynolds had shot Holly Connolly. Pettibone agreed. Laurent questioned that we could prove it beyond a shadow of a doubt in court, however. But with his fingerprint on the bleach jug, his gun at the crime scene, and the circumstantial evidence that placed him there that afternoon, Reynolds was going to be tried as an accessory both before and after the fact. There was also the attempted murder of a police officer with a very expensive golf club, which was not any worse than if he'd swung at me with a knockoff. We had him on gambling charges, too, with Pettibone having tracked down Rico and Derek willing to testify for immunity—a favor I'd pulled for him. Laurent thought it would all end up in a plea deal. I was hoping for twenty years, though our DA wasn't quite that optimistic. I'd have to accept that it was the best we could do, other than me taking him out into the woods and putting him down myself.

The only other shaky moments came at the girls' funeral. In a field past the garden and root cellar was the Village's burial ground. The stones were oblong and random, chiseled by one of their clan as if in the days of the Revolution. Jake's father spoke and read bible verses. A cousin planted beach roses at the feet of their plot. I wore a suit instead of my uniform and stayed back, talked to no one, not even Rory, and left as soon as it ended. All I could think about was how I could have done things differently, starting before I'd heard the names Holly and Maisie Connolly.

I was determined to put my abilities to use and had come up with a plan to integrate the Woodmans, Sampsons, and Connollys into Laurel, Maine. Link Johnson called it foolhardy and overly ambitious. I called it doing the right thing, even if it rose from tragedy and guilt. Kids always being ahead of the parents, I'd already talked to Jimmy Goodwin and Vince Marcucci about it, as well as the principals of Laurel Elementary and the new middle school. When school started, kids from Woodman's would be integrated with others in work and playgroups in every classroom. That left me to develop a strategy for the rest of us—the adults—who were supposed to know better but were the root of the problem. It was something I was working on, and had gone so far as to contact my old sociology professor at Orono for advice.

It was the Wednesday before Labor Day. The town was emptying at a slow and steady rate. The summer folks were packing up and heading south.

College kids were headed back to campuses. Martin, Regan, and Griffin had left on Monday for New Hampshire Tech. They promised to return next year, which I looked forward to after what they'd been put through this season. I was letting Trout fill in while I looked for his full-time replacement. I'd already made my mind up that if I got a decent application from a woman, I was going to hire her. Our department needed to be more than what we'd been.

Suzanne had left that morning for Blink's, her question remaining unanswered. She wouldn't come out and ask if I'd made up my mind, but that didn't stop her from dropping in a "Still thinking?" every now and then. I'd tell her I was, and that was the truth. I think she realized I was still decompressing from the events of summer. But summer was coming to an end.

Instead of calling Rory that morning, I took a ride out to St. Mary's.

I had no reason to be proud of her, yet I was. Boomer hadn't had a will, which I did not find surprising. He also had the entire Village property in his name, passed down in their family since the 1920s. The others had lived there only based on the largesse of that one branch of Woodmans. The farm was also only in his name. Because Boomer did not have a wife or child, everything had gone to Rory Connolly as his next of kin. At my request, Cabot had found a lawyer, Francis Cohen, to help her. He'd gone as far as selling Boomer's truck for her and replacing it with two cars, one for her and one for her husband. Cabot had stepped in and taken over Reynolds' role in the deal for On the River. Rory had gone from the bottom of the Village's social ladder to the top.

She'd changed some things in her new position. She let everyone keep the wages from their jobs, instead of kicking half of it up as Boomer had required. When they relocated to the farm, all the homes would have electricity and phone service. She hadn't moved out of her own place into the regal palace Boomer had constructed. Instead, she'd had Jake and the others burn it down, which I didn't think was allowed without a permit. I had parking tickets to write that day.

We walked out to the bench overlooking the tidal pool behind the convent.

The marsh was filling with blue-green water that looked warm and cold at the same time. August had chased away the humidity. The sun felt good on my skin.

If I hadn't known she'd come from the Village, I would have never believed it. Her face had color, if not a tan. She said it was from eating her lunch outside every day. She'd put five hundred miles on her Cavalier already and donated what clothes the girls had left to a shelter in Portland. She'd driven them there herself, and that made her smile. Her black hair shone. No hint remained of the beaten dog who'd walked into my station.

"You doing all right with Jake and everyone else?" I said.

"They are beginning to get it. What happened, what we can do."

"Everyone thinks the farm is a good idea?"

"I wouldn't say that," she said. "But they'll be okay with it by the time."

"The deal is going through okay?" I asked.

"Glen Cabot is a good man," she said, placing her hand on my forearm. "Thank you for sending him our way. We're getting even a better deal than Boomer. I'm glad I came to you, though I wasn't at the time."

She reached over and kissed me on the cheek. Maybe she'd been watching the soap operas that were always on St. Mary's television. I would have liked to ask her if she missed her daughters, if she thought having them had been worth it considering all that had happened. But I knew her answer would be yes. She gave me a small grin, and we walked back to the nursing home, close but not holding hands like Holly Connolly and Jimmy Goodwin would have been. I was smiling myself.

Author's Note

The places, organizations, businesses, names, characters, and events described in this book are either products of the author's imagination or are used fictitiously. Any resemblance to actual persons, living or dead, is entirely coincidental.

Acknowledgements

I would like to thank Bob and Mary W., whose conversation over the bar one night sparked the story that would eventually become this novel. I can attest that they are quite unlike the Woodmans found in this work of fiction.I am also grateful for the patience of my wife, Kim, during the writing of this book, along with that of our children, Sydney and Aaron. I'd like to thank Josh Bodwell for his support over the years. And I have much gratitude for Celia Johnson's guidance in refining my approach to the mystery novel. Much appreciation goes out to my initial readers, Ray Bartlett, Dan Healy, and Rob O'Regan. They work hard to keep me from writing myself into the ditch.

About the Author

Albert Waitt is a writer based in Kennebunkport, Maine. His mystery, *The Ruins of Woodman's Village,* will be published in 2023 by Level Best Books. Waitt's first novel, *Summer to Fall,* was published in 2013 by Barrel Fire Press. His short fiction has appeared in The Literary Review, Third Coast, The Beloit Fiction Journal, Words and Images, Stymie: A journal of sport and literature, and other publications. Waitt is a graduate of Bates College and the Creative Writing Program at Boston University. Experiences ranging from tending bar, teaching creative writing, playing guitar for the Syphlloids, and frying clams can be found bleeding through his work.

SOCIAL MEDIA HANDLES:
Twitter: @alguschip
Facebook: https://www.facebook.com/albertrwaitt

AUTHOR WEBSITE:
albertwaitt.com

Also by Albert Waitt

Summer to Fall, Barrel Fire Press, 2013